REPENTANCE

TORI FOX

Copyright © 2021 by Tori Fox

All rights reserved.

No part of this book may be reproduced in any form or by any electronic or mechanical means, including information storage and retrieval systems, without written permission from the author, except for the use of brief quotations in a book review.

Editing/Proofreading by Ellie at My Brother's Editor

Cover Design by Juliana at Jersey Girl Design

PROLOGUE

They say when you see death on your doorstep, you see your life flash before your eyes.

But all I see is her.

My angel.

Maybe she is my life. The one that makes me feel alive. That showed me what it's like to really live. But I don't get to keep her anymore.

I played the reaper for so long and now the tables have turned. Now the gun is pointed at me. And I am not afraid. I've never feared death. Death brought me an escape I was so desperately searching for.

Now when I look at death, when I feel the blood escaping my body, I don't feel the relief I used to feel when taking a life. Because my blood is cold. My body weak. My eyes heavy.

Death is not an end.

Death is a welcoming home.

A passage to peace.

But as I fade away, my chest aches with regret. And I only hope those I've wronged find the peace I was never able to give them. That those I love find the peace I was too foolish to hold on to.

Death is a funny thing.

And I do not fear it.

1
MATÍAS

Blood drips down my hands. I watch as it hits the rolled-up cuff of my black shirt disappearing into the fabric.

It's warm.

Thick.

Viscous.

It tells a story the owner of it can't tell.

A story of mistakes and wrongdoings.

A story of regret and downfall.

A story of death.

I watch as the blood soaks into the fabric of my shirt. I watch as it pools in the cuff and drips to the floor.

That's when I look at the body on the ground underneath me.

I don't know anything about him. Just his name.

He was just a target I was given.

Another name to be crossed off a list.

One step closer to my salvation.

"Clean it up," I tell the men behind me. The cleanup crew The Partners always send with me.

I pull a white handkerchief out of my pocket and wipe the blood from my hands and then my gun.

I used to care. I used to hate this. I nearly vomited after my first kill. But after a handful of dead bodies, I began to feel the rush. The power that ran through me knowing I could play God.

I didn't always kill the names The Partners gave me. Sometimes the information the targets possessed was enough to save their lives. Even though I knew they would live in fear for the rest of it. One eye always looking over their shoulder.

This was my penance. I got tied up too deep in this underground criminal organization made up of the richest men in the world. No one knows who leads the group. We only know of them as The Partners and what they say goes. But being involved with them brings you power and riches legal business could never give you.

My brothers, Bastian and Thiago, were involved with them. Bastian made it out alive, but not without almost losing the love of his life and his own life. I tried to fix things but only made it worse. Thiago never made it out. He died by their hand. And I carry the blame for that. A secret I am too scared to tell my older brother. He blames himself but it all falls on me.

I stare out the window of the abandoned construction site. From this high up on the fifteenth floor, I can just make out the marina and the sea beyond.

"Scene is clear, boss."

I nod and turn to look at where I shot the man I was

told to kill. A man who refused to answer the questions I was told to ask. Who let me pummel his face until it was barely recognizable. Blood dripped down his throat onto his white shirt. The rope used to bind his hands and legs to the chair he sat on was also crusted with blood by the time I was finished with my interrogation. He was mostly useless. One name was all I got. A name I already knew.

I put him out of his misery by shooting him between the eyes. Blood splattered across my face and all over the tarp we laid down beneath the chair. The memory of the kill has me wiping the handkerchief in my hand across my face.

"Fiero is ready to bring the body to the dump site," Lastra says as he walks up next to me.

I shove the bloody cloth back into my pocket. I give a quick glance to the spot I tasked them to clean up and find it spotless. "Let's go."

I find Fiero waiting at the lift, the body wrapped in plastic. I can just make out the wooden chair he had been sitting in, broken into pieces wrapped up in the bag.

Lastra grabs one end of the body and Fiero the other. I follow them onto the lift and press the button to the ground level. The wind whipping through the construction elevator clears my mind as we descend.

I can make out the three cars below us. Each of us ready to drive a different way in case anything goes wrong. The sound of sirens in the distance has me tensing up.

I look over at Lastra, who begins to impatiently tap his foot. We are two floors from the ground level when the lights on the construction site turn on.

"Fuck," Fiero mutters just as we hit the ground level.

I slide open the door and pull my Beretta out of my holster. I scoped this building out before choosing it as a kill site. I know the power controls are on the opposite side of the building. But with three cars next to the lift, I can't guarantee we'll be alone.

I cock my gun as I scan the area around me. I'm greeted with silence. Enough to nod at Fiero and Lastra to have them load the body into the back of one of the SUVs.

"Get out of here, boss," Lastra says to me, his weapon drawn, as Fiero shuts the back of the SUV.

The sound of sirens gets closer. "No one should be here."

Fiero looks between me and Lastra and jumps into the SUV.

"Go," Lastra tells me.

I give him one last look before I jump into the back of another SUV.

My driver and bodyguard, Demont, looks at me in the rearview as he swerves out of the parking lot. I spin to look and find two men running toward Lastra. I only hear the gunshots as Demont jumps over a curb and hits the main road. The sirens I heard earlier are closer and I know we made it out just in time. Fiero did too. A few polizia drive past us and I breathe a sigh of relief when they don't turn around.

"You were set up," Demont says to me.

I look at him through the rearview. "The whole thing seemed off."

He grunts. Demont is the closest thing I have to a

friend. He knows more about me than anyone and swore his life to protect me.

"Russo knew nothing. The name he gave me was one The Partners already had. The man fucking pissed himself when I pulled my gun out before I even took a punch to him."

"You're close to getting out."

I run my hands through my dark hair, then remember they still have dried blood on them. "I know."

"Do you think—"

"I'd be a fool to think I could get out so easy."

Demont's blue eyes turn sad in the rearview. The man may be built like a brick wall but has the heart of a puppy when it comes to those he cares about.

"There is a change of clothes in the bag next to you," he tells me.

I open them up and find the gym clothes I normally wear to a fight.

"I'll drop you off and take your suit and burn it."

"Is there a club around here?"

He nods. "Down the road in a rough neighborhood." He glances at my hands. "You'll need an alibi for those."

He's right. I don't normally beat the shit out of my targets. But this time I did. Maybe it was the pent-up aggression I had from earlier or just my need to fight, I can't really say.

We are silent as I change out of my bloody suit and into the gym clothes. I toss the suit into a plastic bag I found at the bottom of the gym bag.

When we pull up to the warehouse, Demont says, "I

paid your fee earlier. They think you are already there. I'll be back in an hour."

I nod at him and shut the door behind me.

I should pay him more than I do. He always has my back, is prepared for everything. I didn't expect to get a call from The Partners as I was scoping out the new hotel construction in Italy. Didn't think I would need to find a place to fight to let out my aggression. But Demont knew.

A bulky man, arms covered in coarse, dark hair, stands by the entrance to the warehouse. He doesn't say anything to me and pushes the door open.

I walk into the smell of sweat and blood. The sound of low grunts and bones breaking.

I smile for the first time in a week as peace washes over me.

2

ALESSIA

The loud beat of hip-hop music beats throughout the room. My hand swipes back and forth across the white canvas, the brush strokes uneven. I bite my lip as I try to figure out what is wrong. I look around the room and find some wilting flowers. I smile as I pick through the buckets of paint and find the black one. I pour it into a bucket and throw some gold glitter in for fun. I dip the flowers into the bucket, then splatter the excess paint against the canvas. I throw my head back in laughter as I feel the paint spray across my face.

I grab the paint-splattered step stool out of the corner of my studio and drag it over to the eight-foot canvas. I walk up the ladder and press the paint-soaked flowers into the fabric. Black glittery paint drips down the painting and I smile at the effect it gives. I use the flowers to shade in the top of the bleeding heart and the crown sitting atop the young woman's head.

I climb back down the stepladder and work on a collage of flowers along the bottom of the painting to give it a softer feel. I toss my wilted flowers aside and go back to the paintbrushes and sponges I was using earlier. I brush feverishly through the flowers, adding knives and daggers throughout the bouquets. I add chains to the woman's wrists that she pulls against.

The deep bass of the music pulses through me as I grab my painting broom. It's one of my favorite tools to create shading and depth in the abstract art. I spin around and dip the broom into a vibrant pink paint, then create giant brush strokes around the shoulders of the young woman. When I am satisfied with the shading, I go back to the flowers along the bottom, adding in finer details and splatter with red paint.

"Is this a self-portrait?"

I jump and drop my paintbrush at my feet. The red covering my toes, looking like blood. I turn to the intruder. "Why did I give you a key again?"

"Because I'm your bestest friend and someone needs to check in on you every now and then to make sure you haven't drowned in paint." Bianca turns the loud hip-hop down as she talks.

"I have three brothers for that." I roll my eyes at her and turn back to the portrait of the crying girl with a bleeding heart. A crooked crown sits on her head, like the weight of it is too much.

"You didn't answer my question, Les."

"No, it's not a self-portrait," I say to her as I study my work. "I had a dream about a girl. She was so sad. Broken. But she fought against the chains that tried to weigh her down, against the crown she was forced to wear."

"Why the daggers?" she asks.

"Because she had to fight her way to freedom." I pick up the paintbrush I dropped and add a few details I don't want to forget. Even though this painting is far from finished.

"And the bleeding heart?"

"Don't we all do crazy things for love?" I ask as I turn to look at her.

She raises a brow.

"Tear down our enemies, fight to the death, just to end up with a bleeding heart." I turn and look back at the half-finished painting.

"Morbid much?" She scoffs. "I think you need to stop reading those fantasy books. Your mind is lost in tales of war."

"Not a chance." I laugh. We have been friends for nearly our entire lives and I don't think I have seen her pick up a book once in her life. Even in school, I had to summarize every book for her.

"I tried," she says with a sigh and a smile on her face. "Have you packed?"

"We aren't leaving until three. I have plenty of time." I turn back to my painting.

"And it's two o'clock, Alessia," she whines.

"It's not…" I look out past my studio into the living room and see the antique grandfather clock that takes up a good portion of the room. She's not lying. "Fuck," I mumble and drop my paintbrush into the dirty pile.

"That's why I came over here. You weren't answering

your phone. And I knew you were caught up in a painting!"

I scramble around the room, picking up my mess and covering up what paint I can. "I lost track of time!"

"No kidding." She laughs as she watches me run around. "Do you want me to help?"

I look up at her and see her tiptoeing around the paint splattered on the floor, trying desperately to keep her designer heels paint-free. "How about you just go help me pack?"

"Oh thank god."

"All the clothes we bought are still in the bags so it shouldn't be too hard."

She nods and walks off toward my bedroom but stops at the door separating my studio from the main living area. "Are you going to shower?"

"I'm covered head to toe in paint, Bianca. Of course I will. But if you don't get out of here, I am going to cover you in paint too!"

She runs out of the studio and I chuckle as I get back to cleaning up my mess.

I throw my wet hair up in a bun as I slip on a pair of flats. I look around for Bianca after I leave the bathroom where she so kindly left me an outfit to wear on the plane but she isn't in my room. I look out through the French doors that lead to my balcony and see her sitting in a chair with a glass of champagne in her hand.

I walk through the maze of my two-bedroom apartment and through the kitchen, grabbing my phone off the table, and head out to the balcony to meet her where I see a bottle of champagne in a bucket of ice.

I love my balcony. It's decorated with original majolica. It complements the baroque-style interior so well. And the view is something I could never grow tired of. The blue water dotted with boats and yachts in the marina. The mountains green and lush, meeting the sea. The colored old-world buildings sunken into the mountains bring life to the small town of Positano. I breathe in the salty air and sit next to Bianca.

"Where did you get the champagne?"

"I brought it, silly. You're turning twenty-five tomorrow! We are celebrating!"

I laugh as she pours me a glass and hands it over. "I thought we needed to leave at three."

She shrugs. "Mmm champagne is more important. Besides, we are taking my father's plane. They can wait for us."

I shake my head at her. "That's not really how it works."

"Ugh, fine. But let's take the bottle to go."

I glance at my phone and see the driver that my father assigned to me texted me to let me know he was ready whenever we were. I really hate that I have a driver. I feel bad for the guy because he barely does anything. I much prefer walking all over the town or riding a bike if I feel like biking up the hills. I love the feeling of this small town, it's so full of life. It reminds me of my mother.

"You ready?" Bianca asks as she stands with the bucket in her hands.

I text my driver and he says he is walking up to grab my suitcase.

As I lock the three locks on the old wooden door, Bianca huffs as she makes her way down the narrow stairwell in her four-inch stilettos.

"Want me to carry the champagne?" I ask her.

She scowls at me. "You know it would be much easier if you lived in a building with an elevator."

"Never happening," I joke.

"I would probably have a heart attack if you did." She wobbles on one of the narrow-tiled steps and grabs the wall for balance. I grab the champagne bucket from her as she says, "Of course, that's if I don't break my neck from these damn stairs."

I just shake my head and follow behind her. Bianca is just as well off as I am, her dad an investment banker while my dad is in the shipping business. We grew up next to each other in Naples and have been connected at the hip ever since. Although she is more of a girly girl and I am just the girl next door. While she went to university to meet boys, I went to university for art history. To get lost in paintings and sculptures from other times and other worlds.

After we graduated, we moved to Positano together. But where I found an old Neapolitan baroque-style apartment, she moved into a modern condo. I know she could never live in something like what I have, and vice versa. She likes crisp lines and glass. Where I like paint splatter and patina. But for some reason, despite being total opposites, we are inseparable.

"Are you excited yet?" she asks me.

I take a sip of champagne. "Of course! You know I love Monaco as much as I love it here."

We drink the rest of the champagne and giggle the entire way to the airport.

3
MATÍAS

I sit down at my desk and spin around to look at the Mediterranean Sea that sits outside my window. It looks peaceful, calm. Like it's where I should be. I need a break from this place. From everything in my life. From all the decisions I have made that led me on the path I am on now.

I glance down at my hands. My eyes are playing tricks on me as I see the blood that covered them three nights ago. I pinch my eyes shut and take a deep breath before the anxiety sets in. No matter how much I lie to myself that I don't enjoy the killing, the release it gives me when it happens, the next few days are filled with regret and unease. How easy it is for me to take someone's life, knowing someone could take my life just as easily.

Maybe I should ask Bastian to borrow his yacht. Get out on the sea, clear my mind. Get away from The Partners, away from work. A job I used to enjoy before I got caught up with the parties and the drugs. No, Bastian wouldn't trust me with his yacht. He would be too afraid I would destroy it.

My phone rings. I grab my cell and see my brother calling, as if he knew I was thinking about him at that moment. We don't have the easiest relationship. We never did. I'm ten years younger than him. And he always found me annoying. I always thought he was cool. I aspired to be him when I was young. He was successful, brilliant, innovative. He grew our family investment business into the billions. Between him and my older brother, Thiago, they knew what success was, they knew how to get power. And I wanted that success. At least that's the lie I told myself. Deep down, I knew I was selfish and wanted the power for myself. They gifted me the Montford Hotel project when it was coming to fruition. And I finally felt that power I always wanted.

Then two years ago I made a bad decision and nearly ran this hotel group into the ground. I was stupid and naive. I got caught up with the very people that my brothers tried to break away from, The Partners. A crime syndicate run by the richest men in the world. I learned quickly from The Partners that control was even greater than money. And the greatest power came from running legit businesses and the black market. Drug cartels, money laundering, weapons trading, sex trafficking. I am ashamed I got involved. Thiago lost his life seven years ago trying to break free from them. He left his wife without a husband and children without a father.

But I craved the power after I was given a taste and I wanted more. I fell deep into the criminal underground. I felt myself getting close to rising up in power. Getting to the next level with The Partners. Then I threw it all away when I got lost in the party life, more so than before. I started fucking up. I almost exposed them. So they did what they do best. Destroy those that do them wrong.

They created a fake scandal that nearly tore apart the hotel group. Almost ruining the family business. I got thrown into prison by Interpol while Bastian had to put the pieces together and fix what I nearly destroyed. It almost got him and his girlfriend killed.

Sometimes I wish I rotted away in that prison. Because life out here isn't much better. And now I have a bounty on my shoulders I need to fulfill.

I hit the answer button on the phone just before it goes to voice mail. "Bastian."

"I need to get that report about the expansion to the investors."

Business as usual. "I'm finishing it up right now."

"I needed it yesterday, Matías. Some want to pull out because they don't think we are moving fast enough."

I sigh into the phone. "We are on schedule."

"With construction?"

"Yes."

I hear him shift in his seat and mumble something to someone. "What about with the prebooking?"

I run a hand through my hair. "I'll have to check with sales on that."

"I asked you to begin the prebooking last month."

I sigh as I lean my elbows on the desk and put my phone on speaker. "I must have forgotten."

"We need to ensure we have the interest of the

people with these hotels before we can move forward with construction on phase two."

"I'll work on it."

"Do I need to find someone else to fill the CEO position there? I have candidates, Matías. I have people in my office that are more than ready and willing to take on the project. You told me when you came back that you would be fine running the business again. That nothing would get in your way. I held back on creating a separate team for the expansion in my offices. Now I am not so sure that was a good idea."

I grit my teeth as I listen to my brother. He's kept a noose around my neck ever since the scandal. He doesn't trust me. And I don't think I will ever earn that trust from him.

"Your silence speaks volumes, Matías."

I clear my throat as I stand. "I'll make sure everything is taken care of by the end of the week."

"Good."

I walk over to the bar in my office and pour a glass of bourbon.

"Are you sure you are okay?" he asks me, his voice softer, less harsh.

"Fan-fucking-tastic, brother." I throw back the glass of bourbon and pour another.

He sighs into the phone. "You know I do worry about you, Matías."

I swish my drink around in my mouth. I know deep down he cares about me. Or at least he thinks he should. I'm just not sure how genuine his care is. I swallow. "I'm fine."

"Right. Well, get that report to me by noon."

"Sure thing." I hang up the phone and stare at the blank computer screen in front of me. I haven't started the report. Hell, I've barely gotten any work done since I got back from Italy. My mind too preoccupied with what happened in Naples. I spoke with my contact with The Partners the next morning. He seemed uninterested in the fact the police came and more annoyed with the fact the only name I got from Russo was a name we already knew. Not that I know much. I'm given a brief dossier about a hit and the information the organization needs. I was just happy to find out Lastra made it out before the cops came.

But with the way that both Lastra and Fiero were surprised by the police and that Russo had no new information to give us, I can't help but agree with Demont. I was set up. But I can't go against The Partners. They will kill me if I try to figure out what happened. And who's to say they wouldn't go after Bastian again.

I'm lost in thought when I look up and see Elyse, the head of marketing, standing in my doorway.

"I just wanted to drop off… are you okay, Matías?" she asks. She seems to be the only one in the office concerned about me since I came back to the hotel after being in jail. Where I used to be a party animal and carefree, I am now more uptight. The last two years have taken a toll on me.

"I really wish people would stop asking me that."

A blush forms on her cheeks. "I'm sorry… I didn't mean—"

I hold up a hand. "It's fine. I'm fine, Elyse."

She nods and then steps farther into the office. "I have that file you asked for regarding the marketing plans for Naples and Málaga."

I sit back in my chair and gesture for her to bring it to me. "Thank you."

"I talked with Celine. She said she is ready to go with the press releases for the prebooking."

I breathe a sigh of relief at that. "Has she been working with sales?"

Elyse gives me a curious look. "You asked her last week to work on it."

Fuck. Maybe I am losing it. "Right, I forgot."

"Are you sure you're okay, Matías?" Her voice is etched with concern. I go to speak and then see her eyeing the bourbon sitting in front of me. "It's not even noon."

It's barely ten I want to tell her but I keep my mouth shut. "Just one of those days."

"I understand that."

She walks out of the office and I want to say something to her but once again I don't know what to say.

Somehow, I managed to get the report Bastian wanted done by noon. I even got work that needed to be done the last few days completed. By the time I make it to my villa down the road from the hotel, I'm exhausted. I put in more work today than I have the last three days.

I walk into the kitchen and find a warm plate of pasta sitting on the counter from my housekeeper. I don't know what I would do without that woman. She is more useful to me than my assistant.

I head over to the bar and pour a drink. I didn't even finish the bourbon that was in front of me this morning after Elyse said something. I felt guilty. Like the man I was before my world fell apart. I didn't want to feel that reckless again.

I grab my dinner and head out to the terrace. I feel secluded out here. It's the reason I bought the villa. A lush yard filled with greenery. It's quiet. Only the trickle of the water in the pool that adds more of a calming effect than anything else. My bedroom sits off the pool too, almost like a guesthouse separated from the rest of the house. On the nights I can sleep, the water brings the calmness I need.

Claudette, my housekeeper, walks out of the house holding another drink. "Bonne soiree, Monsieur Montford. I thought you may need another. I saw your glass was nearly empty."

I smile at her as I take the glass. "Thank you, Claudette."

She grins at me. "How is the carbonara?"

"Delicious as always."

"I tried a new recipe this evening."

"Your own?"

She nods with an even bigger smile.

"You really should write a cookbook. I would buy one."

She laughs and grabs my empty glass. "We both know you wouldn't be cooking, Matías. So what good would that do?"

"I'll buy one for all my friends," I say with a charming smile.

"Or you could find a woman for yourself. Someone that would cook for you."

I shake my head as I sip my cocktail. "Now you're pushing it, Claudette. You know I am not the type to settle down."

"Neither was your brother, and look at him now. He's happier than I've ever seen him with Cameron."

My smile breaks at her statement. She's right though. He was a hardened man until she broke that armor around him. "I don't think that's my fate."

She picks up my empty dish and turns toward the house. "That's the thing about fate, dear, you never know when it's going to strike."

My phone rings at that exact moment.

"Maybe that is fate calling you right now."

I look down and see the number calling is definitely my fate, just not the kind she was talking about. I watch her walk into the house as I answer. "Montford."

"Matías, so good to hear your voice."

"I wish I could say the same, Charles."

He chuckles into the phone and I can't help but want to punch the man in the face. He acts so jovial most of the time but won't second-guess putting a bullet between your eyes.

"I have an assignment for you."

I lean back in my chair, my fingers running along the edge of my glass. "I just got back from one. Seems too soon for another. Not without any new information."

"About that. We did think Russo knew more. Pity

really. His wife now all alone with three kids." I clench my fist. I hate knowing more about the targets than I need to. Charles knows that too. Just another way to stab me in the chest. "Not to mention the police showed up. I thought you knew to be more careful, Matías, when choosing a kill spot."

"It was a coincidence. The construction on that building at been halted for permit issues. I made sure of that."

"Well, at least you are still with us." He chuckles into the phone like the gamble on my life is a joke.

"Just tell me where you need me to be. And the target," I say sternly into the phone.

"After I was given the report on your last assignment, we have decided to change your agreement."

I swallow down the rest of my drink, wishing I had another. But Claudette knows not to interrupt me when I am on the phone. "And you didn't think I should be privy to the change in the agreement?"

"Oh dear boy, that is why I am telling you now."

"It's not much of an agreement when you change the terms without my consent."

"Do you really think you have a choice in the matter?"

I clench my jaw, knowing he's right. "Continue then."

"We have a client that is in need of our protective services."

"I don't do that shit."

"I would watch your tone, Mr. Montford." He waits for me to calm down before continuing. "Lorenzo Calvetti has had threats made to his daughter's life. We need someone to watch over her but she won't go willingly."

"You mean I need to kidnap her," I say flatly.

"Some may call it that."

"Why doesn't her father just tell her to come with us?"

He takes a minute to speak. "Haven't you learned it's better not to ask questions?"

I run my hand through my hair as I think about what he told me. And I have a gnawing feeling this isn't about protecting her. But I am not one to question The Partners.

"All the information you need will be in the file in the post office box tomorrow morning. She arrived in Monaco this evening. She'll be there for three days."

"Got it."

"Don't mess this assignment up, Mr. Montford. You have a lot riding on this."

He hangs up before I can say anything or ask any more questions. But I could tell from his tone it's complete this, or it's my life on the line.

I throw my crystal tumbler at the wall of the house and scream as the glass shatters across the terrace.

4

MATÍAS

I flip through the file as I sit on my hotel room's balcony in Monaco.

Alessia Calvetti.

Brown hair. Whiskey-colored eyes. Petite frame.

She's fucking beautiful.

Five foot two. One hundred and five pounds. Born in Naples. Twenty-five years old.

Damnit, today is her fucking birthday.

I skim over the details. Daughter of Lorenzo Calvetti of Calvetti & Sons Shipping. They are a pretty large shipping company in the Mediterranean and recently expanded into the Middle East and India. The company is worth nearly a billion dollars with massive expansion happening in the last five years. I snort at that. I can only guess that's when Calvetti got in with The Partners. And a shipping company? One of their favorites to do business with. Pretty cheap to move drugs and weapons when you have a shipping company in your control.

I don't see anything of interest with Alessia. She seems boring. She doesn't work. Lives off her dad's money. I wouldn't be surprised if she was a whiny daddy's girl.

I shut the file and text Fiero to make sure everything is set up on his end. He assures me the safe house is ready and secure. I throw back the last sip of bourbon and head back into my room.

"Burn this," I tell Demont as I pass him the file and head toward the front door.

"I don't like this, boss."

I grab my white suit jacket off a chair in the sitting area and slip it on. "Neither do I."

"Something feels off."

I run a hand through my hair. "I don't have another option."

"I know, boss." He hands me my sunglasses I left on the table as I slip on a pair of brown loafers. "I'll have your back this time."

I nod to him as I slide the sunglasses over my eyes and open the door. "Let's get to work."

We've been to two lounges and we haven't spotted her. Lastra had been sitting in the lobby of the hotel waiting for them to leave but they got into a limo instead of walking and he lost them. He has been checking with bouncers but not all are willing to give a beefy Italian with tattoos on his face any information.

I curse at The Partners for giving me this fucking shit.

I don't want to be involved with kidnappings. And I know this is exactly what it is. Not some stupid bullshit about protection. I still don't know what they are playing at but I am sure I'll figure it out as time goes by. They haven't given me any kind of timeline on how long I need to keep the girl either.

We went to two of the nicer lounges but it's getting late so she must have moved on to a club by now.

"Jimmy'z or La Rascasse?" Demont asks me as we sit outside at a small pub, drinking.

I turn to Demont. "La Rascasse. It's next to the marina. We can watch to see if she goes in from there. I'll have Lastra head to Jimmy'z."

I finish my drink and we head toward the marina. It's not far from here and it should be early enough that we didn't miss her. I read that she tends to go to lounges and restaurants before hitting the clubs.

We get to the marina with a clear view of the entrance to La Rascasse. It's an exclusive place. Only the rich and famous get in. Unless you can afford to dress the part enough. I find humor in watching people that clearly don't belong there get turned down to get in. Demont spits out sunflower seeds as he watches, surely just as entertained as I am.

I look down at my watch and yawn. I am tired of sitting around and waiting for someone who clearly isn't going to show up. No word from Lastra either. I bet they got drunk early and are back at the hotel.

I'm about to call it a night when I hear screaming girls. I turn my head and see two blonde females with a bottle of champagne hanging out the top of a limousine.

I shake my head at the obnoxious behavior and start walking back toward the hotel.

But Demont grabs my arm. "Look, boss."

I look over to where he's staring and see a group of five girls. All of them in short dresses that scream money. The only brunette I see is too tall to be Alessia but then one of the blonde girls moves and there she is. Much shorter than the rest of the girls, even with the diamond-encrusted heels she has on.

I take her in as they wait near the bouncer, skipping the line that is formed outside the club. She's wearing a slinky silver dress. One wrong movement and she would be giving everyone a show. She laughs carelessly with her friends and her smile is gorgeous. She turns to face me and that's when I notice a damn tiara on her head.

Fucking typical of a daddy's little princess type.

I near the street crossing, Demont on my heels as we watch them gain access to the club.

"Two muscles are catching up to them."

I look at the two men following the girls into the club. This just complicated things. Daddy must be worried something is going to happen to his little angel.

We cross the street and I pull my glasses onto my face from where they were tucked into my open black button-down. I've been here before and there is no way I won't get in. I'm wearing a white custom-made Italian suit. Gucci loafers. Tom Ford sunglasses. And a watch that costs more than any of these bouncers make in a year.

The bouncer looks at me, then behind me at Demont and nods, pulling back the red velvet rope to let us in. Another man greets us at the top of the stairs and directs us to a VIP table. I smirk at Demont and he shakes his head. I don't even need to give my name to get the service I expect.

We sit at a table with the perfect view of the dance floor. It doesn't take me long to see the girls ordering drinks at the bar. I'm surprised they don't have a table.

"Should I invite them over?"

Demont looks around. I can only presume for the bodyguards. "It might be hard to get her tonight."

"Oh, I think I am just going to have some fun tonight. Tease her. Tempt her."

"Gain her trust."

I nod. "Unless she's easy. Then it will be effortless."

A waitress comes over to our table. Demont glances at the girls and then orders a bottle of vodka. I get up after the waitress leaves and head to the bar. Three of the girls have walked to the dance floor and it's just the tall blonde and Alessia.

I scoot up beside them and flag the bartender down. "Bourbon neat."

The girls giggle next to me and I can't help but roll my eyes as the blonde takes me in without a care. I give her the smile that wins everyone over and she licks her lips while looking at me.

I shake my head as I turn to the bartender to grab my drink. I throw some money down on the bar and turn to face the ladies. Alessia's back is against the bar so I can only see her profile.

"Let me guess, birthday or breakup?"

Alessia snorts and I find it charming.

Her friend cuts in. "It's her birthday. And she's

getting over a breakup so maybe she needs a prince to kiss her."

Alessia's eyes go wide as her friend blabbers on. I stop listening to her when Alessia turns toward me with shy eyes. I thought she looked gorgeous in pictures but in person she's breathtaking. Almond-shaped whiskey eyes are framed by wispy bangs that graze the top of her lashes. Her chestnut hair is pulled into a loose braid and thrown over a shoulder. My eyes travel down her body to the dress that is barely covering her. Her olive skin dusted with gold glitter.

"I'm actually not getting over a breakup, so no need for a kiss," she says quietly before taking a sip of the pink drink in her hand.

"I just got here with a friend of mine. We have a table in the VIP section if you ladies would like to join us. Call it a birthday treat."

She chews on her straw as I ask the question, her eyes getting bigger with every word. "Oh no, I don't think—"

"That would be fantastic!" her friend shouts. "We wanted a table, but they were all reserved. Our other friends are dancing. Can we bring them over too?"

"Why not," I say as I take one last sip of the bourbon and set my glass down.

I hear the blonde girl shriek as I head to the table. Alessia is saying something to her but I can't quite make out the words. I glance to the side where I saw her bodyguards and see one moving as we move.

"Ladies first," I say as I gesture to the table. Demont slides over and Alessia sits down cautiously. Before I can let her friend in, I sit next to her.

Our vodka bottle arrives just as we sit down. "A bottle of champagne, ladies? We are celebrating, aren't we?" I ask with my charming grin.

"Of course!" her friend agrees.

"A bottle of your most expensive champagne please."

The waitress nods and I see the friend mouth oh my god to Alessia.

"I'm Matías. And this big old brute of a man is my friend Demont. But don't worry, he's a gentle giant. He won't bite."

"What about you?" the friend asks me.

"Bianca!" Alessia shouts.

Her friend shrugs. "What? I'm just curious."

I smirk at her friend, then glance at Alessia. "Only if you beg."

Alessia bites her lip, a flush hitting her cheeks, before sipping on her drink.

"Well, since Alessia here so rudely screamed my name. I'm Bianca. This is Alessia. And it's her birthday. She doesn't think she is getting over a breakup but the rest of us do."

"I broke up with Antonio three months ago. I'm more than over him."

Maybe that's why I don't recall anything in her file.

"Let me go get the girls. I'll be right back," Bianca says as she bounces up and out of the booth.

Alessia goes back to chewing on her straw and I can't help but guess that she is nervous around new people. She seemed lively around the girls.

"So where are you from, Alessia?"

"Italy."

I laugh at her answer. "I could tell by your accent. What part?"

"Positano."

"Ahh, the Amalfi Coast. One of my favorite places."

"Really?"

I nod.

"I grew up in Naples. But after college, I moved to Positano."

"Where did you go to school?"

She sips on her drink and I can't help but stare at her full pink lips as she does. I barely listen as she rambles on about Florence and art. I like that she is loosening up to me. It will make everything easier. Her words are lost on me as I'm mesmerized by her eyes. They seem almost too large for her face but they're captivating. The whiskey color almost gold when the light hits them. The way her bangs get stuck in her eyelashes when she gets animated. I like that she has barely any makeup on, unlike her friend. She's naturally beautiful.

"This is Emilia, Tina, and Maya."

I'm startled when Bianca returns. It takes effort to pull my eyes away from Alessia's lips. "Pleasure," I say to the girls.

They squeeze in around the table. Bianca sits to the right of Alessia, the other girls next to me. I slide closer to Alessia, our thighs nearly touching.

The waitress arrives with our champagne and I pour glasses for the girls. "To the happiest of birthdays," I cheers.

The girls giggle and laugh, talking among themselves. I sit back in the booth, laying my arm on the back of the cushion around Alessia. I see her gasp as my arm brushes against her shoulders and a blush creeps up her neck as I move even closer to her, our thighs pressed against each other.

"Did you get anything good for your birthday?" I ask her, my voice low and gravelly.

She turns to look up at me and must be surprised when she sees how close I am to her. Our faces inches apart. She bites her lip as her hand goes to her neck. I look down and see a single diamond teardrop hanging from a silver chain that hits just below her clavicle. "My father got me this."

I move her hand from the necklace and run my fingers along the chain before gliding them along her clavicle. I drop my lips to her ear and whisper, "It's beautiful. Just like you."

Her head snaps up and she looks at me with surprise. She pushes my hand away from her body. I can tell she is nervous. "I… uh… thank you."

I smile at her stuttering. I casually rub my thumb along her shoulder from the arm that's wrapped behind her and it makes her jump.

"Bianca, want to dance? I love this song," Alessia says out of nowhere.

Her friend breaks away from her conversation with the others. "You hate this song."

She shakes her head and gets up. Squeezing between Bianca and Demont to leave the table.

"Okay, I guess we're dancing," Bianca says dramatically. She pours herself a heavy-handed vodka drink and follows Alessia to the dance floor. The other girls following.

I rub my thumb over my lip as I watch her walk away. For a petite thing, she has an ass that I would love to get my hands on.

"I think you are coming on too strong for her."

I look over at Demont, who is smirking at me.

"You might need to take the charm down a notch."

I laugh at my friend and take a sip of water. "She'll cave. They always do."

"The muscles are watching you closely."

I shrug. "I'm sure daddy is getting a full report. But I am Matías Montford, billionaire and playboy extraordinaire. What else do you expect?"

"I expect you to never say that ever again."

I throw my head back and laugh. "I'll put it on a shirt for you."

"Great. I'll be sure to send you video of me burning it." He chuckles as he says it.

I turn my head back to the girls and once again my eyes are focused on Alessia. Not because she's a target. There is something about her. Something that I can't quite place. I lick my lips and set my glass down. "Phase two."

Demont shakes his head at me. "You are trying too hard."

"I'll win her over."

I walk to the dance floor and grab her hips, pulling her into me as she sways to the music. She jumps as I do it and tries to turn around. I lean into her ear. "You looked so gorgeous out here I couldn't stay away."

She relaxes at my words and places her hands over my own and continues to sway to the music. I tower over her by over a foot. But I can't help but lean down to breathe her in as we dance. She smells like lavender. Sweet and innocent.

I run my hands up her body, stopping just below her breasts. To my surprise, she wraps her arms around my neck, pulling my head down so I'm closer to her. I spin her around so we are facing each other. Her hands move down to my chest and I can't help but drop my hands to her ass. She looks up at me as I do it and I give her a half smile.

I try to pull her closer to me but she keeps a small space between us. Bianca cuts between us and tells Alessia something I can't hear.

"I'll be back. Just going to the restroom," Alessia says to me as Bianca pulls her away.

I lean down and whisper in her ear. "Come back to the table when you're done."

She blinks as she looks up at me. I squeeze her hand and walk away.

I don't think she is coming back to the table. It's been well over twenty minutes. She didn't leave though because I can still see her bodyguards near the bar.

I finish another glass of water. I still don't see her and I'm getting bored of the game. "Let's head out," I tell Demont.

We walk to the door when I hear my name. I turn around and see Alessia behind me.

"Hi. Sorry. Emilia got sick."

I nod. "We are heading out."

She bites down on her lip and I can tell she is trying to find words to say. And that's when I know I've hooked her.

I step closer to her so I don't have to shout over the crowd. "I enjoyed our night together. Although I do wish it ended differently."

She looks at me with wide eyes and brushes a piece of loose hair behind her ear. "How did you wish it ended?" she asks quietly. I barely hear it.

I ignore her question. "Are you still in town tomorrow?"

She smiles at me. "Yeah, one more night. I think we are going to Jimmy'z."

I lean down to her ear and wrap my arm around her waist, pulling her flush against me. "Maybe I'll see you there."

Her hand moves to my chest as I pull her into me. "Okay," she whispers.

I drop my hand on her waist and lightly run my finger up the back of her bare thigh. "You wanted to know how I pictured the night ending?"

Her hand grips on to my shirt as she nods.

My lips make their way from her ear to her jawline. I clasp my hand to the back of her neck as I pull her lips to mine. "Like this."

I suck her bottom lip into my mouth and hear her gasp as I do it, her fist getting tighter on my shirt. I then press a firm kiss against her lips and pull back quickly.

"Maybe tomorrow night will end differently," I say as I let her go and walk away.

5

ALESSIA

"I know, Daddy… we will be fine, I promise."
I roll my eyes as I listen to my dad drone on about my safety.

"It's just me and a few girlfriends."

I watch Bianca as she mouths at me to get off the phone and hold back a giggle.

"We've been here two nights and been fine. Besides, we are tired after all that partying for my birthday." I lie. "We are just going to stay in."

"Is that a promise?"

I groan into the phone. "Dad. You've had Mo and Larry following us around the entire time. I think you would know if we left. Besides, it's hard to have fun when they are watching us the whole time."

"I'm doing it for your safety."

"I've never needed them around before."

"Things change."

I pinch my brow in confusion. What does that even mean? But before I can ask, he changes the subject.

"Who was that man you were with last night?"

"What man?" I pretend.

"Alessia Arianna Calvetti," he speaks sternly into the phone.

I groan. I hate it when he uses my full name. "He was just a guy I met."

"Be careful. You don't know what kind of men are out there."

"Dad, please. I'm twenty-five. I know how to take care of myself. And I know when someone is being a creep."

"I just worry about my baby girl."

"I'll be fine, Dad. Like I said, staying in. Bianca is still hungover." She glares at me when I say it.

"Alright, well, I'll talk with you tomorrow. I look forward to seeing you next week for a birthday dinner."

"Night, Dad."

I hang up the phone and join the girls in the bathroom, where they are getting ready.

"You are such a daddy's girl."

I roll my eyes at Tina.

"It's just because he gives her everything she wants. I'm sure if he acted like any of our dads she wouldn't be that way."

Bianca scoffs at Emilia. "Your dad literally paid for you to go on a month-long wellness vacation. Where all you did was get drunk, do blow, and sleep around. I wouldn't talk if I were you."

She sticks her tongue out at Bianca and goes back to curling her hair.

I pull her into the living room and sit on the floor to do my makeup. "My dad is acting weird. Like he's worried about me. More so than usual."

"He just wants to protect his only daughter." She sits next to me and hands me a glass of champagne. "But it is weird he had the bodyguards with us. That was new."

"Ugh, I know. And of course they told him about Matías."

"Oh girl. He better show up tonight. He is so dreamy."

I blush at the thought of his hands on me last night. And the way he sucked my lip into his mouth and then gave me a quick kiss. It sent chills down my entire body. I can almost still feel his lips on mine. "He seems like a player."

"So… who cares? You need to get out of your shell. Find someone new, even if it's just for a night. Cleanse your body of Antonio."

I snort at her. "I don't think having sex with a random guy is how one cleanses themselves."

She leans into me and whispers. "It apparently worked for Emilia."

I throw my head back and laugh. "You know I've been over Antonio since before I broke up with him."

She gives me a look that says she doesn't believe me but it's true.

I never loved Antonio. He didn't love me either. Sure, we had fun when we first got together. And he was undeniably handsome. But I never felt a strong connection with him. I felt like we were together more to make our families happy than anything else. It made my father happy that I was going to settle with a good man. And Antonio could pretend to his family he wasn't sleeping with every woman in Italy. I don't know why I didn't break things off sooner. I stopped having sex with him after I found out about the first affair. But I wanted to keep up appearances. I wanted my dad to think I was ready to settle down and start a family like he wanted. He and Mom were married with one kid and another on the way by the time they were my age.

It finally came to a point when I knew I had to end it all when one of Antonio's floozies threatened me. I don't know why she was so mad we were together. I even told her that I had no problem breaking up with him but he would never settle down for anyone. She slapped me and I slammed my door in her face, then called Antonio and broke up with him. He tried to fight it, asking me what he was going to tell his parents. I told him to grow a pair and let them know he was a whore.

I haven't spoken to him since then.

Bianca nudges my shoulder. "Hey, get out of your head. Drink your champagne. Put on the hottest dress you brought so Matías can't keep his hands off you. And let's celebrate."

I sip my champagne. "Since you packed for me, I have no doubt there is an even skimpier dress in my suitcase than last night."

She grins at me, and I know I'm going to need a lot more boob tape to keep this dress on.

I sit with my legs crossed as tight as I can make them. I love the dress Bianca picked out for me but it's tight as hell and the cutouts on the side made me unable to wear any type of underwear underneath it. It's a red halter dress that actually makes it look like I have cleavage. I hate my tiny boobs. The sides are cut out and kept together with strings of Swarovski crystals. It's a sexy dress and it makes my ass look perfect but it sure as hell sucks to sit down in it.

We managed to sneak out of the hotel without the stupid bodyguards knowing. Thanks to Maya's flirting, she got us through the kitchen and out a back door. They think we are in our rooms watching movies.

I don't understand why my dad is so worried. I am not doing anything out of the ordinary. Bianca and I go out all the time at home. We even take a few trips a year and he's never cared at all. This past year we've already been to Seychelles, Ibiza, and the Maldives. We love the beach and sometimes I think I need to move to an island. Just the sun, sand, drinks, and my art. The thought puts a smile on my face until I think about the painting I left half finished at home.

That dream I had sends a chill down my spine. I never could see the girl's face in the dream. Even after having it nearly every night for a month. But I could feel her pain, her sorrow. Like her broken soul was becoming my broken soul. I would wake up in sweats every time. My heart beating so rapidly I thought I was dying. At first, I thought nothing of it but as the days dragged on and it only got more intense, I knew I had a connection to the girl somehow.

"Earth to Alessia. That man has got you tied up in knots."

I look over at Maya. "What?"

Bianca answers for her. "Maybe you should have gotten his number."

"Huh?"

"You keep looking toward the entrance. I know you are hoping he shows up tonight."

I look at my friend, not wanting to tell her my mind keeps going back to that damn dream. "I don't care if he shows up or not."

"What other lies are you telling yourself?"

I push her shoulder and shake my head at her. I really wasn't thinking about him when I have so many other things on my mind. But now that they brought it up, it's all I can think about. Which is a welcome reprieve to the dark thoughts in my head.

I try to push my mind somewhere else but all I can think about are his hands on me and that damn kiss. I almost chased after him last night after he kissed me like that. It was barely even a kiss. But it was enough to leave me craving more. My fingers dance along my lips as I think about it.

I finally stop looking at the damn entrance and join my friends on the dance floor. The vibrations of the song flowing through my body as I shake my hips to the beat. Every thought disappears as I get lost in the music. That reoccurring dream, the painting, the beautiful stranger Matías, the odd worry from my father. All I can think about is letting loose, dancing my cares away. Living the life I should be living. Wild and carefree.

I don't know how long I dance for but I just know I feel truly happy. Bianca eventually asks me if I want another drink and I nod, so we head back to the VIP table we were able to reserve for the night. I pour a weak vodka drink. That's my stupid mind thinking that if he does show up, I don't want to be completely hammered. I'm a lightweight. Two drinks I'm tipsy, three I'm drunk, and four I'll be crawling onto a couch, ready for a nap.

I yawn as I finish my second drink. Half tempted for a third to erase all the thoughts from my mind when I hear that gritty voice behind me.

"Tired so soon? I wish I could have gotten here earlier."

A smile hits my face and I bite my lip before turning around and taking in the man that has consumed my thoughts in just twenty-four hours. He's more casual tonight. Gray slacks and a white button-up. The top few buttons opened, giving me a glance of deep olive skin. The sleeves of his shirt rolled up to show his forearms and the ink that covers them.

This man is ten times sexier than Antonio. He has an air about him that makes him dangerous and mysterious. And even though the warning bells are going off in my head that I should keep away, I'm too drawn into his blindingly blue eyes that I can't look away. Maybe I have had one too many drinks.

He slides around the side of the booth where I am sitting alone and that's also when I notice he is alone too. His friend nowhere in sight.

I gasp as he slides right up next to me. His arm wrapping around my shoulders and pulling me flush to his side. He whispers words into my ear in a foreign language. The cadence of his voice sending a chill down my spine.

I have no idea what he said to me but it sounded hot as hell. But before I could even ask him, he captures my lips with his own. This kiss not a tease like last night. No, this kiss is intense, needy, passionate.

I manage to pull away from him, breathless. Our lips only inches from each other. "What did you say?"

He smiles and I swear it melts all my fears of him being dangerous. "I said 'I couldn't stop thinking about you. Your beauty, your eyes, your smile, your lips.'" He grips the back of my head and presses his lips against mine.

Those words do something to me and I feel reckless. I don't even recognize myself as I crawl onto his lap, straddling him, not caring how short my dress is or the lack of garments underneath. I became wanton as he grips my ass, pulling me into his hips. I can feel his need as our hips touch, the thickness in his pants turning me on.

His hand drops to my thigh and slowly glides up until he hits the hem of my dress that is barely covering my ass. I am suddenly aware that he will find me pantyless and wet, so I sit back on his lap.

"Getting shy on me now?"

I shake my head and bite my lip.

"I wouldn't do that," he growls.

I look up at him through my bangs. "Do what?"

His thumb rubs over my lip. "Bite this because it has me wanting to do very dirty things to you."

I blush at his words just as Bianca returns to the table. "Am I missing a show? Is there an admission charge?"

Matías chuckles as I crawl off his lap and return to sitting next to him. My neck and chest matching the bright red of my dress.

"Oh please, don't stop on my account. I was getting rather turned on by it."

"Bianca!" I shout at her. She just shrugs and Matías laughs.

She pours another drink and offers me one but I decline as does Matías. His hand makes lazy circles on my shoulder and it's driving me insane.

Bianca studies the two of us. "Well, I think I am just going to go back to the dance floor."

"Okay," I squeak out.

She raises her brows at me a few times and makes a crude gesture with her hand before sauntering off to the dance floor.

"Not interested in dancing tonight?" he asks me as his other hand drops back to my thigh.

I shake my head.

"Want to talk?"

I peek up at him through my bangs. But can't find any words to say, my shyness returning at warp speed.

He pushes a strand of hair behind my ear. "Interested in getting out of here?"

I look at him, then look out to my friends.

"Or we can stay and hang out with them. I'm just going to have a hard time keeping my hands off you."

His sexy voice has me clenching my thighs as he whispers into my ear.

I take a deep breath before turning to him. "I don't think we should be seen making out in public."

He grabs a piece of my hair and twirls it between his fingers. "Mmm. Probably smart." His lips find my neck, then trail up to my ear. "Where are you staying?"

"Hotel de Paris."

He smiles against my neck. "Me too." He licks along my jawline. "We can go to your room."

He licks along my jawline and I squirm in my seat. "We can't," I say breathlessly.

His hand glides up my throat and cups my jaw, turning me to face him. "Your friends sharing a room?"

I nod.

"Good thing I am not sharing a room with anyone."

His lips find mine again and I moan against his as his hand glides down my side and under my ass. He smiles against my lips as a whimper falls out of my mouth.

"Let's go."

He stands and offers me his hand. I take it and stand up, adjusting my dress before grabbing my clutch. I watch his eyes as he devours me, seeing fully what I'm wearing for the first time tonight. He growls as his arm slides around my hip, pulling me into him.

He pulls me quickly through the VIP area and onto the crowded dance floor.

"Wait, I need to tell my friends—"

"Text them."

I see the hunger in his eyes and understand completely that there is no reason to delay what's coming.

He rushes through the front door, handing his ticket to the valet.

He turns me in his arms while we wait, my chest pressed firmly to his own. His hands sliding down my back until he grabs my ass in both his hands. "You're teasing me right now."

I smile into his shirt. "It's just a dress."

"More like a scrap of fabric meant to get the attention of every man in this town."

Before I can answer, the valet pulls up in a blacked-out Bugatti. Matías pulls away from me and hands the valet a tip before walking to the passenger door and opening it for me. I slide into the sleek, expensive car and take in the features. I can even smell the scent of Matías in here, is heady cologne mixing with the smell of leather.

He gets into the driver's seat and smirks at me. "Buckle up."

I do as he says and we fly out of the roundabout and onto the main road that takes us back to the hotel. The ride is silent and I begin to second-guess everything I am doing. This isn't me. I don't go home with strangers. I am the safe one, the responsible one. Yet here I am being reckless, all because a few kisses with one of the hottest guys I've ever seen have left me wanton.

I pinch my lips together tightly as I try to think of an excuse to go back to my room. Anything to keep myself from being careless. I know that Bianca would be cheering me on right now, telling me I am finally doing what she would do. But in the back of my brain, I have this weird inkling. Like something isn't right. Like this man is dangerous.

But all those thoughts quickly fade away as his hand lands on my thigh and he squeezes before slowly dragging his fingers up and down the inside of my leg. He makes it until he is inches from my wet, throbbing center, then runs his fingers back down to my knee. I know he can feel the heat between my thighs, feel how turned on I am without even touching me. I bite my lip as his fingers inch even closer.

When we get to a stoplight, he leans over and whispers in my ear. "Don't forget to text your friends."

The words snap me from the pleasure trance he was putting me in and I quickly open my clutch, entering in the passcode and shooting a text to Bianca. I can feel his eyes on me the whole time and it sends another burst of shivers down my spine.

A minute later, we are pulling up to the magnificent hotel. Matías jumps out of the car and I watch as he rounds the front to open the door for me. Maybe chivalry isn't dead, even though we were close as hell to fucking in the damn club.

I grab Matías's hand as he helps me out of the sports car and I watch as he tosses the keys to the valet. We waste no time walking through the lobby until we make it to the bank of elevators.

When the door opens, I step in first, Matías's hand on my lower back. An older couple steps in after us. Matías's hand drops to my ass as he pulls me against his side. The sexual tension between us so intense that I am sure the other couple can feel it in the air. He leans down into my ear and starts speaking to me again in the language he was speaking earlier. I have no idea what the words are that he is saying but I'm worried if we don't make it to his room soon, my arousal will start to leak down my legs.

When the elevator chimes for our floor, Matías is practically pulling me down the hall. He scans his key card and before the door even shuts behind me, he picks me up and slams me against the wall in the entrance to his suite. My legs wrap around his hips as I grind against him, while his mouth attacks me with hot, brutal kisses. I don't even know who I am. This man is doing something to me I never felt before and all I want is more.

His hands run up the bottoms of my thighs until his thumb finds the wetness in my core. I whimper at the feeling of his thumb. One light touch and I swear I am going to melt into the wall.

"Fuck," he mutters as he realizes I have no panties on and pulls back.

Disappointment etches my face. "Is there something wrong?"

He shakes his head. "I think we just need to slow down before I fuck you against this wall."

I blush at his directness and nod.

He slowly slides me down the wall and pulls my dress down until it's more decently covering me.

He runs his hands through his hair as he takes a step back and then another. "You do something to me, Alessia."

"You do something to me too."

He sighs deeply. "I think… I think I need a drink. Want one?"

Even though I already had two tonight, our wild make-out sessions have sobered me up. "Sure."

"Champagne?"

"That would be great."

He nods, and it almost looks like anger or pain flutter over his features. I barely know him, so I can't be sure. Maybe it's sexual frustration.

"I'm just going to use the restroom," I say to him. He nods and I head to the bedroom en suite.

I splash water in my face to try and cool down. I am so confused with myself. This is not the Alessia I know. This is a totally different girl and I am not sure if I like her. I quickly use the toilet and then head out to the living area. I see Matías on the balcony, looking out over the sea.

I step out behind him and he hands me a glass of champagne. I take a small sip before leaning against the railing.

"Sorry I got so carried away."

I giggle. "I think it went both ways."

He smiles at me before taking a sip of a dark liquid, maybe scotch or whiskey. "For some reason, I can't keep my hands off you. But fuck, you're gorgeous. And your lips taste like cherries."

I down a huge gulp of champagne at his words. I thought he was trying to mellow out the sexual tension but his words only make my body yearn for him.

We are both quiet for a few minutes. I finish my glass and he asks if I want another. I shake my head as a burst of fatigue hits me. Maybe the make-out sessions didn't sober me up as much as I thought.

I stumble, and he catches me. "Whoa there, are you okay?"

I nod. "Sorry, I just got dizzy for a second. I think I just need to sit down."

He doesn't say anything, just wraps an arm around my shoulder and directs me to the couch in the sitting area. I think he is going to sit next to me but he doesn't. My mind starts to fade in and out and I swear I hear him on the phone as he walks into the bedroom.

I close my eyes briefly when I hear the click of a door. I look up and think I see his friend but maybe it's just Matías. I swear there are two of him.

The sound of deep voices fades away as I close my eyes and slump over on the couch, letting sleep take me over.

6
ALESSIA

I cry as the dream overtakes me. The girl trying to crawl her way free. Except where before I was watching the girl. This time it's me. I feel the chains pulling me down as I sink deeper into something almost like quicksand. But when I look down, it's a pool of thick blood, so dark, it's almost black.

I scream as I try to break from the chains, the metal cutting into my wrists. That's when I notice the blood pouring from my wrists, like it's my own blood drowning me, holding me captive.

I stop struggling and start to sink into the pool. My waist, my chest, my neck. I take a deep breath before my head goes under.

I gasp for air and wake up screaming. I glance at my wrists and see them free of chains. I pull the sheets up around me as I fight the wet cold I felt in my dream. It feels like a weight is on my chest as I try to breathe, like I was really drowning in the blood.

When my breathing is finally calm and I can center my energy, I look down and don't recognize the blankets. My mind feels like pieces are missing, huge gaps of time I can't remember.

Blue eyes flash in my mind and I remember Monaco. My birthday. The hotel.

I start to panic again as I look around the room and realize it's not the hotel. I don't recognize the decor. There is a balcony off to the left but that view doesn't overlook the water. It overlooks green hills.

Fear creeps up my throat and I start clawing at it, thinking I am still in a dream. I scramble out of bed and run to the only door in the room besides the balcony. I pull on the knob and twist but it won't budge.

I bang across the door. "Help! Is there someone there?" I hear no sounds on the other side. Even after I bang on it for nearly ten minutes. I run to the balcony but find those doors locked too. Bolted together at the top. There are no other windows in the room. No other doors.

I run back to the door again and try pulling and twisting and turning. But to no avail. It won't budge. I start to bang again, begging for help, for anyone to hear me, but I am greeted with silence. It's then I decide to move on to the walls. Hoping someone on the other side can hear me. I bang until my arms give out and the tears are flowing freely down my face.

Where am I?

What happened?

I try to be logical. I try to piece together my night as

best I can. I remember sneaking out of the hotel with the girls. The red dress.

I look down and realize I am in a T-shirt I have never seen before and a pair of sleep shorts a few sizes too big, the string drawn tight around my waist. I don't remember changing. I look around the room and don't see my dress either. My throat dries out as I start to peel the clothes off me. Looking for signs of bruises, cuts, blood. But my body is clean. No one touched me.

I slide down the wall across from the lone bed in the room. A toilet sits in one corner with no sink. There is no other furniture in the room except for a small bedside table with a paper cup sitting on it.

My throat is dry from the screaming, and I crawl across the floor, hoping for water. I'm surprised to find the cup full. I bring it to my lips, but just before I taste it, a memory passes through, I can almost grab it, almost see it, but it's like a fog is lying over my mind. All I remember is a glass of champagne. I throw the cup across the room, scared of whatever is in the cup.

I crawl back to my spot in the corner of the room across from the bed as more tears fall down my face.

Think, Alessia, *think*.

But it's no use. My mind won't let me remember a thing. Only vague flashes of a club. A man. Laughing and dancing.

I pull my knees up to my chest and wrap the T-shirt over them like I am a child. I sink as far into the corner as I can. Fighting my shame and regret. I bite hard on my lip as I wipe tears from my eyes.

Think, Alessia, *think*.

I remember my birthday night. One too many cosmos. A silver dress. A booth. A man with blue eyes.

I gasp when the memory hits. I remember him. Matías. I remember the way he looked at me. The way he touched me. I remember telling him to meet me the next day. But I don't remember seeing him again. He never showed.

I lay my head on my knees as I force my brain to work. A headache forming in the front of my head as I try to recall anything. My eyes closing as the terror in front of me lives behind my eyes too.

Think, Alessa, *think.*

The sound of a phone ringing jolts my eyes open. I stay perfectly still, hoping to hear it or a person or anything. But it was only in my head.

A phone call. My father. The bodyguards. His warning.

I didn't listen to him. I didn't take him seriously. I lied about going out.

He has to be looking for me. I know he will be.

I'll be okay. I'll be okay.

I tell myself that over and over in my head as I watch the sky turn to twilight, then to darkness.

The tears that were running down my face turn into sobs as I realize I'm alone. Like the dream. In the dark. Cold and alone. Chained to one place and unable to break free.

I'm startled awake by the sound of a door. My eyes fly open but I don't move. Too scared to see who my captor is. My cheek is pressed into the cold tile floor where I must have fallen asleep. I glance toward the balcony and see the hint of morning light breaking across the room.

I glance at the door but find it closed. The sound that woke me must have been someone leaving.

I slowly push myself off the hard floor. My throat hoarse and tight. And my stomach growls as I sit up.

I don't know how long I have been here. Did I wake up the day after I was taken? Or did I sleep for days?

I grasp my head as the headache I had the last time I was awake comes back full force. I groan as I sit on my knees. How is it I feel worse than before?

I pull myself on shaky legs to my feet, resting my hands along the wall for support. I move slowly toward the door and find a tray with a glass of water and a croissant. I move quickly to the door and try the handle, finding it locked.

I scream and bang against it, but still no one answers. I know someone was just here. Just brought me this food. I give up on the door and my cries for help quicker than yesterday, knowing no one will come to my rescue.

I look down at the food and although my stomach rumbles, the fear it's drugged overtakes my need to eat. But I do drink the water this time. My parched throat in desperate need of hydration. I swallow the entire cup down, then curse myself for doing it as the need to vomit threatens my stomach.

I crawl onto the bed, lying across it on my side.

Hoping the position will calm my stomach and keep the water in me. I don't know when I will get more.

Eventually the nausea passes. And my headache slowly fades as I watch the light outside change from dawn to day. At some point, I move and close the heavy curtains to block the light before falling asleep once again.

The next time I wake up, I roll over and see a new glass of water and a new plate of food. I sip the water slowly this time. I move to the curtains and open them to find it's nighttime. I leave them open and sit on the floor, leaning against the glass. I can see a sliver of the sky from this angle. Bringing me a bit of peace. As much peace as one could ask for after being kidnapped.

The next two days, I follow the same pattern. I never see my captor. Never hear a sound other than my own breathing. I ignore the three meals they bring me and only drink the water. My stomach hurts from lack of food but the fear of what could happen to me if I eat keeps me from touching it.

Not eating helps me sleep. The lack of nutrients shutting my body down. And just when I am about to fall asleep, the sound of voices has me jolting up from the bed.

7

MATÍAS

"She hasn't eaten?" I stammer into the phone as I walk across the jetway to my private plane. Demont gives me a disappointed look before climbing up the steps to the jet.

"She's mostly been asleep. She refuses to eat but drinks the water. We were able to put tasteless nutrient tabs in there," Fiero tells me.

"Merda," I mutter into the phone as I take my seat on the plane. "I'll be there in a few hours."

Demont stares at me, and I force myself to look out the window.

"I didn't want this," I mutter to him as I stare off outside.

"I didn't say anything."

I groan as I rub my hands over my eyes. "Fuck," I yell even louder. My hands itching for a fight, anything to get this rage inside of me to go away.

I was told to kidnap her. Bring her to a safe house.

Those were my instructions. But I know The Partners don't play fair. They never have. My entire life has been one fucked-up mess since I got involved with them.

I contacted them after I dropped the girl off in the room. They said they would be in touch. The next day I got a callback from them telling me they would let me know when I was to let her go. I swore up a storm with them. Argued. Tried to fight against it. But it was no use. They wanted me to oversee her captivity.

It's not my job. It's not what I agreed to do for them. I agreed to interrogate. To maim. To kill.

But kidnapping someone who is innocent crossed a line for me.

"What are you going to do, boss?"

I glance up at Demont. "I don't have a choice. If I let her go, I'm as good as dead. Or worse."

He nods at me, and I go back to my thoughts. She was asleep for two days and then I got called away on business when there was an issue at the building site in Málaga. It's taken me three days to get back to France. And now I need to face her.

"What are you going to tell her when we get there?"

I snap my eyes back to Demont. "Act the part I always do."

"Even after that night?"

I clench my hand into a fist. "That was a game, Demont. That's not the man I am anymore."

I let the mask fall over me as we descend into the airport. The mask of a coldhearted man with no feeling, no remorse, no regrets. The mask of a killer.

I walk through the front door of the three *pièces* flat a half hour west of Saint Tropez. The guard inside the entry nods his head at me before I head up the stairs to the second floor. As I walk into the apartment, I see Fiero and a few of the other men who were sent to guard the girl playing a game of poker.

"Has she eaten?"

Ficro looks up at mc and shrugs, thcn turns back to the game. "Lastra is up there. But last I saw she still hadn't eaten a thing."

"When was that?"

He throws his cards on the table. "I fold." He stands up and walks over to me. "A few hours ago. Lastra took over watch at six."

I check my watch and see it's after ten. "Has she said anything?" I ask as I walk over to where the security monitors for the building are set up. She's lying on the bed, not moving.

"Not a word. We've only been in there when she's asleep. And that's all she does besides look out the window."

I study the screen and sigh before running my hand through my hair. Frustrated and annoyed over this damn situation. I shut the monitor off.

"What are you doing?" he asks as I walk back to the front door of the flat.

"Going to have a talk with her."

"Is… did they ask—"

"I don't give a fuck what their rules are." I slam the

door behind me as I climb the stairs to the third floor. My instructions were to feed her and hydrate her, but to leave her alone. I don't know what they plan on doing or what the game is they are playing but if she isn't eating, I'll do what I need to, to keep her alive.

I push through the door of the apartment we are keeping her in and see Lastra rise to his feet. "Anything?"

"No, she is still refusing to eat. I've checked on her when I know she's asleep, but she doesn't wake up. She hasn't spoken in days," he says quietly.

I walk into the kitchen and find a tray of food sitting there. "Her dinner?"

"Lunch. I haven't pulled her dinner tray yet. She only lay down half an hour ago."

I curse as I bang around in the kitchen and make her some toast and soup. If she hasn't eaten in days, she probably won't be able to keep a thing down.

"She won't eat it," he says to me as I grab a spoon out of a drawer. "And we were instructed no utensils or dishware."

I shoot him a stare that makes him freeze. "She weighs a hundred pounds. Even if she broke this bowl and tried to stab me with it, she would barely puncture the skin. She's like a wounded animal. There is no fight in her."

I grab the food and head down the hall.

"You are going to risk your identity?" he asks me as I walk down the hall to her room.

"Is there a choice?" I say to him, but don't turn around. I pull out the key I have and unlock the three deadbolts and open the door.

I take one step into the room and immediately I am attacked by her. She pushes against my chest with more force than I expect and the bowl clatters to the ground. She curses as hot soup hits her legs, which gives me enough time to slam the door behind me and press her against the wall by the throat.

Her eyes bug out and she tries to claw at my hands. But I grip both of her wrists and slam them against the wall above her head. I push my hips into hers to immobilize her legs and tighten my grip on her throat. Her eyes closing tight as I cut off her breath.

"I would be careful what you do, Alessia." Her eyes snap open at the sound of my voice and I see her brow crease in confusion. "You wouldn't want to upset the wrong people."

I see the panic forming in her eyes as I speak.

"Now are you going to be a good girl if I let you go?"

I swear she snarls at me.

"Because I could easily say you had an accident." I apply more pressure to her throat as I say it.

She gasps for breath and I swear I hear the word asshole on her breath.

I tighten the grip on her wrists as I let go of her throat.

"Let me go, you arrogant bast—"

She shuts up as I pull the switchblade out of my pocket and press it to her throat. "What was that, angel? Were you going to call me a bastard? Because I have news for you, I already know that."

She stays still as I press the blade more firmly against her neck.

"I remember you," she mumbles. "I remember your eyes."

I smile at her, the one that brings women to their knees. "And what was your favorite part, angel?"

"Fuck you."

I laugh as she says it, running my nose along her jawline and up to her ear. "That never happened, sweetheart. But I know you wanted it. I remember how wet you were. I can still feel you on my fingers when I think about it."

She fights against me and I press my hips farther into hers. Telling my dick to stay down because this game I'm playing is too much of a turn-on. I click my tongue against my teeth. "I'd be careful, angel, wouldn't want you to accidentally slice your throat. And I'm wearing white. I don't particularly like getting blood on my white clothes."

"You aren't the man I met," she huffs as she stops fighting.

"And you aren't the woman I met either. That one was docile. But I do have to say I much rather like this one. The fight in you is an even bigger turn-on."

"Fuck you," she growls as she pushes against my hips with her own.

"I'm sure we could arrange that." This time I shift my hips against hers so she can feel the semi growing in my pants.

"You're sick."

"Mmm, I've been called worse." My mouth is to her ear before I pull back and lick her cheek. "Much worse."

She tries to turn her face away from me, the pressure

of the knife keeps her restrained. Fear builds in her eyes like I wanted. I laugh as I pull the knife away from her neck. "Now, are you going to behave or do I need to keep you pressed against this wall?"

She whimpers as she looks down, her hair falling in her face. I use the knife to lift her hair up. "I'm sorry, I didn't hear you."

"I'll behave," she whispers.

"Good girl."

I take a step away from her, her arms still trapped by my hand and see if she tries anything but she remains calm, her head still hanging down. I slowly release her hands and let her arms drop. She grabs her wrists and starts rubbing them.

"You should eat," I tell her as I move across the room and fold my arms over my chest.

She looks up at me, her eyes laced with a deadly combination of anger and fear. She swallows before pushing her hair behind her ears. She looks at the door, then back at me, before focusing on the door again.

"I wouldn't try it if I were you."

She looks back at me, a fierceness in her eyes I didn't expect. "Why would a billionaire be kidnapping people?"

"I'm not sure what you mean."

"Why would a Montford kidnap someone?" she says through her teeth.

I raise a brow at her. "You know who I am?"

She nods.

I ignore her question and ask another. "Why would someone ask for their daughter to be kidnapped?"

Her eyes snap up at me. "What did you say?"

I give her a sinister smile and head over to the locked balcony doors. I pull the key out of my pocket and undo the locks that keep it bolted shut. "Beautiful night tonight. Warm salty breeze. Almost tastes like freedom."

I hear her feet pattering across the floor as I grin at the hillside view.

"You bastard. Why did you do this? Why are you keeping me locked up? Let me go. Let me go!" she screams as her fists bang across my back. It doesn't hurt. I've felt far worse. I give in to her and let go of the doors I am holding open. She stops hitting me and pushes past me to the small balcony. She looks over the side, her shoulders slumping when she realizes there is no way out from here.

"Did you think that screaming would change a thing?" I ask as I take in the view. Nothing spectacular but the fact we are in the middle of nowhere. No one for kilometers around us.

"What about my father?" she asks with a clenched jaw.

"Hmm. Was I saying something?" I see murder in her eyes as I speak. I laugh. "Oh yes. Your father is not a good man."

"You lie. He is a good man. He's always taken care of me. He would never do this."

"Maybe you don't know your father as well as you think." She frowns at my words, her face falling as if she is remembering something. "Not everyone is as they seem."

She looks up at me, the anger I saw earlier prevalent in her whole body. "Like you?"

"Precisely."

She lunges for me but I scoop her up, pulling her legs around my waist as I bring her back inside and push her back against a wall. I press my dick against her center. Because arguing is my favorite type of foreplay and my dick is hard as steel.

"Why are you doing this?"

I shrug as I take her in. My jaw clenching as I see her beauty even through the layer of filth covering her. Those smoldering almond-shaped eyes, the slight dusting of freckles over her nose and cheeks, the plump rosy lips that have me fighting control.

"Did you even want me or was all that a game too?"

I smirk at her. "I just want control."

"You're a monster," she says as she tries to fight against me.

"Ding ding ding. You finally got it right."

"What's wrong with you?"

I press my nose into her hair, the woman in desperate need of a shower. "Oh, angel, you should be asking yourself what's wrong with you. Because if I remember correctly, this monster had you so close to an orgasm you were practically begging for my dick."

She slaps me across the face. I smile at her. "Bad move, sweetheart."

"I hate you."

"Welcome to my world."

She looks at me strangely and I hide my features, trying not to give away the truth in my words. That I hate myself more than she hates me.

"You need to eat. Daddy dearest wouldn't want you to starve."

"I won't touch that food."

"I'll have someone force-feed you," I growl.

"It's drugged. Just like you drugged me."

I bring my lips to within inches of hers. "Now why would I do that, angel. I've already got you where I want you."

"Stop calling me that!"

I give her my deadly grin before slamming my lips to hers. She fights like hell against me. Her nails clawing at my chest and face. But I just keep my lips on hers, the monster inside of me enjoying the tastes of her lips, her resistance.

I go to pull away but she bites hard on my lip. The metallic taste of blood hitting my tongue. I only smile at her as I drop her legs to the ground.

"Eat," I say as I walk to the door.

"No."

"Then next time I come, I'll make sure that door stays locked." I gesture toward the balcony I didn't shut.

I open the door to her room as she stares at the balcony doors and I slip out before she notices. As I slip the locks in place, she starts banging on the door but I just walk away.

"Bring her more food and clean up the mess inside," I tell Lastra as I walk out the door.

My soul aching at what I just did.

8
MATÍAS

I sit on my deck and stare out at the pool before me. A warm bourbon sitting in my hand, untouched. The last seven years of my life filtering through my head. The mistakes I made that landed me here. My drug addiction, my need for power, my failures.

I am not a good man. Alessia called me a monster yesterday, and she wasn't wrong. I am a monster. I've turned into a man I never thought I would be. I didn't grow up thinking this would be my life. I spent my summers as a kid in Mallorca with my brothers. They were older than me and all I wanted was to be like them. But the men they were in Mallorca were not the men they were at home in England. I vowed not to become the hardened men they were in London and lived a careless lifestyle. One that eventually led to addiction and failure.

But I was tempted with forbidden fruit. A man I didn't know came to me while I was still at Cambridge and asked if I wanted the power my brothers had. My jealousy took over. Of course, I wanted the power they seemed to embody. But I didn't bite right away. Something didn't seem right. I didn't talk to the man again. I went to work for my brothers at Montford Holdings. Then I was sitting at a pub one day and Kilian Bancroft sat next to me. He tempted me like the other man did but I trusted Kilian, he was a good friend of my brothers.

I remember walking into a meeting with Kilian, the man that approached me a year before sitting at a table. I felt so unsure of what I was doing at that point. It all sounded too good to be true. Helping out with minor crimes, filtering money in and out of Montford Holdings so quickly it wouldn't even be noticed. Then Thiago walked into the room. The disappointment written over his face. I didn't know at the time that he and Bastian were trying to get out of The Partners' hold after being involved with them for ten years.

After the meeting, Thiago brought me back to his penthouse. He was livid. He actually punched me in the face. We argued for hours. He told me to choose, decide if I wanted to be a part of the organization. He said there wasn't much more he could do. He just hoped that what he told me resonated inside my head and I would make the right decision.

He and Bastian offered me a position as CEO of the hotel group a week later. I knew Thiago did it in hopes I wouldn't join. That I would stay on the right side of the law. But I was too tempted by it all. Thiago fought like hell against them, trying to make them not accept me.

He died two months later by their hands. But I still hold all the guilt, knowing it was my fault.

I let that guilt eat away at me for a year, every day I worked in our offices in Saint Tropez while we built the first hotel. I was given the hotel project to stay out of the criminal world. That's when I snapped. The realization that the power my brothers held came from a crime syndicate that they were involved with rather than their actual business savvy. I made contact with The Partners after that, became obsessed with the power as I let the guilt gnaw away at everything inside of me. The drugs helped quiet the guilt until it was too late.

I fucked up. I owed them money but refused to pay, thinking I had more control and power over them. But I was just a lowly pawn on their chessboard. They framed me, put me in jail. It took me too long to realize it was all on purpose. They wanted Bastian back in their reins.

Then they let me go. At the time I was released from prison, I didn't know it was because they had Bastian back in their clutches. But I had been stabbed in the yard one day, turns out it was to lure my brother back into their hands.

After I was released, they told me they would let my brother go from the torture they were putting him through if I brought them someone. A woman named Cameron Wilder. I thought she was a reporter that dug too deep into the organization but then realized she worked for Bastian as a PR consultant. It was an easy decision for me. Some woman I didn't even know. All I had to do was deliver her to them and me and Bastian would both be free.

I followed her for days until I had the opportunity to intercept her at a restaurant. But as I spoke with her, I saw that look in her eye. She was in love with my brother. And I refused to hurt him again. I already led him into a trap to get him back in with The Partners. I couldn't take her too.

But now, as I look at the blood on my hands, the remorse and regret I feel, maybe I should have done it. Gave Cam to them. Maybe I wouldn't be the killer I am today.

I drink down the entire glass of bourbon at those thoughts. Weak thoughts from a weak man. I barely know Cam but I know that I have never seen my brother happier. I could never have taken her from him.

I drop my elbows to my knees and lean over in my chair. Who is this man I've become? What happened to the man I used to be?

I run my hands through my hair, then pull out my phone. "Tonight?" I ask the man on the other end. He mumbles off an address and I move quickly through my house and get ready for the warehouse.

I spit out blood as a right hook nearly cracks my jaw. I duck before the next punch comes and slam my fist into the beast of a man's stomach.

Booing comes from around the ring as I give a quick uppercut and then a side punch, causing the man to fall against the ropes. He shakes his head out, then pushes up and lunges for me. I block a few punches but he surprises me with a cross punch I didn't see coming, then follows it with a sharp hook into my side I didn't anticipate. I stumble a few feet and he takes the opportunity to hit me with an uppercut, then a jab under my left eye. He gets in three more punches and I fall into the ropes. The crowd cheering around us. My vision is spotty as I try to focus on the man in front of me I now see two of.

"Done yet?" he asks.

I smile a bloody smile at him. "Not even close."

He chuckles as I say it. I take that second to swing at him but I completely miss as I stumble on my feet. I get hit with another hook and fall to the ground. Blood drips into my eye and I feel nausea start to overwhelm me. Before I can find something to focus on to clear my head, the man sucker punches me with a jab to the face, my head bouncing off the floor. I pinch my eyes shut as the pain reverberates through me. Then feel a sharp kick to my gut, causing me to cough up blood.

I wait on bated breath for another punch but a man picks me up from my shoulders, setting me down on unsteady feet.

"You weren't ready for this fight, Matías."

"I needed it."

He shakes his head at me. "When will you ever learn?"

I look at Bernardo, the man I always call when I need a fight, need a release. "Not anytime soon."

"Let's get you out of here."

We start to move but the guy I was fighting shouts, "We weren't done."

Bernardo turns to him. "You were done."

"That's not fair. You know I get paid more for a KO."

"And I handle the money. You'll get what you deserve."

His words are harsh as he pulls me between the ropes and out of the ring. I barely remember getting to his office as I collapse onto the beat-up leather sofa.

"How much did you drink before you came here?" he asks me as he hands me a wet towel and a pack of ice.

I try to glare at him but my eye is swelling fast. I know it was stupid for me to come. I shouldn't have. Not after I drank those two glasses of bourbon. But the thoughts churning in my brain wouldn't quiet down from the alcohol. It only made it worse.

So I came here for my repentance. To feel physical pain, to make up for all the pain I've caused every person I know. It's the only way I feel anything anymore.

"I know I shouldn't intrude, Matías. It's not really my place. But I think you should get help. See a therapist. Fighting isn't therapy."

I groan as I roll onto my back, the pain slicing through my ribs with the movement. I hold the bag of ice up to my eye and sigh. "Therapy isn't going to fix me, Bernardo. Trust me, I've tried."

He pulls a chair across the room and sits in front of me. "Not enough."

I try to sit up but he pushes me down. "Just let me do this. Let me fight. Let me feel something."

He sighs, almost like a sigh of parental disappointment. The man is reaching his midsixties and I have no idea why he keeps up the illegal fight rings. He's made enough money. He should be living on a beach somewhere.

"I worry about you, Matías." I feel the harsh burn of alcohol on my forehead as he tries to clean up my cuts. Yet another strange thing about him. I'm the only one he cares for after a fight. The only one he takes care of. "You've been different the last few years. More aggressive but you lack emotion. Almost like you feel like you deserve every hit."

"Maybe I do."

He applies bandages to the cut above my eye. "Look, I know you hate my advice. But you need to realize something. All that shit that happened to you two years ago, the false accusations against you and your brother, you need to let it go. It was taken care of. Interpol publicly apologized for wrongdoings when it came to your family. You need to move on. Letting that shit build up inside of you is just going to destroy you."

I sit up at his words, letting the pain flood my body at the movement. He has no idea what really happened two years ago. No one does. Except for those involved. "If only my family felt the same way," I mutter under my breath.

"Your father is a good man. He forgives you."

"Then he should tell me to my face," I hiss as I stand.

Bernardo gets up and attempts to support me but I push him away. "Anger and guilt will get you nowhere."

"It's gotten me this far. And I'm doing just fine." I look up and see Demont standing in the office doorway. I pull on the T-shirt I came in but took off for the fight, wincing as I do it.

Bernardo releases a deep sigh from his chest. "Take care of yourself, Matías. Think about what I said."

I don't say anything as I walk past Demont. We exit through a back hallway so the crowd won't see me. They love when I get the shit beat out of me. And I don't give in to them when I leave, the pleasure they would find with me walking out bruised and broken. Sometimes with Demont helping me walk. I could win if I wanted to. But that is a secret I keep well-guarded. I don't try to win. I never have. Maybe Bernardo knows it. I train with him some days. He knows what I'm capable of. But he keeps his mouth shut every night.

I wince as I pull open the door to the warehouse and another wave of nausea comes over me.

"You okay, boss?" Demont asks.

I nod. "Yeah."

"You took a bad hit to the stomach. You want me to call the doctor?"

I shake my head. "I'll be fine. Fucking pussy kick. Asshole knew I was down and not getting back up."

"Bruno always has it out for you."

"Maybe one day I'll actually take him down." I laugh but regret it immediately as the pain in my ribs becomes unbearable and I start coughing.

Demont holds open the back door of the SUV. "Maybe one day you'll actually fight back."

He knows I hold back, he's sparred with me, he knows what I'm capable of just as much as Bernardo.

He shuts the door behind me and climbs into the driver's seat. I stare out the window as we drive the winding road back to Saint Tropez.

"Stop," I tell him. "Turn around. Head to the safe house."

"Sir, I don't think—"

"I wasn't asking for your opinion."

He doesn't say a word. He turns the car around and heads toward where Alessia is being held. I clench my fist and accept the pain as the broken skin on my knuckles starts to bleed again. I finally look down at myself. Blood drips from my face onto the T-shirt. My hands are marred and red, the scars from previous fights covered by the new cuts. I touch my face and feel the bump swelling under my eye. I know within a few hours I won't be able to see out of it. I don't want to look at my face in the mirror. I don't want to see the evidence of what I've done to rid myself of my shame. Because in all honesty, this is more shameful. A man so broken he lets others break his body, so he can feel anything.

I pull out of my thoughts as we arrive at the safe house. It's tucked away in a small village. A four-story building that once was a single-family villa on a small amount of farmland. Now it's divided into four separate apartments. A larger main house sits near the road and a few smaller buildings are scattered on the property for farm work. It's remote enough that the neighbors are far away.

I open the door and climb out of the SUV. The guards on the first floor giving me strange looks as I walk inside. The climb up the stairs is brutal, my muscles aching with every step. By the time I make it up to the third floor, I need to lean against the wall, my breathing uneven and strangled as I close my eyes.

"Here." I open my eyes to Demont handing me a water bottle. "I'm going to have the doctor waiting at your house in an hour. You're pale, Matías. You need medical attention."

He's right. My body is aching in a way it never has. "Tell him midnight."

Demont nods. "I'll be in the car."

It's just after ten and I want to spend time here. I don't want to be in and out. I don't even know why. Maybe I want to talk with Alessia. Not that she will speak to me. Not after the way I treated her. But we have a connection. I felt it the first time I touched her in Monaco. A slight brush of my fingers along her shoulder and it felt like I knew her for years.

I see Fiero sitting in the living room when I walk in. He gives me the same look the others gave me and I know I must look as bad as I feel. "She eat?"

He nods. "She wouldn't touch anything last night. But ate some toast this morning. And some dinner tonight."

"Good," I mutter. "She asleep?"

"Yes." He raises a brow at me. "You okay? You look like you're going to pass out."

I ignore him, grab a chair, and walk down the hall to her room. I forget that I don't have the key with me. My energy is waning and I don't want to walk back down the hall. Luckily, I turn around and find Fiero behind me.

"Need the key?"

I nod and he hands it to me.

I try to enter as quietly as I can, carrying the chair in with me. I shut the door, the lock clicking into place. I step quietly across the floor and set the chair in the corner of the room. I slump into it and watch her as she sleeps. The balcony doors are still open, bringing in a light cool breeze across the room. The moonlight shines across her face and even through everything she's been through in the last five days, she's still beautiful.

I close my eyes as I remember that night. The way she fell asleep so easily after she drank the champagne I drugged. I watched her for a while before I called for Demont. Her breaths even like she was having a pleasant dream. Too bad she would wake up to a nightmare.

I was careful with her. I removed her clothing so no one else had to do it. For some reason, I feel like she would rather have had me do it than anyone else. I remember the feeling of her soft skin under my hands as I pulled the dress over her head. I tried to be a gentleman and keep my eyes off her naked form but it was hard. The woman is a goddess. I pulled one of my T-shirts onto her body and a pair of shorts Demont had picked up at the store. The shorts came with a sleep shirt but I wanted to see her in my clothes. I wonder if she knows it's mine.

Demont then placed her under the room service cart and wheeled her out of the building. He brought her here while I stayed an extra day in Monaco. We paid a girl that resembled her to be seen talking to me in the hotel lobby, kissing me goodbye before I left.

I open my eyes and watch her. It was so easy to take her. An unfamiliar ache hitting my chest at the thought. I shouldn't have kissed her, shouldn't have seduced her. I'm charming as hell and can use my smile on anyone, hell, that was part of the plan. I just didn't think I would feel something for the girl in the process. Maybe I should have just fucked her and gotten it over with. Then maybe I wouldn't have the regret I have now. Would think of her as just another target.

Instead, I need to fucking look at her every time I come to the safe house and remember what those lips tasted like. How that pussy felt as I teased it for a brief second. Fuck, this woman gives me a hard-on just thinking about her. Yet I have her locked up like a damn prisoner. Maybe that's my connection to her. We are both prisoners. I'm imprisoned in my own mind, fighting a battle with myself for a freedom I'll never have. And I'm the monster taking her freedom away from her.

"What happened to you?" she whispers.

I look up to find her eyes on me, studying me. I don't say anything and just stare right back at her.

"You're bleeding."

At first I think she is talking about the dried blood on my hands. But then I feel the warm drops hit my swollen eye and cheek. I bring my hand up to the cut above my eye and find the butterfly bandages are not keeping the wound closed. I use my shirt to wipe away the blood. But I don't say anything to her. What could I possibly say? I'm sitting in the room I have her locked up in, thinking about her body, the way it felt, the way I want to feel more of it, taste more of it. I truly am a monster.

She shivers as a strong breeze floats across the room. I stand up, moving slowly toward the bed. She winces as my hands move toward her and it just reinforces the fact

I'm a monster. I pull up her blankets, her eyes wide as I do it.

Then I lean over and kiss her forehead. I think she is going to hit me but she stays frozen as my lips caress her skin. I walk out of the room without a word.

I'm silent as we drive home. When we get to my house, Demont tells me the doctor is waiting for me in the study.

He starts to walk toward the guesthouse he lives in but I stop him. "I think I need to go to Scotland."

"Tomorrow?"

I nod.

"Ainslie isn't going to be happy with your face. Not to mention with the kids around."

"I know." I look toward the house where the doctor is waiting for me. "Demont?"

"Yeah, boss?"

"Stay here. I want to go to Scotland alone."

"Okay."

"Take watch over of Alessia. Give her more freedom. Let her have the apartment. As long as someone is always around. She needs a shower. She needs…" My words fade out because I don't know what she needs other than to go home. But it's my life on the line if I let her go.

"Got it, boss." He walks toward his house as I turn to head into mine.

I really hope the fresh air in Scotland will clear my mind.

9
ALESSIA

I wake up with aching bones. My body in desperate need of nutrients. I push the covers back and flashbacks of Matías sitting in the room hit me when I see the chair in the corner. I thought maybe it was a dream. Why would he come visit me, then just sit there and watch me? He looked like he had been beaten up pretty good. But it didn't seem to faze him. I saw the dried blood on his knuckles too. I also didn't miss the ghost in his eyes. Who is Matías Montford? He isn't the man whose image had been strewn across the gossip magazines years ago.

A shiver goes down my spine as I remember his lips pressing to my forehead. I nearly want to vomit at the memory it brings back. The way his lips felt on my skin in Monaco. The way he touched me, illicit feelings I never felt before.

I get up to use the toilet to vomit when I notice the door to my room is open. Within seconds, I am out of bed and through the door, running down the hallway, looking for a way to escape.

But my feet come to a halt when I see a familiar man sitting in a recliner reading a newspaper.

"Good morning," he says with a smile and a thick French accent. "Want some breakfast? Coffee?"

I feel like I am in the twilight zone. What the hell is going on?

He must be able to tell I am in shock. "Matías requested you receive more freedom."

I swallow, my voice cracking as I speak. "Wh-what do you mean more freedom?"

The man folds his newspaper and stands up. Memories flashing through my mind. I don't remember him being so tall. He's a few inches taller than Matías. And Matías has over a foot on me. Thoughts of escape fade away as I take in the beast in front of me. He is huge, solid. No doubt the man can bench press over three hundred pounds. His shaved head makes him look scary but his sapphire eyes are soft as they look at me.

"Mr. Montford said you have freedom to use the entire apartment."

I look toward the door that I think is the front door.

"Not that much freedom, Ms. Calvetti." He has a kind smile as he says it and I am taken aback by it. "There is a larger balcony off the kitchen. Plenty of food in the kitchen. A bathroom with a shower down the hall. Mr. Montford said you could use a shower."

I snort. "I'm sure he did."

"If you need anything, just ask."

I bite my lip as I watch him sit back down in the chair and grab the newspaper. "Why?"

He glances up at me. "Excuse me?"

"Why is he doing this?"

"I'm afraid I can't tell—"

I shake my head. "I mean this." I gesture around me. "The freedom."

"Mat—Mr. Montford didn't say." He studies me as I pull on my shirt, twisting it in my hands. "But he has a good heart. He doesn't show it to many people. I wouldn't question his actions and be happy he gave you this."

I keep back my retort and turn to look for the bathroom. The Matías I saw two nights ago did not have a kind heart as he held a knife to my throat. Or as he assaulted me with those lips. I smile as I think about how I bit down so hard on his lips I tasted his blood on my own.

I find the door to the bathroom and shut it behind me. A sigh of relief leaving my body as I slump against the door. I shouldn't feel relieved, but just being able to walk around the house makes me feel slightly better.

I look around the bathroom and find it has no windows. Not that I think I could get past that man in the living room. I look on the counter and find a handful of toiletries. Nothing special, but any kind of soap and shampoo sounds amazing. A fluffy robe hangs next to the shower. I run my fingers down it and realize I have nothing to change into.

A knock on the door causes me to jump but the gruff voice of the man actually soothes me. "Ms. Calvetti, I forgot to bring clothes in for you. I have some here if you don't mind opening the door."

I push the panic down of being in this tiny bathroom with such a large man, remembering nothing happened to me over the last five days. I crack open the door and he hands me a pile of clothes. "Thank you."

He nods and walks away. I shut the door and secure the lock just to be safe. I set the clothes on the counter and find a pair of lounge pants, a shirt, as well as a bra and underwear. I turn the water to scalding and let it heat up as I undress. I take in my body. Looking for bruises but I don't see any. No marks, no cuts. My ribs poke out a bit, my stomach growling as I run my fingers down them.

I grab the things I need for the shower off the counter and slide into the scalding heat, letting it wash away whatever happened to me. Not that it can do much, I am still being held against my will. Maybe I can find a way to escape. Although I don't think Matías would have given me freedom if there was a way out of here.

My mind goes back to that kiss last night. It was tender, sweet. Not the man that had me pinned against the wall with his hands around my throat. But that night, he also left the balcony door open for me. A taste of freedom I hadn't had since I woke up in that room. I don't understand him at all. Is this all a game to him? What is with the hot and cold?

I soap up my body, trying to push Matías out of my mind, but I can't. He is a mystery. And I don't know which side of him is the real one. Maybe they all are. I want so many answers. I just don't know if I will ever get them. I guess it depends on the version of Matías I get. The quiet one from last night, the flirty and teasing one from Monaco, or the rough, intense, dominant man from two nights ago. Each one different, each one with weaknesses. I just need to figure out what they are.

I stay in the shower until the water runs cold, thoughts clouding my mind.

When I exit the bathroom, the smell of bacon and syrup infiltrates my nose. I pad barefoot across the hall and into the kitchen to find the man flipping pancakes on a griddle. Over on the small kitchenette, I see a bowl of fresh berries, a cup of coffee, and bacon. My stomach growls again, even louder than before.

The man chuckles. "Go help yourself. But eat slow since I've been told you haven't eaten much."

I freeze before I go to the table. "What do you mean, you've been told? Haven't you been here the whole time?"

He shakes his head as he places pancakes onto a plate. "No, miss. But Mr. Montford has me watching over you now."

"Who was here before?"

"Someone else."

"Matías?"

"Go take a seat."

I know I won't get answers from him so I walk over to the table and shove a handful of berries into my mouth. I pour a glass of water from a pitcher and swallow the whole thing down. The man brings me over a plate of pancakes and then sits across from me with a plate of his own. I grab a slice of bacon and nearly swallow the thing whole. I had no idea how hungry I was. I drown my pancakes in syrup and shovel a forkful into my mouth. I groan at the flavor. God, I missed food.

The man laughs as I annihilate my plate. "So much for eating slow."

I wipe my mouth with a napkin. "I remember you."

He doesn't say anything as he sips his coffee, then bites into his breakfast.

"You were at the club. The night I met Matías."

He sets his fork down. "I was."

"Was he going to take me that night?"

He sighs and rests his elbows on the table. "Would it have made a difference?"

I purse my lips as I think about it. "I guess not."

"Ms. Calvetti, I'm sorry for what has hap—"

I hold up my hand to stop him. "Please don't tell me you're sorry. If you meant it, we wouldn't be here."

He nods.

"I don't remember your name."

"Demont."

I nod as the memory comes back to me. "You work for Matías. Are you his bodyguard?"

"More or less."

"Then if you are here, where is he?"

He sips his coffee before answering me. "He had business to attend to."

"Without his bodyguard?"

"He doesn't always need me around."

I think of his bloody face from last night. "Because he can take care of business himself. Fight for himself."

"I'm more of his driver."

"You're his bitch then."

He starts choking on his food when I say it. "Uh, no Ms. Calvetti. I'm not. But I assure you Mr. Montford can take care of himself."

I finish my pancakes and grab another slice of bacon off the plate. Contemplating things as I chew. "You know my family and friends are probably looking for me." I probe him.

He eats his breakfast but doesn't say a word. Just stares at me as he chews.

I shove another piece of bacon into my mouth. "I wouldn't have just disappeared. My friends are probably freaking out. I never came back to my room. My dad would definitely have people looking for me. And I am sure my brothers are too."

He says nothing, just goes about eating.

"It has to be all over the news."

"It's not."

I smile in victory, glad I got him to talk. And clueing me in more on what happened. "So it's not headline news that the daughter of a millionaire is missing?"

He pierces me with his blue eyes, the kindness in them gone. Yet he says nothing.

"Matías made it sound like my father did this." I hope my words will startle him.

They don't.

"And when did he tell you this?"

"When he had his hands around my throat," I snap.

He nods his head.

"That's it? You have nothing to say? I just said one of the richest people in the world had their hands around my throat. A man that kidnapped me. A kidnapping that doesn't seem to be on the news! Like no one cares!"

"Maybe no one does care," he says with venom in his words.

It shocks me. The tone of his voice nothing like how he acted earlier. I'm at a loss for words. Instead of finding something to fight back with, I just stand from my chair and go back to my room.

I curl up on the bed. Suddenly tired. I stare out the open balcony windows until I drift to sleep.

It's been two days since I was given 'freedom.' I don't know if you can actually call it that, since I am still a captive. But instead of being in a twelve-square-meter room, I now have an apartment to wander around. Not that there is much to do. There are a handful of books but they are all in French but I am not fluent enough to read them.

The one thing I have been able to do is gain Demont's trust a bit more. I only hope it will lead to the opportunity for me to escape. I even told him yesterday to stop calling me Ms. Calvetti and to call me Alessia. I also learned from him two days ago that he sucks at poker. Not that it's much fun with only two people. But it keeps me entertained.

And that's where I am now. Another game of poker. "Maybe we should invite the other guards to come up and play."

Demont raises a brow at me. "No."

"Oh come on. Why not?"

He doesn't say anything and just goes back to his cards. I learned yesterday there are more people in the building. I should have known. But it's only going to make my escape attempt that much harder.

"Are you ever going to tell me what my father has to do with this?"

He sighs and drops his cards to the table. I've asked him a hundred times in the last two days but he never says anything. But he also doesn't deny what I'm saying so I know there must have been some truth in Matías's words the other night.

"He wanted you under protection," he says quietly.

I'm shocked he actually answered me. "From who?" I ask.

"We don't ask questions."

"But why kidnap me?"

He looks at me with a smile on his face. "Would you have gone willingly?"

I think back to all the warnings from my father over the last few months that I've brushed off. The defiance I had in going to Monaco for my birthday when he begged me not to go. How he told me not to go out in Positano. To stay home all the time. At one point, he wanted me to go to his estate in Naples, my childhood home, but I hate feeling like I am constantly under watch, even if he isn't there. One of my brothers would be there or the men that watch the property. I guess you could call them bodyguards. Though I never understood why he needed them. He's just a businessman.

I look at Demont. "No."

"And that's why."

I frown at him, then go back to my cards. I can tell by the way he said it that he isn't going to tell me anything else.

I win three hands in a row and start yawning.

"Maybe you should go to bed," Demont says to me as he shuffles the cards.

I shrug. "I'm just bored."

"Want to play a different game?"

"Like what?"

He looks to the front door. "I think there may be some board games downstairs."

My ears perk up at that. "Please, for the love of God, anything besides more card games."

He smiles at me. "Can I trust you to not do anything stupid if I run down there?"

"You mean like jump off a three-story balcony? I haven't done it yet."

He rolls his eyes at me and I can't help but laugh. Despite being a prisoner in this two-bedroom apartment, I actually like spending my time with Demont. He may look scary as hell with his shaved head and tattoos and beast of a body but he makes me feel safe.

"Be right back."

I watch him as he walks out the front door. I listen for the click of the lock, then scramble out of my chair. I run to the kitchen balcony because it really could be my only chance of escape. I've already looked over the one in my room and there is nothing below it. I lean over the balcony and see another below me but I know that is where the other guards are, so that won't work. I look to the right and notice a lattice wall covered in ivy. Cliché, but useful. I lean over the side of the balcony as far as I can, but can barely reach the wall.

I grab a chair from the table and set it against the rail. My hands start to sweat as I stand on the chair and lean over, trying not to look down at the rocks below, which will lead to death, or at least a very broken body. I am able to grasp the lattice and find it semi sturdy. I don't know if it will support my weight. But it's worth trying.

I slowly pull myself back toward the balcony. Just as I put the chair back where I found it, I hear the click of the front door.

Heavy steps stomp down the hallway until they stop in the doorway to the kitchen. I dump chips into a bowl and pour myself a glass of lemonade.

"Want one?" I ask Demont.

I can tell from the look on his face he thought I tried to escape. But I'm not that stupid. I can't do it the first time I'm left alone. I need to wait until he trusts me more. Because right now I don't trust him enough to leave me alone for more than a few minutes.

"Sure."

I hand him the bowl of chips and pour another glass, then follow him into the living room. "So what did you bring to play?"

It's been two days since I found a way to escape. Demont has left me alone again, but only for a minute or two and I always hear him on the other side of the door on the phone. I even checked to see what happens when he is sleeping in the other bedroom. But I found a guard in the living room at night.

At least we've had more exciting game nights. Board games make the time go by much faster than card games. I even learned a few things about Demont. He grew up in Northern France, he's worked for Matías for seven years, and he hates broccoli. Maybe it's not much, but it's better than nothing. I can't stand the silence and I need someone to talk to. Maybe it helps me feel less like a hostage and more like a person under protection. But I still don't know what to think.

I haven't seen Matías since Demont got here four days ago. Which means I have been here for nine days. Nine days! How could no one be looking for me? Demont still won't say a word to me about it. I asked him if I could talk to my father since it was apparently his idea to do this. But I was told I would have to talk to Matías about it. Too bad he seems to have disappeared.

We are in an intense game of Monopoly when Demont's phone rings. His brows scrunch together as he looks at the phone and excuses himself outside. I sit in my chair and wait patiently for him to come back but this call is longer than the others. I look at the clock on the wall and see it's been five minutes.

I get out of my chair and tiptoe over to the door. His voice loud as he yells at someone on the other end of the line. I cross my fingers this argument lasts a little longer.

I run across the apartment to the kitchen balcony. I drag the chair to the railing and stand on it. I look down just once to the rocks thirty feet below me. I send a quiet prayer to the heavens that my plan works. I lean over the railing, my hands and feet both sweaty as I do it. My fingers grasp onto the lattice and I slowly step up onto the railing. I lean over even more so my other hand can reach my ladder to freedom. I close my eyes, ready to let go and hope the woodwork will hold me, when I feel a pair of thick arms wrap around my waist and pull me back onto the balcony.

"Where do you think you're going?" Demont's voice is filled with ice.

I struggle against him but it's no use. This man has over a hundred and fifty pounds on me.

"I trusted you," he says into my ear as he walks me into the kitchen and down the hall. "All you had to do was behave and now look what I have to do."

I kick and scream as he carries me into my room and throws me on the bed. Fear washes over me, thinking the worst. But nothing happens. He doesn't come near me. He walks to the balcony doors and shuts them, locking them in place. He storms out of my room, slamming the door behind him. The unmistakable sound of the locks on the door clicking into place.

I am a prisoner in this tiny space once again.

10

MATÍAS

I speed around the green hills of Scotland in a rented Maserati. The cooler fall air chilling my veins as I weave in and out of traffic on the country roads. There has always been something about this place that calms me. Maybe it's the quietness or the seclusion. Maybe it's the lush green hills of the Highlands filled with history, more violent than my own. Whatever it is, the last three days here have brought the weight off my shoulders. It's a relief even if only temporarily.

My brother's widow, Ainslie, lives on her family's estate near Inverness. A sprawling mansion larger than what I grew up in on the outskirts of London. Her family is old money and full of tradition. They always loved Thiago, but they have blamed me for his death. Luckily the house is so large I only need to see her mother at dinner. Her father is in Glasgow on business, making my timing impeccable. Despite her family's hatred toward me, I always got along with Ainslie. She was like a big sister to me.

I was only eight when Thiago and Ainslie met at university. She was always kind to me. Sometimes she even acted like a mother. My parents divorced when I was only five. My mom moved to Paris and I barely saw her between my time at school in London and my summers in Mallorca. But Thiago would take me to Scotland on the weekends whenever he and Ainslie went to her home. I loved her giant house, full of secret passages. Not to mention the sprawling acreage where I was able to run free.

She is part of the reason I feel like a different man here. She understands me for some unknown reason. She knows I haven't made the best decisions in my life but unlike Bastian who criticizes me for them, Ainslie always listens and supports me, telling me that the choices I make will lead to consequences I have to deal with and that is the only way to grow and become a better man.

Rain starts to fall so I take a turn that leads back to the estate. I grimace as I pull into the roundabout and see her father's car in the drive. I thought I would leave before he returned. In order to avoid him, I use the kitchen entrance to the house and make my way up a back staircase to my room. It's been my room ever since I was a kid. Secluded from the rest of the family wings. It's at the very end of a hall with beautiful views of the Highlands.

I don't join the family for dinner. Knowing well enough, I won't be welcome. Ainslie has a butler send me a plate of dinner. I don't eat much as thoughts of Alessia flood my mind. Instead, I start drinking bourbon.

A knock on the door startles me from my thoughts.

"Matías?" Ainslie's voice singsongs through the door.

"Come in," I tell her.

She walks into the room and joins me at the seating area by the window, helping herself to the bottle of bourbon. She's silent for a few minutes as she sips her drink, her eyes studying me the whole time. "I didn't think he was going to be home until the next week."

"It's fine," I say quietly as I watch the sky turn dark.

"I wish you would have come down to dinner. The kids would have like spending one last night with their uncle."

I close my eyes. I hate the gap I've caused between her family. The kids love me and they always want me around. Her mother despises it though. "I'll have breakfast with them."

"Thank you."

"We've barely talked much these last few days, Matías. And I can tell by the look in your eyes that you aren't doing well. You have that same look that Thiago had the months before he died."

I clench my fist around my glass because I know what words are coming next.

"How deep are you involved with them, Matías?"

I stay silent.

"Don't lie to me. I've already lost my husband. My children lost their father. I don't want to lose a brother-in-law and my kids don't want to lose an uncle. It's a dangerous game you are playing."

"I'm well aware of that."

"You are going to get yourself killed. I don't know the reach of The Partners. I don't know how deeply seated they are in this world, but I know they are dangerous. And if you upset them in any way, your fate will be the same as Thiago's."

I clench my jaw. "There are things that I have to take care of. Things you don't understand."

"I'm not asking to understand." She pleads. "I am asking you to make the right decision."

"It's not as easy as you think."

She looks off toward the green hills. "Do you even want to get out of this world, Matías?"

I pinch my eyes shut. I wish I could tell her yes. But I don't even know if it's an option. I feel trapped by them. Chained to men with power who are unwilling to break my chains. The guilt and truths of my past like a stone on my chest. She has always blamed Bastian for Thiago's death. And I want to tell her it was my fault. I am the reason he is dead. But I know she will never forgive me. And right now, she is the only support system I have.

She reaches over and grabs my hand. "I don't want to lose you too."

The blood of the men I've killed flashes through my mind. All I can think about is all the things I've done. All the wrongs I've committed. The deaths and deceit that lie in my hands. And there is nothing I can do to change my path.

I squeeze her hand back. "I promise you, I'll always be here."

"Don't make promises you can't keep. Thiago did the

same thing and look where we are now. A broken family."

"You aren't broken, Ainslie."

Tears crest her eyes as she downs a good amount of her drink. "I cry nearly every day thinking about the life I could have had."

"You had a good life with him. He treated you like a queen. He gave you everything. Don't be mad that you couldn't have more time with him, but be happy about the time you did have."

She wipes away a tear. "You should remember that too, Matías. Don't waste your life like Thiago's was."

We sit in comfortable silence after that, both sipping on drinks until late in the night.

I stomp up the stairs when I get to the safe house. My anger at an all-time high. I thought I could trust her. Give her more freedom. I didn't think she would take advantage of my kindness and try to escape.

I slam the front door open. Fiero back to watching her now that she is locked in her room.

"She's pretty livid, boss."

"Not as livid as me," I growl as I rush down the hall and open the locks to her door.

As soon as I barge through and slam the door behind me, she just scurries to the corner of the room.

"Do you have a death wish?" I yell at her.

She bites her lip as her bangs fall in her face, avoiding eye contact with me. "I just wanted answers. And I am not getting a damn thing. What else was I supposed to do? I'm a captive. A prisoner. I just want to go home."

"I told you your father hired us to protect you." I lie.

She sniffles at her next words. "Then why can't I talk to my father if he's the one that hired you to protect me?"

"It's not safe."

"From whom? Who is trying to hurt me?"

I shake my head at her. "That's confidential. But know that I have your best interests in mind."

"I don't trust you," she says weakly.

"I wouldn't trust me either, sweetheart."

I see a tear fall down her face. "Don't cry. It won't get you anywhere."

"I just want some freedom. Fresh air. Can I at least have that?" she cries.

A cynical grin washes over my face. "I'm sure I could arrange that."

"Really?"

I rush toward her as I pull her into my side. I keep her tight against me as I use my other hand to undo the locks. "Is this what you want? To breathe in the farm air, ripe with the smell of manure?"

She doesn't answer me so I push her in front of me, hard into the railing. "Is this what you have been needing?" My words seductive along her ear.

"I-I—"

I grip her hip bones, digging my fingers into her flesh. "I can give this to you."

"W-why?" she stutters.

"Maybe I've had a change of heart."

She looks over her shoulder at me and I smirk at her in a diabolical manner as I push her to the ground, slapping handcuffs onto her wrists around the railing of the balcony.

"Now we both get what we want. You get fresh air and I get peace of mind that you won't do anything fucking stupid."

She pulls against the handcuffs roughly, wincing as they pinch against her wrists. "I thought I wasn't a prisoner."

"You're not."

"Then why are you handcuffing me to the railing?" Her words a throaty plea.

"To keep you where I asked you to stay. In this house." I start to move back to the door.

"You're supposed to be protecting me."

"I am."

"Then take these off me. Don't restrain me," she screams.

I stride over to her, my toes touching hers as I lean over so we are face to face, my breath on her lips. "You better learn to behave. Or the next time I use those handcuffs it won't be to the railing but to my bed."

She gasps and I can't help but laugh. "And I'm not sure you could handle that, sweetheart."

I see the fight in her eyes, the need to do anything to get out of those handcuffs. So I pull her chin to my face and bring my lips down hard on hers. Biting hard on her lip before backing up again to leave.

"How long are you going to leave me here?" she begs.

I have to say I like the begging just a little too much. I give her a diabolical grin. "Oh, I don't know, a few hours. Maybe a few days. Depends on how long my business trip will take." I turn to the door to her room, unlocking the handle. "It really just depends on how well you behave."

I don't look for her reaction. Instead I walk out, slamming the door and locking it. "Don't feed her. She needs to learn a lesson."

I then storm out of the building and into the car Demont has parked out front.

My trip to Naples is short. A few permits needed to be signed off on before the final stages of construction could be finished. My brother will be happy to hear that construction is ahead of schedule and the resort should be finished early. I make a call to the design team to plan a trip out here in two weeks to start finalizing the plans as I step back into the back of the SUV.

"Did you want to get something to eat, boss. Or head back to the airport?"

"Let's eat. We can't fly out for a few more hours."

He nods at me through the rearview and drives to the outskirts of the city to a small café that isn't overcrowded. The weather is much warmer than Scotland but a cool breeze floats in from the sea, cooling down the heat.

We both eat sandwiches in silence. My mind is spinning. Alessia once again at the forefront of my brain. Not my business. Not my questions about The Partners' motives. But Alessia, the girl with honey-colored eyes, I cannot get out of my head no matter what I do.

"You'll get through this."

I look up at Demont, the look on his face tells me he's been watching me this whole time. "You sure about that?"

He rests his arms across his chest. "You've been through a lot. I've been there for most of it. And every time you pull through. You take a lot of risks. I don't think you should but you always come out ahead. This thing they are making you do. It's just another stepping-stone. You'll cross it and come out fine on the other side."

I run my hand through my hair. "And what if I don't?"

"Then we figure it out from there."

I clench my jaw as I think about my future. The bleakness I feel every time I picture it. Because I don't picture it at all. My dreams always telling me my life will end soon.

"What are you going to do about Alessia?"

I unclench my jaw and look over at Demont. "What do you mean?"

"Are you just going to leave her in that room?"

"I haven't thought about it." I lie. I've thought about it a lot. It's all I think about. And after watching her defiance as I handcuffed her to the railing, I thought about doing a lot of other things to her that I will force her to agree to.

"She was doing fine while she had the entire apartment."

"Until she tried to escape. And you have yet to tell me how that even happened." My voice thick with anger.

He leans forward and rests his elbows on the table. "I stepped outside to make a phone call. I was next to the door the whole time."

"Then what the hell happened?" I never asked for the details earlier. I was too angry with everything that I didn't even care to ask.

Demont sips on his water. Despite my rage, he is calm and collected. The reason I hired him. Nothing gets to him. His emotions so tapped down in his body, I sometimes wonder if he even has any. "She tried to climb over the kitchen balcony railing and climb down the ivy lattice."

I smirk at him. "How the hell did she even reach it? She's barely five feet."

"Hell if I know. She barely had one hand on it. That's when I found her and watched her try to reach with her other hand. Once I was convinced she was going to fall, I pulled her inside and threw her into her room."

A smile takes over my face. "Always wanting fresh air."

Demont gives me a curious look. He has no idea that I handcuffed her to the railing on the small balcony in her room. It's even more fitting now that I did.

"What's so funny?"

A vision of her sitting on that balcony chained to the railing in that skimpy tank top she had on flashes through my mind. Then I picture her handcuffed to my bed, struggling against the restraints as I take my time licking and tasting every part of that delicious body until I fuck her so hard she will never forget who she belongs to.

I run my thumb along my lip as I think long and hard about the fact that she is mine right now. I don't care if I'm under orders of The Partners. She's mine and I will do with her as I see fit. And part of that will be to finish what we started that night in Monaco. Because I know she wants me despite everything I have done with her. I will have her begging on her knees for me to take her.

"Matias?"

I blink as I look up at Demont. "I'm sorry, what were you saying?"

He shakes his head at me as if he knows exactly what I was thinking of. "She's bored, you know."

"I'm sure she is."

"Maybe we should get her a few books here. She can speak French, but she isn't able to read it very well. And all the books there are in French."

I shrug. "What did you do with her?"

"Found out she can whip my ass in poker."

I let out a light chuckle at that.

"But she sucks at Monopoly. No wonder she isn't a part of her father's business."

"What else does she like?"

He finishes the rest of his water. "She didn't tell me much. She said something about art but I was interrupted by Lastra."

I look at my Rolex and see we still have plenty of time before the jet is scheduled to leave. "How far are we away from Positano?"

He shrugs. "An hour maybe."

"Let's go."

"Sir?"

I give him a look that says don't ask questions. He just nods and heads toward the vehicle.

By the time we make it through the winding roads of the town, I know we won't have much time. But I don't care. I want to know more about her. I want to know what draws me to her. What is so special about her that I can't get her off my mind.

"You really want to be doing this?"

I nod.

"Someone could be watching her house."

"It's a possibility. But doubtful. Her father knows we have her. I don't think he is concerned about anyone coming here."

I tell him to wait in the car as I walk through the gate that leads to the old building. I pick the lock and walk up a winding staircase made with majolica tiles. I know from reading about her that she lives on the third floor. The door to her house is old and antique looking, a wooden door with brass details. I slip my lock pick into the lock and easily get in. For a man so worried about his daughter's safety, maybe he should have put better locks on her door.

I am surprised as I step through the entrance. The home nothing like I expected even with the door and the staircase leading up to it. I can't even imagine how old this building is, but this house has so much detail in every corner it looks original. Baroque design, if I recall, from an art history class I took.

I walk into her living room and find a bookshelf filled

with art books, history books, and a few fantasy novels. I run my fingers along the walls of the house as I pass through into the kitchen. A small kitchen with a marble sink and an even more ornate ceiling than the last room. I look out the balcony doors that lead to a beautiful balcony adorned with more tiles, like the ones in the staircase.

I move to her room, looking at her vanity and clothes. Abstract art hangs all over her walls, none of it familiar to me, though I am not much of an art person. I find a necklace laying on the table next to her bed, a locket. I open it and find a picture of a young girl and her mother. There are words written in Latin on the back but I don't know what they say. I pocket it before I even know what I am doing.

I walk into the next room expecting another bedroom but am surprised to find a studio. I remember she told me she went to school for art history and her excitement over art but I didn't know she was an artist herself. I am blown away by the giant mural against the wall. It's unfinished and from the paint splatter on the floor, I am guessing she was working on it before she left for France. The picture is almost fitting of her. A woman with a crooked crown trying to break free of her chains. I wonder what the bleeding heart means.

I look around the room and find a few piles of smaller canvases leaning against the wall. I flip through them, stunned by the beauty in the pictures. Portraits of faces, some happy, some sad, but all of them created using other objects. Birds, flowers, and feathers used to create different features. They are stunning. I find one that draws me to it more than any other one, besides the large unfinished mural. A woman crying as she reaches for the hand of a faceless person who is being carried off by birds. The emotion in the painting screams at me, begging for me to take it.

I grab the artwork and make my way back through the house, quickly stopping to look at a few pictures of Alessia with her friends and family. The girl so alive and happy in these photos. And I tore her from this world. All for a debt of mine that I somehow can't find a way to repay.

I curse myself as I leave her apartment. I feel as if I have an obsession with her, one that won't go away easily. I shut the door behind me and carry the artwork down the winding staircase. Once I get to the car, I place it carefully on the floorboard.

"What's that?" Demont asks me.

"Nothing. Just drive."

He doesn't say a word, but gives me a look as we head to the airport. I know that look. It's the one he gives me whenever I let my feelings get in the way.

I shove my hand in my pocket, my fingers tracing over the locket and the words etched on the back.

11

ALESSIA

I gave up hours ago trying to get out of the handcuffs. I even tried kicking the metal railing, hoping I could snap it. It didn't work. But the sun has passed over the building and is beating directly on me. It's hot and I'm thirsty and not one person has come to the bedroom. I swear the second Matías gets back here, I am going to curse him and kick him in the balls.

Bastard.

I groan as I adjust to turn my back to the sun. The heat causing sweat to drip down my back. The tank I have on sticking uncomfortably to my skin.

Who knows when he is coming back. He told me a few hours or a few days. Days! That asshole better not leave me here for days. I will bite his dick off if it comes to it.

I yank against the metal again but nothing happens except for an aching in my wrist I wish would go away. I blow my bangs out of my face as I slouch against the railing. Uncomfortable and fuming with rage.

Hours pass, and the sun is finally behind a hill, giving me a reprieve from the heat. I'm exhausted and tired so much so I am surprised my eyes start to close.

But the sleep isn't welcome as the dream hits me like a Mack truck. The pull of the chains on my wrist feels more real than before. The weight of the crown on my head, bringing my neck down. I don't struggle this time though. I just let the chains pull me down into the pool. This time it doesn't look like blood. Just an unknown darkness pulling me under. But this time the murmurs of a man float across the air, caressing my body in an unwanted warmth.

"I see you behaved."

My eyes snap open at those words and I look up to see Matías leaning against the doorjamb, staring at me.

"I knew you could be a good girl. Just takes a little restraint." I want to slap the smirk right off his face.

"Fuck you," I spit at him.

He laughs at me like he is some sort of evil villain. "Are you not even going to struggle?"

"And where would that get me?" I hiss.

He just stares at me as he runs his thumb along his lip. A hint of desire flits across his eyes, like he finds pleasure in me being chained to the balcony. I haven't forgotten his words from earlier either. The ones about handcuffing me to the bed. I would never want to do that. That is not the type of woman I am. But for some reason, the thought of him devouring me while I'm restrained turns me on more than I want it to. I pinch my eyes shut, trying to get my mind to turn off the thoughts of him and me alone in a more compromising position.

When I open my eyes, I find him squatting in front of me. He reaches out his arm, his hand caresses my face, his fingers dance over my lips. His other hand drags up my thigh until he reaches my hands, that are resting against my hip.

"What are you thinking about, angel?" he whispers.

I don't answer him and he laughs, leaning in closer so I can feel his breath against my ear. His hands run over the metal on my wrists. I try not to breathe him in but he smells like a dangerous man who likes to play with fire. A man who knows how to control others and make them fall easily to his demands.

I fight the urge to reach up and touch his lips with my own as he moves his lips near mine. I turn my head away from him to protect myself from the desire beginning to course through me.

I hear the click of the cuffs and feel the metal slide off my wrists. I go to grab my wrists but he takes them first. His hands massaging them with the gentlest of touches. I swallow when I look up and find his eyes on me. Lust and desire etched across the azure of his eyes and I am sure he sees the same in my own. I don't know how this turned sexual but the tension between us is palpable. I feel the wetness between my legs, the heat in my belly growing just from the light touch of his fingers on my wrists. But his stare is more intoxicating than anything.

"Matías." The words come out in a mix of a whisper

and a moan as my body moves closer to him on its own accord.

"Fuck," he mutters as he closes the distance between us. Our bodies inches apart but still not touching minus his fingers on my wrists. "What are you doing to me, angel?"

Before I can answer, his hands move from my wrists to my hair, pulling me to his mouth. I give in immediately, my need for him desperate. Our lips and tongues collide. Forceful, intense, angry kisses. I bite his lip and he pulls my hair. Soon my hands are clawing up his chest and into his hair as I pull him harder into my mouth. He groans into me as his hands slide down my body and grasp my hips.

He pulls me into his lap and I push him onto his back and straddle him. He grins at me as I do it. Then pulls a gun from the back of his pants and tosses it on the floor. His hands land back on my hips as his own hips thrust up into mine as I grind down on him, feeling the rock-hard steel of need in his pants. His hands move up and under my shirt, pinching my nipples hard. I throw my head back at the sensation as heat floods through every nerve of my body. He sits up and I feel his tongue licking up my throat as I bask in the pleasure from his kisses alone.

"Have you been a bad girl?" he whispers in my ear before taking the lobe and sucking it into his mouth.

A chill goes down my spine at his words and I shake my head.

"Are you sure? I had to lock you up. Was that enough punishment for misbehaving? For trying to escape?"

His words cause more need to flood through my body, his name a moan on my lips.

"Mmm." He captures my lips before tugging hard on the bottom one until it pops out of his mouth. "I think you need to be punished for being a bad girl and a liar."

"I'm not a liar." I manage to get out.

He grips my hair and pulls it back so I have to look him in the face. "Sweet angel, I know you are. You told Demont you would behave. Then you tried to jump off a balcony. That sounds like a liar to me. And someone so reckless with their life deserves to be punished."

I gulp at his words, scared yet thrilled about what he may do to me. Before I even know what's happening, he has me flipped over on the tile floor. My face pressing into the cold stones. He has my hands gripped by his above my head as his other hand slides down my back and over my ass. He squeezes it hard, then slides his fingers under the edge of my shorts.

"How wet are you for me?" he asks with strain in his voice.

I whimper as his fingers run over my center on top of my panties.

"I can feel how much this turns you on and I haven't even touched you yet."

He pulls his hand out from under my shorts and pulls them down, along with my panties, just under the edge of my butt cheeks. His hand caresses me and I bite my lip in anticipation of what I know is to come.

He leans over me, his lips in my ear. "I think you are enjoying this far too much. Hard for it to be punishment when you find so much pleasure in my touch."

I groan as his hand slips between my legs again. This time he glides one finger through the wetness pooling between my legs. But he stops abruptly just as he reaches my clit, causing a guttural moan to leave my lips.

"Mmm. I think I found a way to punish you."

Despite everything inside of me telling me this is wrong. That he is my captor and I shouldn't feel this way toward him, I groan at the loss of his fingers.

Without any warning, his hand slaps across my ass. The pain causing me to wince. He does it a second time so hard that I bite into my arm to keep from screaming.

"Now that wasn't so bad," he says as the grip he has on my wrist tightens. "I am sure you can handle a few more."

I pinch my eyes shut as I wait for the next blow but it doesn't come. Instead his fingers dip inside of me and I groan from the pleasure, sweet heat flooding every inch of my body.

He leans over me again, his lips against my ear as he pulls his fingers out of me. "I knew you could be a good girl."

I go to speak, but the sound of gunshots and yelling pulls us apart. His hands let go of my wrists immediately as he jumps off the ground, picking up his gun that fell to the floor. He walks to the balcony and peeks over the side.

I scramble across the floor and push myself against the side of the bed as I pull my shorts up. My heart nearly flying out of my chest. I reach for the locket that is usually around my neck, but forget that I haven't had it since Italy. I try to take deep breaths as the panic sets in.

But surely we are safe in this room. I know the door locks automatically. Matías always needs a key to get out.

"Shit," he mutters as he walks toward me and pulls me off the floor. He pushes me into the corner of the room near the toilet. "Don't move."

I nod because I am too scared to do anything. This isn't my life. I'm a homebody. I'd rather spend my days alone, covering myself in paint as I work on a mural. I don't deal with secrets and guns. And now I am beginning to wonder if this is exactly what my father warned me about.

The sound of someone unlocking the bedroom door makes me scream. Matías is on me in seconds, his body blocking mine, his hand over my mouth.

"Boss, we got to go." The sound of Demont's voice relaxing me slightly as I loosen my grip on Matías's shirt.

"No shit," he says as he reaches behind him to grab my hand. "How many?"

Demont holds the door open as Matías pulls me behind him. "Four came in through the front door, three through the back of the main house. Fiero said they are able to hold them there. No one has come here yet."

"Loss?"

"Two of ours."

I freeze at that. I can only guess by those words that whoever is here is coming for me. Matías pulls on my arm hard but I can't move.

"Alessia." His voice soft but commanding. I also realize it's the first time he's called me by name since I became his captive.

I shake my head as I clam up, chills covering my

body. He turns to face me, his body so close to mine. He brings his hand to my jaw. "We need to move before you get taken."

"W-why?" I stutter, unable to talk.

He presses his lips to my forehead. "I don't know."

The sound of banging below us has Matías pulling away from me.

"Back entrance," Demont mutters. "Two men are in the hall."

A noise comes out of me somewhere between a scream and a wheeze and Matías quickly covers my mouth with his hand. "You need to be quiet."

He turns to Demont. "Let's go."

I'm pulled down a hallway, tears streaming down my face in fear as we reach the door to a linen closet I found the first day Matías let me have freedom. Turns out it's not just a linen closet, the back panel moves to reveal another door that leads to a dark staircase.

Just as Matías goes to pull me down the stairs, the front door bursts open and the sound of gunshots has me letting go of his hand. A bullet whizzes past my head and hits Demont in the arm. He fires back at the men that are trying to take me. I hear one fall to the ground as another man shoots again, hitting the wooden door to the closet.

Matías's arms wrap around my waist as he pulls me back into the dark staircase. Demont squats as he fires his weapon, giving me a split second of a clear view of the attackers before I am pulled into the darkness.

I must be in shock or my brain confused over the lack of food and water as I sat chained to a balcony in the hot sun all day but I swore I saw my father's assistant standing in the doorway of the apartment.

I don't have time to think about it, as Matías pulls me down the stairs at a grueling pace. My bare feet sliding on the stone steps as I try to keep up with him. The sound of yelling and a door slamming above us makes me grip onto him harder, worried that we are being followed.

The air turns musty and the ground damp as we make our way to a flat walkway. I realize we must be underground. I slip and stumble on the wet floor.

"We need to keep moving, Alessia."

I grip his arm as I keep up with his grueling pace. "Wh-what about De-Demont?"

"He knows how to survive."

I stop asking questions and keep up with Matías as we make a turn around a bend. The path starts to go slightly uphill and soon enough we run into three steps that lead to a door. Matías lets go of me and fishes keys out of his pocket for the door.

He turns to face me. "Be quiet. Don't cry or sniffle. Don't say a word. I don't know if there is anyone on the other side of this door. Stay here until I come back."

I nod as he presses me into the wall. He turns the key in the lock, then cocks his gun before pushing the door open and steps out onto the other side.

I hold my breath, digging my nails into my hand as I wait for him. The air coming in from the other side of the door smells like lavender and jasmine. I go to take a step closer to it even though Matías hasn't come back.

But a large hand grabs my arm as I reach for the door, pulling me back.

I bite back a scream when I see Demont next to me. He shakes his head at me and I push back against the wall.

He goes to walk through the door when Matías reappears. "It's clear. They haven't found this place yet."

Demont pushes past Matías with his weapon drawn as Matías reaches for my hand again. I keep quiet as I follow him. The darkness is soon illuminated by moonlight as we walk into a greenhouse filled with vegetables, flowers, and herbs. We walk through it quickly and make our way to the door. As we exit, I can see two houses in the distance. I must have been in the smaller one. I try to look around and figure out where we are, but I am quickly being pulled through a cropping of trees to the left.

"Ouch," I whisper as I trip over a root. The crunch of dead branches on my bare feet causes sharp pain across them. Matías must feel me slowing down. He turns toward me and picks me up before I can even say a word.

We run for maybe a hundred yards, then come out to an old dirt road. A car is parked along the side and Demont unlocks it. Matías sets me into the back before getting into the driver's seat. Demont in the passenger seat. The engine starts and we pull onto the road.

I start to shiver and my breathing becomes labored as I sit in the back. The night air is cool and all I have on is a pair of shorts and a tank. Anxiety sets in as I think about what just happened? Who was after me? What does this have to do with my father? Would they have killed me? Why was my father's assistant there? Or at least I thought it was him. My eyes were probably playing tricks on me. Or is Matías lying to me and that was someone coming to rescue me?

    I lie down in the seat as the panic attack takes full effect. I hear Matías speaking to me but I can't make out any of his words. I close my eyes, hoping that sleep will come and take me away from this place. That I will wake up in my bed in my apartment. All of this a bad dream. I can get back to painting and my boring life. Not this nightmare that I'm living.

12

ALESSIA

I must be in some sort of trance because I don't remember how long we drove. Or getting out of the car. Or walking into whatever house we are in.

All I know now is I hear the sound of water running. My head is leaning against a wooden cabinet and I feel cold marble under my legs. Or maybe I'm just cold. All I do remember is the constant shivering that won't seem to leave my body.

Flashes of the last few hours hit my mind. Yelling. Gunshots. Running.

The feeling of warm hands on my body. The pain and pleasure I felt moments before everything changed.

It's like I can still feel those hands on my body. Rough, calloused hands on my arms, my legs. I lean forward and my head hits something hard. I try to focus on what it is because it's soft despite the firmness. I press my cheek into it, the sound of beating hitting my ears.

How strange for a wall to sound like a heartbeat.

"Shh, you're safe, angel. Don't cry."

Matías.

I try to lift my arms to wipe the tears I didn't know I had but I feel weak, unsteady.

"I've got you." The soft and smooth cadence of Matías's voice relaxes me. Even as I feel his hands run under my shirt. He holds my head back so he can pull it over my head. The thought of him seeing me naked doesn't even faze me as I try to get my mind to focus on the present.

He lifts me up with one arm as the other pulls my shorts down. This time I do realize the marble is cold that I am sitting on. I feel him peel my shorts and panties down my legs. I wonder what he is doing, what game he is playing now when he lifts me off the counter. One arm beneath my knees and the other across my back.

The smell of lemon verbena and lavender overwhelms me as I feel myself being placed in warm water. The feeling shocks me into the present. My eyes flying open and my arms covering my chest.

"You're in shock, Alessia."

I look around the room. This place very different from the apartment I was being kept in. This place modern luxury, clean lines, and minimalist color. The tub I am sitting in is a deep soaking tub. Effervescent bubbles float around me, bringing me a sense of calm.

Matías kneels next to me and I chance a look at him. His sapphire eyes laced with concern beating into me. His hands are in the water. The edges of his rolled-up dress shirt dipping into the warm bath. He runs a hand up and down my bare back, the other resting on my knee. "Relax."

"Wh-what happened?" I ask through shivering lips. Despite the water being so warm, I can't stop shivering.

"Not now, angel. I just need you to warm up. Relax. Calm down. You had a panic attack and then went into shock."

I bring my knees up to my chest and wrap my arms around them. "Where am I?"

"Safe," he whispers as his hands move to my shoulders, massaging the tension out of them.

"I-I thought I was sa-safe at the other place."

"Me too. Me too."

"How am I safe here then?" I ask as my voice gets slightly stronger.

"No one will find you here."

I rest my cheek on my knees. "How can you be sure?"

"I just am."

I feel too weak to fight him. To demand answers I know I will never get. Instead, I close my eyes as I take in the warmth that starts to defrost my bones. His hands never leave my body. I should push him away. But I don't. His voice and hands soothing.

Once the water starts to turn cold, he steps away from the tub and grabs a fluffy robe. I try to push out of the tub but my limbs still feel weak. He notices my struggling and lifts me up out of the tub until I am standing on my feet, completely naked. He grabs the robe and wraps it around me, tying the belt against my waist.

"Can you walk?"

I nod as he wraps an arm around my shoulder and

leads me out of the bathroom and into a bedroom. I shiver as I take in the room. The cold whites of the walls and the sheets. No art lines the walls. The only colors in the room are the gray armoire and dresser along the walls.

"You can sleep here."

I shake my head.

"You don't want to sleep?"

I bite my lip as I look at the bed. It reminds me of the apartment where I woke up a captive. I know I still am one but the memories are too fresh in my mind. "Cold."

"I can turn the air off."

I pull on his hand and he turns his face to look at me. "The colors are so cold."

He nods as if in understanding and guides me out of the room and into a gray walled hallway with a glass ceiling. I try to remember things as I pass. A few closed doors. A library. An office.

We walk until we hit an open space. This room as white as the other but at least it has black and white abstract art on the wall. I look around as Matías slows down so I can take in the space. A kitchen sits off to the right. A sleek modern design that feels cold but fits the space. I look out through the floor-to-ceiling glass windows to the deck outside. It's too dark to see what lies beyond it. I turn toward the way we were heading and Matías takes the cue to keep on walking. We pass a hallway of glass and I can see water all around us.

We enter a room of dark grays and rich garnets. A large bed sits facing more floor-to-ceiling windows that look out onto another deck. This one has lights on it and

I can see the pool surrounding it. Just beyond the bed, I see an open door that leads to another bathroom. I can tell this must be Matías's room. The dark decor and colors suit him, not that I know much about him, but it just feels like this is where he belongs.

"Wait here," he says as he heads toward the bathroom.

When he comes back with a T-shirt, I realize his closet must also be in there too. He pulls on the tie of my robe and it opens, revealing my naked body. I suddenly feel self-conscious as he peels the robe down my shoulders and lets it fall to the ground. I go to cover up my body but he leans into my ear. "You're beautiful, Alessia."

I look up at him and see the sincerity in his face that I heard in his words. He pulls the T-shirt over my head and I slide my arms through. I watch him as he pulls back the blankets and fluffs a pillow. I climb into the bed and he pulls the blankets over me. He sits on the edge, his hand brushing away a piece of loose hair from my forehead.

"Sleep. You're safe here."

Maybe I am still in shock or just losing my mind. But I let myself trust him this time as I close my eyes and fall asleep in his bed.

I wake up as daylight begins to dance along the edge of the sheer black curtains of the floor-to-ceiling windows. I roll over in the bed and wrap my arms around a pillow, taking in the masculine scent coating the pillow. Why does the man have to smell so good? Like worn leather mixed with the warmth of the sun.

Reality sets in as my mind wakes up. I was almost kidnapped last night. Well kidnapped again because it already happened once. But for some reason, I was more scared of being taken from Matías. I know I saw one of my father's men there but maybe it was my fear and adrenaline playing tricks on me. Daddy wouldn't go to such lengths to get me. He would negotiate for my safety, not put me in harm's way.

Not to mention that I am supposed to be under the protection of Matías on Daddy's orders. But the more I think about it, the more far-fetched it seems. And I don't know who to trust. What could my father have done that would have put me in this predicament. What is he hiding? And what does Matías have to do with any of it?

I stretch as I sit up in bed, taking in the view from the sheer curtains. I have a much better view of the outside now. A deck sits directly off his bedroom with a pool beyond it. I look out past the yard filled with lush greenery and can just make out the soft waves of the Mediterranean beyond.

I climb out of bed and walk toward the deck. I slide it open and breathe in the cool salty air. Summer is on the brink of turning to fall and I can smell it on the air. I wrap my arms around me as the cool breeze sends goose bumps over my arms. I take in the massive pool that covers the length of the house. How peaceful it must be to be able to step right out of your room and into the comforts of a warm pool. I run my toes along the water and am tempted to jump in but I have more important things to do. Like demand answers from the man holding me captive.

I head back inside and creep through the house, looking for Matías. I don't see any guards, which makes me think I could easily just walk out the front door. But after last night, I have no intention of running until I get answers.

I hear voices down the hall and stop outside the office I remember passing last night. From the sound of the voices, I know it's Matías and Demont.

"Are you sure you don't want to put her in a different safe house?" I hear Demont ask.

"No." Matías's voice is harsh, angry. "She will be safer here."

"Are you just going to stay holed up in your house?"

I peek into the room and catch a glimpse of Matías nodding. "I'll work from home. I can keep my eye on her."

"The hotel would be safer. Put her up in a suite. Enough people around, no one would try to take her."

There is grit in Matías's voice as he answers. "And the hotel was where I got dragged into a mess two years ago. It never should have happened. But I was a fool then, just like I am now. They have their control over me. If anything were to happen, I would rather it be here than the hotel. If my name is in the headlines, I don't want it to tarnish my brother's reputation again."

Who has control over Matías?

"I understand, boss. Let me know how many people you need and I will have them here."

"I've already got three at the gate—"

"You shouldn't be spying on him."

I jump at the sound of a woman behind me. I turn and find an older woman with a large bag slung over her shoulder. "I wasn't—"

"Yes, you were." She smiles at me. "Now you must be Alessia. Mr. Montford said we would be having a guest."

"I am," I say in confusion.

"I'm Claudette. Mr. Montford's housekeeper. If there is anything you need, please don't hesitate to ask."

I scrunch my hands in my shirt. "Thank you, Claudette."

"I'll take it from here." Matías's harsh words cut into the space as he steps behind me. His hand comes to the back of my neck and squeezes, not too tightly, but enough to warn me to keep my mouth shut.

"Bonjour, Mr. Montford."

"Morning, Claudette. We'll take breakfast on the deck in an hour."

She nods at him and scurries off toward the kitchen.

His grip on my neck tightens as his mouth comes down to my ear. "I thought I told you to stay in bed."

I reach for his hands but he pushes them away. "You didn't. You told me to sleep. I did. Then I woke up."

He pulls me into the office, letting go of my neck, and pushes me into a wall. "Leave," he commands to Demont. Demont walks out, shutting the door behind him.

I look up at Matías and see anger in his eyes. "I didn't—"

"Just because you are in my home doesn't mean you have freedom."

I clench my jaw. "You didn't see me walk out the front door this morning, did you?"

He growls at me, then pushes off me and walks toward his desk, running his hands through his hair.

"Am I really safe here?"

"Yes."

"How? There are fewer guards here than you had at the other place. Actually, the only person I've seen is Demont, so really that means that there are no—"

"The men that tried to take you won't come here."

I want to ask why but I have more important things to ask. "Who tried to take me?"

He leans against his desk and folds his arms over his chest. "It's not important."

"Like hell it's not. This is my life we are talking about," I yell at him. "If it's not important, then why did you take me?"

"I didn't take you."

"Yes you did!" I yell, throwing my arms in the air. "My father wouldn't have asked for me to be kidnapped. Meaning he is doing something he shouldn't be involved in. And from the sounds of your conversation this morning. It sounds like you are too."

I can see the anger building in him with every word I say. The way his eye twitches, the clench in his jaw, the tightness of his knuckles on his biceps.

"Whatever is going on, I need to know! Why am I here? What did my father do? What did you do? Why was one of my father's men there last night? Was he trying to take me back? Or was he—"

"What do you mean, one of your father's men?"

I swallow down my words. "Um... I mean—"

Matías crosses the room in two strides and grabs me by the arms. "Tell me what you know, Alessia."

I bite my lip and look down at the ground. Panic starts to set in at the harshness in Matías's tone and the grip he has on me. I don't know why I felt safer here. This man is more dangerous than I thought.

"Tell me," he demands.

I let out a whimper. "You're hurting me."

He glances down at his hands on my body and lets go. "I'm sorry, angel. I-I lost control."

I look up at him and see remorse in his eyes. "It's—"

"It's not okay," he says as his hands wrap around my waist and pull me into him. "Tell me. Please."

I push a piece of hair behind my ear as I look into his eyes. I don't know why I tell him what I know. This is just another one of his games. His soft caresses that make me trust him. "My dad's assistant. He was there. He came into the room after Demont was shot." My eyes widen at my own words. "Oh my gosh, he was shot. Is he okay?"

"He's fine." His words soft as his hands slide down my back and over my ass. "What is his name?"

"Nicolas. Nicolas Di Masio."

"And how do you know what he does for your dad?" His hands glide under my shirt, his shirt, and over my bare ass. His lips leave a trail of warm air down my neck but they never touch me.

I know what he is doing. He knows what his touch does to me. The undeniable attraction we have toward each other. And I snap out of it, pushing against his chest to force his seduction for answers away from me. "I don't know."

He grabs my wrists on his chest as I try to pull away. "Liar."

He backs me back into the wall. "I know this game you're playing. Seduction to get me to talk. It's not going to work anymore."

He pins my hands to the wall on either side of my head. "I don't know about that, angel. I wasn't asking for answers yesterday when you crawled on my body and ground your pussy into me."

I roll my eyes at him as I try to slip out of his grip. "Momentary lapse of judgment."

His hand lets go of my arm and grips my chin. "We both know that wasn't what it was."

I use that moment to take my free hand and pry his fingers off my other wrist. I slip under his arm and head to the door.

"Who is he?" he asks me.

My hand rests on the doorknob as I look over my shoulder at him. "You'll just have to figure it out," I snap.

He growls and is on me before I can leave the room. He presses me against the door so my front is flush to it. "Where do you think you're going?"

"Somewhere other than this room with you."

"You didn't give me answers yet."

I squirm against his body that is pressed against mine. "Neither did you. So I guess we're even."

"I don't think so, sweetheart."

I fight against his hold on me, my face pressing hard into the wood of the door at my cheek. His lips come to my ear and he bites hard on my lobe. "Answers," he commands.

"No."

His hand suddenly slides between me and the door, his fingers sliding into the wetness between my thighs. I curse my body for being turned on by the argument between us. Two thick fingers slide into me and I let out a moan at the sensation that overtakes my entire body.

"See, I know you can be a good girl." His lips slide down my neck as he pumps his fingers into me. I can feel his length pressed into my back and I fight the urge to rub myself against him.

His thumb starts to tap against my clit and I feel so close to coming. My eyes close as I bite my lip, soft moans escaping my mouth as I try to hold them back.

Just when I am about to explode, his hand disappears.

"What the hell?" I groan.

"Tell me what I want to know and I'll give you what you want."

I know I shouldn't say anything, let him think I know more than I do, but I am tired of the games.

His lips press a kiss to my shoulder. "Alessia…"

I sigh. "I really don't know. I know nothing about his business. I've always stayed out of it. I just know that the few times I went to the office to see my dad Nicolas was there. I assumed he was an assistant. But maybe not. He's always with him. At the house, the office, vacations."

"How long has he worked for him?"

I shrug. "Maybe six or seven years. I don't remember seeing him until I went to college."

Without warning, Matías presses his fingers back inside of me and the sudden intrusion has me screaming his name as I come harder than I ever have. He pulls his fingers out of me and spins me around so my back is pressed against the door. His lips crash to mine and I pull him into me as I ride out the wave of my orgasm. He lifts me up and I wrap my legs around his hips. He grinds into me, making me ache for more of him. My hands go to his belt buckle and he doesn't stop me. I moan against his lips, needing more of him, all of him. This attraction to my captor undeniable. My hand slips into his pants and wraps around his thickness.

He bites down on my lip as his hands push my shirt up over my breasts. His hands grip my nipples hard and my head falls back against the door. I slide my hand over the tip of his cock just as his phone rings.

"Fuck," he mutters into my neck. He slides me to the ground and buckles his pants before pulling his phone out of his pocket. "Montford."

I adjust my T-shirt to make sure it covers me and go to grab the door, but Matías pulls me against him. His hand sliding between my legs again as he talks on the phone. I don't even know what he is talking about, all I can focus on is the pleasure he is giving me. I hold in my groan as best I can as another orgasm hits me and I collapse against his body.

He smiles down at me as he pulls his fingers from me and sucks them into his mouth. I watch him as he closes his eyes as he tastes me and a sudden urge to kneel before him comes over me. But before I can do anything crazy, he leans into my ear and whispers. "Later."

He steps away from me and walks over to the window of his office. I watch him for a second more before I slide out the door.

I have no idea where to go. I can't walk around in his T-shirt all day, especially with Demont and Claudette around the house somewhere and no doubt more guards will show up.

I walk down the hall to the first room he showed me and open the armoire to find a selection of clothes in my size. I have no idea when he did this, maybe while I was sleeping. I walk into the bathroom he bathed me in last night and turn on the shower.

After what I just did, what I wanted, I need the heat to wash it all away. What am I thinking? I can't be with him. He kidnapped me. Lied to me. Handcuffed me to a balcony. Matías Montford is a dangerous man. And I need to remember that.

13

MATÍAS

I watch Alessia as she lays out by the pool. Her dark hair glistening in the afternoon sun. I close my eyes as I remember what she tasted like. The sweetness I sucked off my fingers as I talked to my brother on the phone. The look of need in her eyes even after I got her off twice. If Bastian hadn't called, there is no doubt I would have fucked her against my office door.

But I need to get her out of my head. I shouldn't be doing this. She is just a target. And here I am picturing her naked in my bed or fucking her in my pool. This will just lead to trouble if I keep up with it. I never should have touched her. Even when I was trying to seduce her back in Monaco.

I open my eyes and watch her take her top off as she sunbathes. Fuck, she's gorgeous. I turn away from her and sit at my desk. Looking at her makes my need worse.

I told her she could do whatever she wanted in the house. After she left my office yesterday, she avoided me most of the day. By dinner, I could tell she was bored out of her mind. Demont went to the store and came back with board games. I watched them play for hours but didn't ask to join. I knew she didn't want to be near me and I knew I needed to stay away from her.

She slept in her room last night too. I didn't even have to tell her. But as I lie down well past two in the morning, I found myself inhaling the sheets where she had lain alone the night before. Wishing she was in my bed again.

I spend the rest of the day working, not even noticing as day turns to night. I only notice the time when the phone rings. My fist clenching at the unknown number on the screen.

"Montford."

"Matías, how are you doing? Keeping our favorite person under your watchful eye, I hope."

I grit my teeth. "Of course."

"Good, good."

The Partners didn't have much to say after Alessia's attempted kidnapping two days ago. Not that they would let me know until it's necessary.

"We have a job for you."

"What do you mean you have a job for me?" I growl into the phone. "I thought my agreement was changed to playing babysitter."

Charles laughs into the phone. "No Matías, that was just your punishment. Check the box in the morning. You have forty-eight hours to complete the assignment."

"Fuck you."

"Oh Matías, you know we can't be fucked over.

Besides, just think after this one you only have one more job."

Charles hangs up and I slam the phone onto my desk, cracking the screen. This is not what I wanted. I joined them to have power, control. To be more than my brother. But now I wish I'd listened. Got out when I still could have. Now I owe them my life.

I walk out of my office and see Demont and Alessia in the dining room playing Risk. Both of them concentrating hard on the board. If only war was that easy.

I pour myself a drink, grab the bottle, and step outside onto the deck. I sit at my usual spot at the table and sip my bourbon. It's pouring rain and I watch it fall, the pergola above me keeping me mostly dry. I study the raindrops as they hit the water of the pool. My eyes focusing on the splash as the water bounces up as the rain hits the pool. I drain my bourbon and pour another glass.

"You're going to get sick if you sit out here in the rain all night." Alessia's soft voice fills the air.

I don't look at her. "I'll be fine."

She pulls the chair across from me out and sits on it.

"I thought you were playing a game."

"We were. Took a break."

I nod at her and go back to looking at the water as I sip my drink.

"You weren't at dinner."

"I was working."

"Do you want something?"

I look at her this time. "All I want is for you to leave me alone."

She stands up. "Look, I was trying to be nice."

I scoff at that. "Why would you be nice to me? You're here against your will. I'm an asshole. And the last person you should be nice to."

She sweeps her bangs out of her eyes. "I—well—"

I grip her wrist and pull her between my legs. "Is it because I made you come twice yesterday morning?" I cup my hand between her legs. "You think that if you're nice to me I'll do it again?"

She pulls out of my grip. "You're an asshole."

"I told you I was." I don't say anything as I sip my drink. She stares at me like she is trying to find something to say, then stomps into the house.

I need her to hate me. Because if she ever finds out the truth, she will kill me.

I slam a wrench into the side of the man's face that is sitting in the chair in front of me. I let the anger inside of me overtake me. My anger with The Partners, with Alessia, with myself. I thought I was done with this. Done with the interrogations and the torture and the killings. But I should have known that I would never get out of this.

The man, I don't even know his name, spits out a tooth and turns and grins at me. I've been at this for two hours. And I haven't gotten shit from him. The only information I know about him is that he has something to do with Calvetti & Sons. He knows some secret I am supposed to get out of him but I wasn't given any direction as to what that secret was.

"You think I would tell you anything?" he asks me, the bloody grin on his face demonic.

I use a towel to wipe the blood off my hands. "No. If the secret is good enough to take it to the grave."

"I know who you are. I know who you work for," he hisses at me. "You are just like me. A man tasked to do the dirty work of men much more powerful. Men who make you think you have control. When really, you are just as weak as me. Soon enough you'll be tied to a chair and questioned too. Until one of those men you work for puts a bullet between your eyes."

I crack my knuckles but keep a straight face. I know the words he speaks are true but I won't give in, won't let him know I know what my future holds.

I look at Lastra, who is leaning against a wall behind me. I toss him the wrench in my hand. "I'll be back."

I don't miss the smirk that lands on his face. I know Lastra enjoys the torture. He'll admit it to anyone. I keep the fact that I enjoy it to myself. A secret I will never tell a soul.

I walk into the dim, wet hallway of the old warehouse I was told to find the target in. I don't know who brought him here or how long he's been sitting tied to a chair. I can only guess since the night Alessia was almost taken from the safe house. This man knows something about that night, he gave that away at least.

I pull my phone and flip through the pictures of the documents I was given. I don't find anything of use. The pictures attached to it are mostly just him working at the docks. But then I see a picture of a woman I know. Some girl I met years ago and only see at social functions. I look her up on social media and find her page with a few pictures of the two of them that I know means they are more than friends. I find out his name and after some digging, find out he has a wife and a kid. Asshole is a fucking cheater.

I storm back into the room and watch as Lastra breaks one of the man's fingers. He looks up at me and steps away from him. "Bastard talks a lot of shit."

I nod at him and he goes back to leaning against the wall. I pull another chair up and sit across from the guy I now know is Eddie Strauso. The bloody grin is back on his face as I lean back in my chair and cross my ankle over my knee.

"Seems like you've been through this before, Eddie."

He raises a brow at me.

"See, I know who you are too. I could give a shit if you know who I am. Most do. Matías Montford. Billionaire playboy. The ladies love me just as much as most businessmen hate me. I'm smart, calculated… rich."

He spits at me but it misses. "Most men hate you because you were handed everything on a fuckin' silver platter."

I shrug. "True, but I'm still rich and powerful."

"You're just an asshole who's gotten lucky. Everyone knows you would have run that damn business to the ground if your brother didn't save you."

"Maybe." I grin at him in the same demonic way he grinned at me. "But at least I still get world-class pussy." I rub my thumb over my lip. "Want to know which one was my favorite? Mallory Mast."

His eyes widen as I say her name.

"Mmm. She sure knew how to suck my dick the right way. She even let me stick it in her ass. She let you do that too?"

"Bitch doesn't mean shit to me."

I smile at him. "Just a nice sidepiece to keep you busy when your wife won't give it up?"

His face falls.

"I'm sure your daughter wouldn't be too happy to know that her daddy fucks around on her mommy."

"You stay the fuck away from my family!" he shouts at me.

I lean forward and rest my elbows on my knees. "You sure they mean that much to you? Or does Mallory mean more?"

"Fuck off," he growls.

"Hmm. I don't think your daughter would like that language. What's her name? Daisy? Cute little girl. Someone may pay a lot of money for her someday."

"No one will find them! They are well hidden."

"Is that so you can keep a sidepiece or is it for another reason? Say fucking around on your boss? Screwing over Calvetti and working for someone else?"

He stops struggling against his chair. "I ain't tellin' you shit."

I nod and pull a switchblade out of my pocket. "Fair enough."

Fiero pops his head in at that moment and I walk over to him. I smile at the name he gives me and circle around Eddie. "You see, Eddie. You think I don't have power. That I am a weak man, controlled by powerful men. Well, what if I told you I was one of those men. The ones who control others. I have a lot of pull in this world. I have seen a lot of things most people don't even know exists."

"Fuck you. I'm not falling for your false threats. Just kill me and get it over with."

I tsk at him. "What good would that do? You would be dead and I would have nothing. It doesn't work that way."

"I don't think you understand, asshole. I have nothing to say to you or anyone that isn't worth my life."

I nod at him. "Honorable." I drag my knife along his neck, hard enough to break the skin but light enough to not cause any damage. "I do have to say that is quite honorable. Too bad I don't have any honor. I bet I could get well over a million dollars for your little girl. Maybe even two. Some men would pay a lot for her virginity."

"You're a sick bastard. But you won't find her."

"You know it's strange for someone who apparently has nothing to say because he is admirable. A trustworthy employee, it's odd that you would hide your family. Unless, I don't know, maybe you aren't as admirable as you say you are."

I press the knife harder into his neck as I lean over and whisper in his ear. "I heard Nici is beautiful this time of year. I think a holiday in Greece would be perfect right now."

Eddie trembles in the chair. I can feel the rage pulsating off him.

"Now, dear ol' Eddie. I won't touch them. Just tell me that little secret you have and I'll make sure no one knows where they are."

He curses and spits at me again. I sigh, tired of this game. I grab a hammer off the table next to me and slam it down on his wrist, cracking it into a hundred pieces of broken bone. He screams bloody murder as I take the hammer and slam it back on his already broken wrist.

"Motherfucker," he yells, the pain evident on his face.

I laugh. "Oh, did that hurt? Just think about how much your daughter is going to hurt if I sell her? Now tell me a fucking name!"

I watch the sweat drip down his face as he contemplates telling me his secrets. I grow bored as I wait. I toss the hammer back on the table and pull my knife back out, flipping it in my hand. I look over toward Lastra. "Make the call."

I see the panic in Eddie's eyes as I say it but he still doesn't say a word. I look over at Lastra. "Can he be there in an hour?"

Lastra's face turns diabolical. "I'm sure he can get to her in thirty minutes."

"Di Masio!" Eddie shouts.

The name sends anger through my veins. The man that tried to steal Alessia away. "And who is that?"

"He-he works for Calvetti… please don't hurt them. Don't hurt my baby girl." He starts to cry and I have to hold back an eye roll. Bastard is a fucking baby that tries to act tough.

"And what about Di Masio? I couldn't care less if he

works for Calvetti." I make a slice down Eddie's arm out of boredom more than anything else.

"He is crossing him. He promised me lots of money and security if I helped him."

Interesting. "And who is he loyal to?"

Eddie doesn't say anything so I twist my knife into his arm near his broken wrist. "One of the Italian families. He never told me who."

Well this changes things. Was Di Masio working for Calvetti when he came to the estate or was he working for the mob?

Eddie's head falls forward. "Please don't hurt Daisy. She's innocent. She's just a toddler."

I don't say anything to reassure him before I take my knife and slice it across his throat. A much messier kill than I am used to, but the information I got pissed me off. What if Alessia was taken, and it was by the mob? I would never have seen her again.

Blood splatters across my shirt and hands as I make the cut. I watch Eddie's eyes go lifeless in the chair.

"Clean it up," I tell Lastra as I wipe my knife clean. I head out the door and tell Fiero to go in and help. I don't stay for the cleanup. Don't stay to make sure there isn't a mess. I walk out of the warehouse and slide into my car. I pull my phone out and make the call I need to make. Not to The Partners, they can find out later. Instead I dial Bernardo.

"There're no fights tonight, Matías."

"I know someone is there training, I can hear it."

"Are you really in a state to fight right now? Remember what happened last time?"

I whip around a corner, fighting the need inside of me. "Bernardo. Please."

He sighs into the phone. "Fine."

I hang up the phone and speed the rest of the way to the warehouse where Bernardo's gym is. I throw the car in park and jog into the building. Bernardo is coaching two guys that are sparring but looks up when he sees me walk in.

I head to his office. I don't have clothes with me. I wasn't prepared for this. Demont is usually with me. But he's watching over Alessia. The only man I trust with her.

I fight or come here after every kill. To me, it feels like a penance. Allowing someone to beat me up, take control over me, repay for the life I just took.

Bernardo walks into the office with clothes, shoes, and a plastic bag. "I figured you needed clothes."

I grab them from him and point at the bag with a question on my face.

"Matías, I'm not an idiot. You've been coming here for two years. I know you aren't involved with something legal. Hell, my fight nights aren't legal. But sometimes your hands are beat up. Sometimes there are traces of blood on you that I know you missed wiping off." He hands me the bag as I stand in shock. "I'm not one to judge. Hell, I was a shit person for a ton of years before I got clean and started this gym. I just need to know that you are careful. That you are taking care of yourself."

I nod. I don't have anything to say to him, anything that would change the situation I am in and he knows it.

He hands the bag to me. "For your bloody clothes."

I take the bag from him and head into his private bathroom. I unbutton my shirt and toss it in the bag. Blood soaked through and is staining my undershirt. I strip it off along with my pants and toss them all in the trash bag. I scrub the blood splatter that I didn't even know was on my face. I wash the blood off my knuckles, then splash water on my face. I lean over the sink and stare at myself in the mirror.

What kind of monster have I become?

I scrub my hands over my face and through my hair. My actions weighing heavily on me, my mind on the verge of breaking.

When I don't think I can take my thoughts anymore, I pull on the gym clothes and change my shoes. I leave the bloody clothes in his office and make my way to the gym. He's coaching the guys that were sparring so I head to the punching bag and start taking my anger out on it.

The anger with myself and the decisions I have made that have destroyed the lives of so many. The kills I've made for people who own me. I don't know if I'll ever get my life back. If I'll ever be able to repay for my actions against The Partners. If my life is what I owe them and one day, I'll be as dead as the man was tonight.

I should have fought that guy that stabbed me when I was in prison. Egged him on so he stabbed me again. Maybe if I pissed him off enough, the blow would have been fatal. And I wouldn't be here, disgusted in myself and my actions. For tearing apart the lives of families. For tearing apart my own family.

I wouldn't have been caught up with Alessia. In some scheme that will surely send me to prison again if I ever get on the wrong side of The Partners. I know that's why they had me do it. An insurance policy on my own life. They could easily have me sent to prison again and it not be their problem. And maybe they will do it. It would be better for everyone if they did.

Especially Alessia. I shouldn't have touched her. Yet all I can think about is the taste of her. She's a drug and I'm addicted to her toxic taste. I'm going to ruin her. I have no doubt about that.

"Matías!"

I turn and see Bernardo waving me over to the ring. I adjust the tape across my knuckles as I walk over. My jaw clenching as my thoughts weigh me down with so much guilt I feel like I might collapse.

I climb into the ring and see the man I am going to spar with. I've fought with him before. He's not the best fighter. I was hoping to get my ass pummeled tonight. Bernardo cues us to start and the man hits me so quickly, I didn't even see it coming.

"Focus, Matías," Bernardo says quietly, as he paces around us. "Watch out for his right cut."

I shake my head and body out. But I get hit with the right cut. I saw it coming, I just didn't care.

And that's how the next twenty minutes go. I get a few good hits in but I let the man in front of me break me down. It clears my mind. With every punch, every hit, I feel the weight falling off my shoulders. I feel like I am paying for my sins. Even more so when I feel my cheek split from a hook, when I spit blood out on the ground, when I fall to my knees in so much pain I can barely keep my eyes open.

"Enough!" Bernardo yells.

I don't move. I don't even look up at the man who did this to me but I know a smirk covers his face. I feel hands grip my biceps and I am hauled to my feet. I slip out of the ring as I walk dizzily to Bernardo's office. I slump into a chair and drink the water he hands me.

"When are you ever going to fight back?" he asks me.

"I do," I mumble.

"Not at the level you are capable of. You're better than this, Matías. I know that. You know that."

I close my eyes as I lean my head back. "I deserve it."

"No you don't. You need to remember that."

"You don't even know," I whisper.

He sighs. "Rest. I know you're alone tonight and I can't let you drive like this."

I nod at him, but don't move out of the chair.

"You're not allowed back here. Not until you learn to deal with your shit outside of the ring."

I don't say anything. I just hear him shut his office door. I eventually move to the couch and lie down. My eyes fighting sleep as his words ring through my head.

The only way I'm going to get over my shit is when I let death knock on my door.

14

ALESSIA

I struggle against the sheets as I feel chains being wrapped around my wrist. "No," I whisper as the cold metal cuts into my skin. "Stop."

Whoever is chaining me doesn't listen. I feel the restraints grow taught and then they start to pull me down. I stumble as I get pulled to the floor, unable to stand. Then I feel the wetness around me. Like a thick sludge, as it starts to cover my limbs. I scream into the void but I know it's no use. I'll be underwater soon enough.

I let the master of my chains pull me through the sludge, the color a deep red, like blood thickening. I close my eyes as I am pulled under. Deeper and deeper I fall into the abyss. My strength growing weaker as I am pulled into the depths of hell.

This must be the end. I won't face death with my eyes closed. But when I open them, I am no longer in a pool of blood. I'm in an endless sea and the chains break free.

But every time I try to swim to the surface, it gets farther out of reach.

A loneliness begins to take over along with a bone chilling cold. I wrap my arms around my body as I hold my breath. I watch as the water begins to freeze. I swim down as I try to get away from the ice but it's chasing me so quickly.

A crown falls from my head and I watch as it sinks to the bottomless floor.

Why am I wearing a crown?

I chase after it to get away from the ice, in search of answers I'm not sure I'll find. But just as I go to grab it, I wake up.

It took me two hours to shake the cold from my bones from the dream. I stood in the shower until the water turned cold, then I wrapped myself in a blanket and sat outside in the warm sun. Claudette brought me hot tea, but didn't ask me anything. I have the sinking feeling she has seen a lot of weird things in this house and has learned not to question it.

By the time lunch rolls around, I realize I haven't seen Demont or Matías the entire morning. I check his office and his bedroom, but both are empty. They are the only two places I've ever seen him. I'm not sure if I want to see Matías though. He was an asshole last night. Not that he isn't one all the time, but he didn't need to degrade me like that.

But aren't you the one allowing him to? I ask myself.

I'm a fool. I don't know why I was concerned with him last night. Who cares if he was sitting out in the rain? He's an adult, he knows how to take care of himself. Maybe I let him degrade me because it makes me feel something other than loneliness. His hands light a fire inside of me. I know it's wrong. I know I shouldn't want him. But I find myself craving him when he gets that look in his eye. The one where he knows he has power over me. I swallow as my thighs clench, picturing that look. It's like he is right in front of me with his hand around my throat.

The sound of a door closing jolts me from my thoughts. It's then I notice my hand between my thighs as I sit on Matías's bed. I jump off the bed and scurry out of his room, closing the door behind me.

When I walk into the main living area, Demont is talking to Claudette.

"Oh, there you are. I was looking for you," she says to me. "I just made lunch."

I nod at her and look at Demont, wanting to ask him where Matías is, but he walks back out the front door before I can get a word out.

I eat lunch by myself on the patio and then decide to swim. But the second I get in the water, all I can think about is the dream and being pulled under, drowning in this pool. I am frozen as all the emotions I felt in the dream hit me. Despair, regret, remorse. I get lost in my head as the dream pulls me under and I think I'm drowning. I try to gasp for breath but water fills my lungs. I try to scream but nothing comes out.

Hands wrap around my shoulders as I'm pulled out

of the water. I cough up water as a towel is wrapped around me. When I open my eyes, Demont is squatting in front of me, concern etched across his face.

"Were you trying to kill yourself by drowning?"

I wheeze and cough as I suck in as much air as I can. "I-I—"

"There are much better ways to kill yourself than drowning. And I don't think Mr. Montford would be very happy if you died on my watch."

I frown at him. "I-I wasn't trying to-to kill myself." Every gulp of oxygen making my lungs stronger. "Where is Matías?"

"Working," he says as he stands.

I know I'm not going to get much more out of him. He holds out his hand and helps me up.

"Get dressed. I want to show you something."

I look at him curiously, but don't ask questions. Instead, I just walk into my room and change like he asked me to.

When I meet him in the living room, he starts to walk to the front door. "Where are we going?" I ask.

"Come and find out."

For some reason, I have always trusted Demont. He may be a beast and I have no doubt a murderer, but his eyes are soft. But right now I am scared to death of leaving the house with him. Maybe it was the dream or my own sense of self-preservation finally kicking in.

He turns around when he sees I'm not following him. "Ms. Calvetti, I have a surprise for you."

"I don't like surprises."

He shakes his head and walks over to me, pulling me

out the door with him. "Mr. Montford asked me to take care of some things this morning."

I swallow at the ominous words. "What kind of things?"

Demont looks down at me. "Well, that would ruin the surprise."

Ice floods my veins at his words. Maybe this is my end. Not drowning in a pool, but being killed by Matías's muscle.

He pulls me across the grass and around the side of the house, where I see a guesthouse and a small shed. I dig my heels into the ground as we make our way to the shed. Is he going to lock me up in there? Chain me to the walls like I'm chained in my dream. Or is this where he kills people?

He shakes his head at me where I am stalled but tightens his grip, forcing me to walk to the shed. When we get closer, I notice there are windows on the side. When we make it to the front, I see two French doors. I breathe a sigh of relief, knowing I'm being dragged to my death.

"Mr. Montford thought you might find this enjoyable."

I look up at Demont, confused, then look into the shed. Blank canvases lie stacked to one wall. Cans and tubes of different paints lie in front of them. All my fears disappear as I see that the shed is an art studio. I fling the doors open and smile.

"I'll leave you…" Demont trails off as I take in the room.

I look around the room, the grin never falling off my

face. A real smile for the first time in weeks when I see the one thing that centers me.

But that thought alone is enough for me to lose the smile.

I've been gone for almost two weeks. Two weeks of being a prisoner to a very powerful billionaire. None of this makes any sense. If I am supposed to be under protection by my father's orders, why hasn't he called or why hasn't Matías let me talk to him? And why was Nicolas in the room that night, I thought someone was trying to kidnap me?

Maybe I am a fool to think that what Matías told me to be true. My father would never have me kidnapped to protect me. Even if Matías says it was so no one knew where I really was. Something isn't adding up. And I don't know why I didn't think about it before. Matías has been lying to me the whole time. It's the reason he is so hot and cold. Why he gets mad when he touches me.

I grab a canvas and slide it over to an empty wall. My anger taking over me. I need to speak to Matías. I need to demand answers from him.

I spend the afternoon painting. Taking my anger and aggression out on the canvas even though I would much rather do it with my fists to Matías's chest. I know he is keeping secrets from me. But maybe I am the biggest secret of all.

After dinner, Demont asks if I want to paint some more or go back to our game of Risk.

I choose the game because the only thing I see when I think of the art studio is red. And I need to keep my calm when Matías gets home.

"Your move," he tells me as I stare at the game board.

"Why do you work for him?" I ask Demont as I move a pawn on the board.

"He's a good man. A good boss."

I look up at Demont to see if he's joking. His face is serious. "He kidnapped me."

"Under orders of your father."

"Bullshit," I stammer as I lean back in my chair, folding my arms over my chest.

Demont slides a pawn across the board and sighs. "You'll have to ask Matías what you want to know because I can't say anything."

"Why work for a monster?" I ask, ignoring the game in front of me.

Demont runs his finger over his bottom lip as if he is questioning telling me. "He wasn't always like this."

I gesture for him to continue.

"Sometimes I feel like he is still a boy trying to prove himself to his family."

"So committing crimes proves that he is a man," I say in a mocking tone.

He shakes his head. "No, he sees it as a penance."

"A penance?"

"Matías has made decisions in his life he isn't proud of."

I snort. "I'm guessing I am one of them."

Demont ignores my comment. "He wants to be the hero. But he doesn't know how."

"Well kidnapping isn't the best—"

Demont cuts me off, rubbing his hands over his smooth head. "He saved me. Saved me from a life of destruction. I was ready to kill myself. But Matías took me under his wing. Gave me a job. Made me remember life was worth living."

I see the ghost in Demont's eyes. "What happened?"

"I lost everything." He pauses and looks out the window toward the lit-up deck of the pool. "I got in with the wrong people. Made bad decisions. My family paid the ultimate price."

I try to picture this man with a family. "Where are they now?" I ask, afraid to know the answer.

He looks me straight in the eye. "Dead."

My heart breaks for him. I know the pain my heart took when my mother passed away. My hand reaching for the necklace that no longer sits on my neck.

"They were five and six," he continues, as if he needs to talk about it to move on. "My baby girls so full of life. My wife was pregnant with our son." His head falls. "I broke their trust and, in turn, they were killed to teach me a lesson. I was so broken. But I met Matías. He had just lost his brother. I took a path of destruction; he took the higher road. I learned from him to be a better man. To not let my guilt eat away at me."

"I-I didn't know."

His head snaps up at me. "How would you? You're just a—"

I know he almost let me know too much. But I don't say anything.

He mutters almost to himself, but loud enough that I can still hear him. "And now he's on the path I was on. I'm afraid to lose him."

I bite my lip, unsure of what to say. Or what to make of that little bit of information I just received.

"I think I am done for the night," he apologizes. "We can play tomorrow."

I nod and watch him leave, head hung low.

I sit outside for an hour, waiting for Matías to walk in the door. But he never shows up. I eventually crawl into bed, my thoughts on Demont and everything he lost. And my heart worrying about Matías. I haven't heard from him since he yelled at me last night. And if what Demont said was true about a path of destruction, I know he can't be anywhere good.

15

ALESSIA

I startle awake, but not by a dream this time. I glance over at the clock on the bedside table and it reads just after three in the morning. The sound of labored breathing scares me. I fly up in bed and find Matías sitting in a chair, staring at me.

"You scared the shit—" I stop my own words when I see a cut on his cheek. I can't tell from here if it's dried blood or fresh. But I can hear his wheezing breaths.

I scramble out of bed and rush over to him. My hand going to his face, finding it bloodied and bruised. I remember him coming to me like this before. Back at the other house. I woke up to him sitting in a chair, watching me. Blood on his hands and face. He didn't say a word to me that night, but gently kissed my forehead like he was protecting me.

I shouldn't care. I should let him fight his own battles. Especially after the way he talked to me the last time I saw him. But Demont's words are stuck in my head. And

I can't help but feel for Matías at this moment. I can tell he was fighting. Memories of my oldest brother coming home like this after Mom died. He was just about to graduate university but he took out his aggressions through fighting and nearly got kicked out of school.

I look into Matías's eyes. He doesn't say anything to me as I hold his face in my palms. He just sits there, lost in thought. That's when I see through him, see past the hardened man I am used to. And I see what I saw in my brother all those years ago. I see a boy hiding in a man's body who has lost control of his life.

"You should take care of this cut," I whisper as my finger runs along the edge of the cut that is slowly bleeding. He just stares into my eyes. I feel his hand run up the back of my thigh and pull me closer to him. I slide between his legs and run my hand through his hair. "Matías."

He doesn't say anything to me, just holds me close to him, both of us unable to take our eyes off the other. He lets out a deep breath and I can't help but wonder if I'm his salvation. Like he can breathe around me, relax when my hands touch him. This broken man in front of me has so many layers. And it scares me that I want to know them all. I shouldn't want to be near him, but the pull between us is inevitable. And will only lead to something catastrophic.

I tug on his hand. "Come, let's get you cleaned up."

He obliges and stands in front of me. I run my hand down his chest and he winces. I close my eyes, feeling his pain. I see a bag next to him and pick it up as I pull him out of my room and across the house to his own room.

I toss the bag on the floor and pull him into his bathroom. I've never been in here. Only peeked at it earlier when I was looking for him. The lights are bright but with them on I can see the worst of his injuries. I push him on to the toilet so he's eye level with me. I grab a washcloth I find in a cabinet and run it under warm water. I gently press it to his face, wiping away the blood on his cheek. His lip is swollen, dried blood covering a cut over the outer edge. He barely winces as I wipe away the blood, his eyes on mine the whole time.

When I finish cleaning up his face, I pull his shirt over his head. He grimaces with the movement and I already know his ribs must be bruised from the way he flinched when I touched him in my room.

Red circles mark the right side of his ribs. I don't think they're broken or else he would be in more pain. Just badly bruised. I run my hand over his stomach, my fingers outlining his hard abs. I bite my lip as I drop my hands to the top of the basketball shorts.

I step away from him, needing to put space between us, and turn on the shower, knowing the steam will loosen up his muscles. I'll get him ice after. When I turn around, he is standing, his eyes laser focused on me. Hungry, needy eyes.

My nipples pebble in the T-shirt I am wearing and I watch as his eyes fall to my chest. "You—you should shower. It will help," I stammer out. His gaze is making my stomach flip and I know I shouldn't want this, want him.

"Are you going to finish undressing me?" he asks as he steps closer to me.

"I... um... I should—"

His hands grab mine as he places them at the top of his shorts. "Alessia." He leans down, his hot breath on my neck. "Finish what you started."

I gulp down my nerves. My hands shaky as I grip the top of his shorts, staring at the V along the waistband, at his arousal visible through the fabric.

His fingers touch my chin, lifting it until he is looking into my eyes. His blue ones pull me in, like a trance. I can't seem to stop looking at them until his lips land on mine, soft and gentle. But as the kiss deepens, I can tell it hurts him.

I pull away. "You're hurt."

"I don't care," he whispers.

His hands are back on mine where they rest on his hips. He grips them and helps me push his shorts down. I take in his naked form, an Adonis of a man. His cock stands at attention, thick and long, a vein running up the side. I swallow as I take him in. I touched him before but never looked at him, never seen him completely naked. And he is glorious.

He pulls at my shirt and I don't have the energy to fight him as he pulls it over my head. His lips crash to mine and I let him have them. "All I need right now is your lips on mine, angel." His tongue dances with my own and I let out a soft moan as the feeling of his calloused hands pull me against him.

"We shouldn't do this."

His lips move to my neck, sucking and biting. "Why not?"

"You're in pain."

He chuckles against my neck. "Is that the only reason you can think of?"

My hands glide up his chest on their own accord. My lips landing on his chest. I shake my head as I fight myself to stop touching him.

"You want me, angel. Don't fight it." His hand slides into my sleep shorts, between my thighs where I am soaking from his touch. "I need to forget everything right now."

I go to ask him what he needs to forget, but he pushes my shorts off, lifts me up and backs me into the shower until I hit a wall. My legs wrap around his waist because I have nowhere else to put them. I shiver despite the warm water splashing us. His dick is pressed into my stomach as his fingers move in and out of me. I am panting with need, with an unwanted desire. I know we shouldn't be doing this but I can't help the shameless need I have for him.

"Hold on to my shoulders," he growls into my ear as his fingers leave my center, leaving me feeling empty.

I'm slow to follow his orders, so he does it for me, pulling my arms up and around his neck.

"Matías," I groan.

"Angel," he murmurs across my lips before he slams into me all the way to the hilt.

I scream at the intrusion of his thick cock. He isn't gentle. He's ruthless as he takes and takes from my body. His mouth lands on mine in a punishing kiss, swallowing my screams. I know this must hurt him. His body already broken. But I realize he is breaking mine in the process. Tearing me in two as he sends white heat through my entire body, an intense pleasure I have never felt with a man before.

I grip his hair as he pummels me, my breathing erratic, my heart beating a million beats a minute. He slows down for only a second and I yearn for the punishing thrusts he was giving me. I rock my hips into his and a feral smile crosses his face. His fingers crush into my hip bones and I know it will leave a bruise. Without warning, he picks up his pace again, slamming into me even more brutally than before and I meet each one of his thrusts. My nails scratching down his back as I scream every curse word in Italian, French, and English. The orgasm hits me so suddenly, my entire body exploding in pleasure, my head falls forward and I bite hard into his shoulder.

"Mmm, I knew my angel liked it dirty," he says as he pulls out of me, dropping my legs to the floor. I nearly collapse, my body unable to hold myself up from the pleasure I just received.

He flips me around and presses his chest into my back so my front is flush against the tile wall of the shower. He pulls my hips back and slams into me, using his hands as leverage to make every thrust deeper. My toes lift off the ground and I feel like I am going to black out. The pleasure too much as another orgasm surprises me in the best way. My limbs are Jell-O as he keeps up his ruthless pace. I cry and moan as my cheek presses hard into the wall. One of his hands snakes up my body and wraps around my neck, pulling me into his chest. The angle makes him so deep it's almost painful. But as he cuts off my oxygen supply, the pain disappears as euphoria takes over. Like I am having an out-of-body experience.

His name falls from my lips over and over. His lips are at my ear, sucking on the lobe. "So beautiful. My perfect angel submitting to my claim on her body."

He twists one of my nipples hard just as he lets go of my throat, air flooding my lungs as he bends me over. I feel his loss immediately as he pulls out of me. But then I feel hot spurts of his cum along my back, dripping down my butt and thighs.

His hand grips my chin as he leans over me. "So beautiful covered in me. You made the pain go away."

I half expect him to walk away. Leave me to clean up and figure out what the hell just happened. But then I feel a sponge caress my back, his arm wrapped around my waist to hold me up, because he must surely know I'll collapse without his support.

After he wipes us both clean, he shuts the water off and wraps me in a towel. I'm at a loss for words. I don't know what to say. Don't know if there is anything to say.

He grabs my hand and walks me into his bedroom. He pulls back the sheets and takes my towel off as he pushes me into the bed. I expect him to leave but he follows, removing his own towel and slipping in behind me. His arms wrap around as he whispers in Spanish in my ear.

I flip over in his arms and run my finger along the cut on his cheek. "You need ice."

He shakes his head and presses a chaste kiss to my lips. "I just need you right now, angel."

I watch him as he drifts off to sleep. Confused and sated all at the same time.

I don't know what tomorrow will bring. If he will go back to being the cold, hardened man. Or if maybe this version of him will stick around for a little bit longer.

I drift off to sleep with a million thoughts in my head. But the only one that doesn't reach me is the one where I remember he is my captor.

16

ALESSIA

I wake up a few hours later as the sun peeks through the balcony doors of his room. Matías is sound asleep next to me, light snores coming from him.

His face is more swollen than early this morning. His lip worse than it should be because of the damaging kisses he gave me.

I slip out of bed and grab my shirt out of the bathroom. I pick up his dirty clothes and throw them in his hamper in the closet. I walk into the kitchen, glad to find it empty. I shuffle around the freezer and find a few bags of frozen vegetables. I grab them and head back to the room, slipping inside and shutting the door behind me before anyone wakes up and sees me.

I set the vegetables down on the nightstand when I see the bag he had with him the night before. I pick it up and find clothes and shoes in it. I pull out his Gucci wingtips and set them in the closet. I go to throw his clothes in the hamper but find them damp. When I pull my hands away, red stains them.

I wouldn't have noticed the blood if I didn't touch the clothes. The black fabric hiding the secrets Matías keeps close to his chest. I put the clothes back in the plastic bag and set it next to the hamper. I need to get answers from him. I have no other options.

I walk back to the bed and find his eyes open. "Where did you go?"

I grab the frozen peas and climb onto the bed. He reaches out for me, his hand gliding up my thigh as I kneel on the bed. "I got you ice for the swelling."

He gives me that look, the one he gave me the night we met. "I'm fine."

"You are far from fine. Your lip is swollen and your cheek is puffy. I'm sure if I pull the covers back your ribs will be bad too."

He smirks at me. "Mmm. How far back will you pull the covers?"

I roll my eyes at him.

He shifts in the bed and I can tell by the movement it hurts him. But he doesn't let it bother him, his fingers hover dangerously close to the apex of my thighs and I have nothing on underneath this T-shirt. "I might need some help with my swollen body after all." He says it as his finger swipes against me, causing me to drop the peas.

"Matías…"

He grins at me. His smile lopsided due to swelling and I hate that I find it adorable. I should find nothing about this man adorable. He kidnapped me, he's keeping me hostage, he gets into fights, he has a bag of bloody clothes. Yet for some reason, my stupid body doesn't care about any of that and only cares about the feeling he gives me.

He pushes the sheets down and I see exactly what he meant by swollen. His dick thick and hard as it points up to his stomach. Before I can protest, he pulls me on top of him.

"Matías, stop."

His hands glide up my back under my shirt, then back down over my ass, squeezing as he does it. "You didn't tell me to stop last night."

"I... you..." I can't form words as he uses his hands to guide my center across his erection.

He pulls me down so his mouth is against my ear. "And I don't think you want me to stop now either."

All I can do is let out a whimper as he slides into me. It doesn't take long for me to start groaning his name in pleasure. He pulls my shirt over my head and leans up to pull a nipple into his mouth. He nips and bites at each one before pushing me up. "Ride me."

I move up and down on him, finding my pleasure but I know it's not enough for him. I know from the way he dominated me last night, he needs control, he needs it rough. My eyes meet his and I can see the pleasure in them. I start to move faster when he grabs my hips, lifting me up and down as he pushes into me.

"Fuck, angel," he groans before flipping me onto my back.

I groan as he pulls out of me and stands up. "What are you—"

I can't even finish my sentence as he pulls me to the

edge of the bed and starts slamming into me. His hands on my hips so I don't move up the bed. His pace relentless and I have no idea how he can keep his stamina up with the shape his body is in but somehow he doesn't stop. I watch him as he watches himself pulse in and out of me. The man is one of the most handsome men I have ever met. He is alluring, dangerous. And I know what I am doing is wrong. I almost want to tell him to stop, but then his hips shift and hits something inside of me that has me crying out his name. "Matías!"

He grins at me, then pulls my legs up so my ankles rest on his shoulders. Stars flash across my vision with how deep he is. I can't remember left from right as he pounds into me. I can barely remember my name.

"Alessia." My name a plea across his lips. "Fuck, woman. You're so tight. Fucking perfect."

My hands grip into the sheets, needing something to hold on to as he fucks me into oblivion.

"I can't. Fuck. I shouldn't," he mumbles as he grinds his hips into mine. His pace slowing down as he lifts my hips to an angle so only my shoulders are on the bed. "Fuck," he screams.

I feel his hot stream release inside of me but he pulls out quickly, dropping my legs and coming all over my stomach.

I close my eyes, not sure what the hell just happened to me but I swear I had an out-of-body experience. Again. I've never been fucked like this before in my life. Hell, the craziest sex I've ever had was on my kitchen table. And now that seems lackluster to the way he owns my body. Drives me crazy with the slightest touch, then pulls all the pleasure from my body with his rough control.

I open my eyes and find him staring at me. The expression on his face unreadable, like he either wasn't satisfied or doesn't understand what happened. He runs his thumb over his bottom lip, then smirks at me.

I prop myself up on my elbows and blow my bangs out of my face. "What?"

He bites his lip and shakes his head.

"Matías," I whisper.

He picks up my shirt off the bed and wipes my stomach clean, then tosses the shirt behind him.

"What are you thinking?" I ask softly as I sit up, suddenly self-conscious of the fact I was sprawled out naked on his bed. I go to cover up my chest but he pulls my hands away.

He cups my face then leans down and kisses me so intensely I am nearly ready for round two. He pulls away but doesn't let go of my face. "What are you doing to me?" he asks.

"I—um—"

His finger drags over my lip before he leans down and sucks it into his mouth. When he pulls away, he flops over onto the bed next to me. "Fuck, woman. I shouldn't have done that."

Disappointment flutters through my system. "I know. We shouldn't—"

"No, angel, we most definitely should have. But fuck, my ribs hurt."

I look over at him and start laughing.

"Don't laugh, it only makes them hurt more."

I bite back my smile as I crawl over the bed to grab the peas that were forgotten about. I jump as his hand slaps across my ass.

"Mmm. I want that ass too."

My cheeks flame at his words but I choose to ignore them as I pick up the peas and press a bag to his face. "This is what you should have done last night."

His hand replaces mine on the bag and I put the other on his ribs. "I don't have a problem with what I did last night."

I sit back on my knees as I hold the ice to him. "Before or after you came home."

He closes his eyes and I know he doesn't want to talk to me about the fact he was fighting. "I need to get the aggression out somehow."

I bite on my lip, not sure if I should say the next thing on my mind. I decide to hold it in because I am not sure what his response would be if I question him.

"I'm fine, Alessia," he says to me. I look down at him through my bangs. Not sure what to say. I can tell from the emptiness in his eyes that he's lying. And I know from the bloody pile of clothes that he tells me more lies than truths.

We are interrupted by a knock on the door.

"Just a minute," Matías yells as he sits up, pulling the bag from his face.

I panic, thinking about the fact that I am sitting naked in Matías's bed when I should be down the hall in my own room. I jump off the bed and start pulling open drawers in his closet, looking for a T-shirt or something to put on.

I hear him laughing as he stands in the doorway. "You know this is my house. I don't care if anyone knows you're in here."

"Well I do." I turn around and yell at him. "What are they going to think? That I'm some stupid girl that developed Stockholm syndrome. This is wrong, so wrong."

Matías's hands land on my arms and he pulls me into him. "Are you sure this is wrong? I'm here to protect you."

"No you're not," I exhale. Knowing there is much more to this than I've been told.

He leans in and whispers in my ear as his hands glide down my body. "Remember the night we met. Remember that pull we had."

I nod.

"Then how is this wrong, angel?" His lips glide down my neck. "None of this feels wrong."

I moan as his words relax me just a bit and his touch turns me to mush.

"It's probably Demont at the door. Why don't you get in the shower? He won't know you're in here."

Doubtful, I think. But step out of his arms either way and walk into the bathroom, leaving the door cracked open. Once I turn on the shower, I hear Matías open the bedroom door and talk to Demont. I tiptoe over to the cracked door, hoping to hear anything that might help me in my situation.

"—wasn't going to leave the house."

"They requested you."

"Why would they call you and not me?" Matías's voice is soft. I can barely make out his words.

Demont mumbles something I can't quite make out.

"I—I shouldn't have gone to the gym last night."

"Did you find anything out from your hit?"

Hit? Like he killed someone? That would explain the bloody clothes. But I don't believe someone like him could do something like that. Yes, he has me as a hostage but he's never acted like a killer toward me. I know he has a lot going on, turmoil he is working through. But a killer?

"Fuck. There is something going on…" Matías's words trail off as I hear the bedroom door shut.

I grab my shorts off the floor then wait a few seconds before I push open the bathroom door, when I am positive that the room is empty. I don't want to risk walking through the hall to his wing so I slip out the balcony door and cross the main doors. I see Claudette in the kitchen but she is bent over the oven so I'm able to slip past her without her noticing. I hear voices behind the closed doors of the office so I know I can make it to my room without a problem. I open the door and shut it behind me. I let out a sigh as I collapse on the bed in front of me.

I don't hear from Matías for the rest of the day. I watch Demont storm off in the afternoon and he hasn't been back since.

I decide to spend my time in the art studio, getting lost in my thoughts, my hip-hop music, and the paint I use to express my hidden feelings. I asked Demont for larger canvases yesterday and he brought me back mural sizes. I have no idea when but I am glad they are here. I even managed to find a closet of cleaning supplies and was able to take a broom and some towels to use as tools to paint. I picked some flowers in the garden since I love the broken pattern they leave on the canvas.

I rarely create self-portraits but this time I have a strong urge to. My head a mess as I try to figure out what is going on in my life. So many questions I haven't gotten answered. But maybe if I get close to Matías, I can break him. Like how my friends aren't concerned about me? Did my father tell them I am under protection? But even I know that isn't true. He never would have done this to me. He would have told me I was in danger. Not that I would have listened. Hell, I snuck out from the watchful eyes of guards in Monaco.

But what does Matías have to do with all this? Why is a rich man with everything he could ever need tied into something so dark? Does he find a thrill in it? And what did Demont mean by the hit?

When I first met Matías, I fell for his charm. Then after I was kidnapped, I thought he was a monster. But I think he is trapped in something so deep even he can't get out of it. Maybe that is why he fights, to feel something. I know that's why my brother did it.

And why am I so attracted to him, even after all that I've been through? It's not like I am locked in a cell. I have more freedom than most captives, at least according to books and movies. Is that why I am attracted to him? Feel the undeniable pull to him? Because he shows me kindness. But isn't that what real monsters do? Pretend to be someone they aren't in order to tempt you and pull you into their web. Entrap you.

I use heavy brushstrokes as I outline the shape of my upper body, jagged and broken lines of different thicknesses and shapes that match the confusion in my veins. I paint myself kneeling in submission, naked and on display. My mouth open, as if in ecstasy, but my hands doing what they can to cover my nakedness.

I don't know how much time passes as I paint. The picture coming together faster than anything I've ever done. I use the lines of my hair to form a bird, like it's trying to lift me to freedom, but I am stuck, tied to the world I was forced into. I add abstract rope to my wrists and more around my waist, trapped like the girl from my dream. But I don't wear a crown, just a feeling of guilt by falling for the man who kidnapped me.

I spill paint across another canvas and use it as a palette. I take the broom and splatter paint across the image. A mixture of grays, white, deep reds, and eggplant purple mixed with the vibrancy of yellow and pink. I feel the paint hit my legs, my arms, and my face as I dance around the room. A freedom I haven't felt in a while. The only freedom I'll have for a while.

The sound of the music abruptly stopping causes me to slide across the floor where the paint splashed.

I turn around, my breathing heavy, when I see Matías standing in the doorway. A curious look on his face as he sees the broom laying in a mess of paint on the floor.

"Now this is a sight to see," he says as his eyes roam my body.

I look down and see myself covered in paint. Not atypical of me to look this way after a day in the studio.

"Do you always paint with household items?"

I look over and see the paint-soaked towels and broom. I nod. "I like to use different mediums."

"Did you get that from the broom closet?"

I blush.

He runs his thumb across his lips and I finally take him in. The way I remember meeting him in that club. A custom suit made to fit his body, accentuating every inch of muscle I know lays underneath. He doesn't have a jacket on this time and his sleeves are rolled up his tanned olive forearms, his tattoos peeking out underneath. He is a magnificent creature. I feel the blush deepen on my face as I remember just how magnificent he is.

My eyes drift back to his face and he smirks at me. Like he knows exactly what I was thinking about.

"I knew you liked to paint. I saw your work in your apartment."

I drop the paintbrush in my hand. "You were at my apartment? When?"

He licks his lower lip as he moves from the doorway and takes a step closer to me. "The other day when I had to go to Naples to sign off on contracts for the hotel I am building there."

I bite my lip as I study him. "Why would you go there?"

He takes a step closer to me. "I wanted to know more about you." He looks behind me at the painting before meeting my eyes again. "I wanted to know why I am so captivated by you." He steps closer to me, his hand brushing a piece of hair behind my ear. "I wanted to know why looking at you makes me feel like none of my problems matter."

"Matías," I whisper.

"I wanted to know if I met you before we ended up in this situation if I would have been as intrigued by you as I am now."

I swallow at his words, at the slight touch of his fingertips as they move down my jaw and neck and across my clavicle. He steps away from me and I feel myself letting out the breath I didn't know I was holding.

"I would have brought you a broom if you needed it."

"I—" he cuts me off before I can say anything more. Not that I was sure what I was going to say. Apologize for using his cleaning supplies?

"Do you use the flowers too?"

I nod, even though his back is toward me now. I watch him as he carefully steps through the mess of paint on the floor, his fingers drag over the paint on the canvas, messing with my lines.

"Show me."

"Wh-what?" I stutter.

He turns toward me. "Show me how you work."

I purse my lips. "Um—weren't you just watching me?"

He shakes his head but from the way his eyes light up, I know he is lying.

I let out a breath and decide to show him. As I walk past him, he drags the paint on his fingers across the back of my hand. A shudder goes through me, and I am pissed that he can see the way he affects me.

Then I wonder if he is using me. For sex and pleasure while I'm under his watchful eye.

I ignore my thoughts as I bend down and grab the roses I picked earlier. I dip them in black paint and use the petals to fix the lines he messed up. Then I start using them to add more detail to the painting in an organized chaos. The curve of her neck, the bindings on her arms, the tautness of her nipple. I feel myself growing wet as I paint the erotic self-portrait with the man that causes those feelings watching me.

"Is this supposed to be you?" he asks me.

I glance behind me and nod, the blush creeping down my neck.

He smirks at me. "Do you like to be tied up, angel?"

I bite down on my lip and turn around, back to the painting.

"I asked you a question." His voice comes out stern.

I shake my head, my hand stuck on the painting. "I... I've never..."

I feel his fingers graze down my arms. "Mmm. But you want to be."

I don't move as he touches me, my body completely turned on and willing to give in to his game.

His words a whisper in my ear. "And who brings that look of ecstasy to your face?" His hands reach around my front, his fingers grazing my nipples.

"You," I barely say the words as I drop the flowers to the ground.

He spins me around so suddenly I barely have time to

catch myself on the paint. His lips crash into mine and I moan at the attack of his mouth as it overtakes me. His hands glide up my shirt while mine reach for his belt buckle.

He pulls back from me and shakes his head. "Dirty girl, what am I going to do with you?"

I don't know where the words come from but I am just as shocked to say them as he is to hear them. "Tie me up and fuck me."

He blinks a few times at me like he can't believe I said that. But then his hands are on me, pulling my shirt over my head. His mouth is back on mine instantly, devouring my lips, pulling me into his hard body. I reach for his shirt, pulling the buttons as I take it off violently, buttons flying off, landing in the paint buckets, others on the floor.

He backs me up to one of the glass walls of the studio, lifting my legs around his hips. Before I even know what he is doing, my hands are tied up with my T-shirt and he has them pressed above my head.

"Such a sight to see," he says as he stares at my naked top half, speckled with paint that must have rubbed off his shirt and onto me.

He bends down and takes a nipple into his mouth, sucking it so hard it's almost painful. I moan as he pops it out of his mouth, then blows cold air across it. My hips buck at his out of need and he grins at me with that diabolical look that I think I like more than I am willing to admit. His hands reach my shorts and he pulls them off me.

"Keep your hands above your head."

I nod as I watch him walk toward the painting and pick up the flowers I dropped on the floor. A shiver runs through me as he stalks toward me like I'm prey. I press my thighs together from the need between them.

He takes the flower and presses it across my clavicle, twisting it in circles. "Is this how you do it? Or soft and gentle like this?" he asks as he drags the flower over my hardened nipples. The wet paint and his soft touch causing a moan to fall out of my mouth.

"I can be firmer." He presses the petals harder into my nipple, his knuckles pinching it. I squirm under his touch. "Or I can be as light as a feather?" He ever so lightly drags the flowers down my stomach, a light trail of paint in its wake. "What will it be, my angel? Soft?" He moves the feather down to my bare thighs, leaving light circles of yellow paint. "Or firm?"

I gasp as he grabs my hips, spinning me around, and presses my front into the glass. It's then I become very aware of the fact anyone can see us. The fading light of dusk turning to darkness and the lights from the studio lighting us up. My paint-drenched nipples press into the glass as his hand drags the flower over my ass and down the backs of my thighs.

"I asked you a question, angel. Which will it be?"

I moan at the friction of my nipples on the window at the same time I feel one of his fingers slide across the crease between my ass and thigh.

"Ticktock."

I don't know what I want from him. All I know is that his touch is lighting a fire inside of me and I don't want him to stop. He presses his hips against my ass and I whimper. "Whatever you want."

I can't see his face but I know that devilish grin forms. "Good girl," he says, just as his hand slaps hard against my ass. My cheek is on fire as he grabs it hard and squeezes. "I love this ass. One of my favorite things about you."

He pulls away from me and I miss the heat of his body against mine. I go to turn around but he commands me to stay put.

I hear his feet walk back toward me and I anticipate the next slap across my ass. But this time his other hand is cool as I feel the paint coating it soothe the sore skin. "I can't wait until I own this ass just like I own your pussy."

I shiver against the glass as I feel his tongue lick up my spine and around to my ear. "Do you want that, angel? Do you want me to fuck you here?"

His paint-covered hand slides over my ass and I let out a groan. I've never done it before but I know Matías would make it feel good. He could make anything feel good. Hell, he has barely touched me in a sexual way and I can feel moisture dripping down my legs.

"But for now, I need this pussy."

I moan at his words. "Yes, please."

He chuckles as he grabs my hips and pulls me against him, my bound hands falling behind his head and against his back. "Look how beautiful that art is you made on the glass. I should have it removed and hung on a wall. Maybe my living room. No one would know that those round circles are from these hard nipples." He pinches them as he says it. "Or that line down the middle runs to the sweetest heaven I've ever tasted."

I gulp at his words. They are turning me on more than I care to admit. His hand slides down from my nipples and his thick fingers slide between my folds. "So wet. Do you like when I talk dirty to you, angel?" He hooks two fingers inside of me. "I think you do."

My whimpers turn into begging. "Matías!"

"So needy," he says as he pulls his fingers out of me. "But you've been a very good girl."

He lets go of me and I turn around as I hear the clink of his belt buckle. I bite down on my lip as I watch him strip out of his paint-stained pants. His cock hard, thick, and at attention. He grins at me and I jump on him. My bound hands slip over his head and my legs hook onto his hips. He growls into my ear before our mouths collide. Teeth and tongues, licking and biting. Our need undeniable.

He lowers me to the ground and I am not lost in the fact we are both going to be covered in paint after this.

He doesn't take his time as he unhooks my arms from his head and uses one hand to pin my wrists to the ground and the other to hold my hips at the right angle as he slams into me.

"Fuck," I scream out at the intense orgasm that grinds through me with just one pulse of his dick.

"That's right, angel, you need this as much as I do."

I beg and plead for him to move harder and faster and he does as he plows us both into oblivion. He flips me onto my knees and presses my cheek into the floor as he pounds into me from behind. My arms tied behind my back keep me from holding my balance as I slide in the paint across the floor.

Matías grunts as he gets deeper inside of me. His control on my hips bruising. He slides his finger along my clit causing me to buck against him but he pulls it away all too quickly. But then I feel his thumb slip between my cheeks and against my forbidden hole.

I squirm as he uses my own wetness to slide the tip of his thumb in. The pain turns to pleasure as he works my ass at the same time his cock destroys my insides. I can barely keep my knees up as the orgasm hits me. I didn't even feel it coming on, but I explode into a million pieces just as Matías frees my arms, then pulls out and comes all over my back.

He flips me over and his mouth slants over mine, coaxing my tongue with his own. I whimper into his mouth, my arms wrapping around his neck. I want this part with him. The coddling. The comfort. Especially after what he just did to me. What I let him do. The thought gives me a weird feeling in my stomach because I know I shouldn't like this. Shouldn't want this. Want him. My captor. But he is becoming so much more than that.

I don't know how long we lie on the floor next to each other after the most intense sex I've ever had. Every time with him, something becomes unhinged in me. And every time it's better than the time before.

His fingers trace the paint on my thighs as we lie in silence.

I want to ask him so many questions but I don't know where to start and I don't know if he'll answer.

He runs his fingers over the tattoo on my hip, pulling me onto my side to face him. "When did you get this?"

I look into his blinding blue eyes and swallow down the hiccup in my chest. He's too handsome for his own good. Maybe this would mean something different to us if we met under better circumstances. "In university."

"What's it mean?"

I look down at where his thumb runs over the words on my hip. *Vir bellator eligit se fati.* "It's Latin for a warrior chooses her own fate. My mother used to say that to me all the time. Ever since I can remember. It came from my name."

His hand trails up my side and over my ribs. "What's your name mean?"

"Alessia Ariana. Defending warrior." I pause as he smiles at me when I say it. "My mother named me. After she had three boys, she wanted me to be the fighter in the family."

"You are."

"Says the man holding a woman hostage."

He smiles at me, then kisses me briefly on the lips. "You like it."

I roll my eyes at him. "I don't."

"You like my dick."

I sigh. "Unfortunately."

He pulls me closer into him and I feel his dick twitch against my stomach. "Tell me about your family."

"Like any Italian family. Strong-willed, loud, and loyal. They are all a bit crazy but maybe I am too. My father wanted to carry on the family tradition of names but my mother wouldn't have it. I got lucky with Alessia.

If it was up to my father, he would have named me Alessandro even if I was a girl."

He laughs. "Why's that?"

"Because every male in this family has their name end in o. My brothers are Angelo, Leonardo, and Emilio. My uncle is Gianno and my cousins are Rocco, Gerardo, Leandro, Aldo, Dario, and Gianno Junior."

Matías cracks up next to me.

"It's not funny. It's annoying. There are so many other names out there. If I ever have kids, I swear I am going to name them the most stupid names just to try and end this Calvetti family tragedy. Like brush, paint, and canvas."

He throws his head back and laughs. A sound that seems so foreign on his lips but I like it. "No one would ever know you are a painter."

I blush.

"My middle name is Diego so I fit right into your family."

I frown as he says it. "Where do they think I am?"

"Your family? Under protection as they asked."

"They don't know it's you though."

He shakes his head. "No one knows what I do besides run Montford Hotels."

I gather the courage to ask him more. "What is it you do, Matías?"

He pinches his eyes shut and rolls away from me. "I can't tell you, Alessia. And not because I'm a dick but I don't want to risk your life even more. If you knew how deep my secrets went or your family's secrets, it could kill you."

I look at him in confusion. "My family's secrets? I know all of them."

A mocking laugh falls from his lips. "You think you know but you obviously don't."

"Then tell me," I stammer.

"I can't."

"What are you keeping from me, Matías?"

He looks over at me, and I see sincerity in his eyes as he speaks. "I really am protecting you, angel. Trust me on that." He sighs when he sees the anger in my eyes. "All I know is there was a threat to your life. Kidnapping you was an easy way to keep whoever made that threat in the dark. They wouldn't have been able to find you as easily."

"But they did."

"Once. They know nothing anymore. Not after I brought you to where I should have the whole time."

"You don't think anyone will look for me here?"

He runs a finger over my brow. "No one knows I have anything to do with this."

I decide to let it go for now. I know I won't get more answers out of him. Yet. But I will try like hell to find out the truth somehow. "Are my friends not worried about me?"

He shakes his head. "I texted them from your phone the night…" he trails off and I know he was going to say the night he drugged me and took me. "They thought you were spending another day or two with me in Monaco. Your father told them you needed to be kept safe after that."

"Bianca would be biting at the bit to find out what is going on."

He shrugs. "And your father can tell her what he wants."

"When am I going to get out of here?"

He pulls me back into him and presses his lips to my forehead. "I'm not sure. But I'll do what is necessary to keep you safe."

"And after all this?" I ask curiously. My mind not wanting to believe he is a bad person.

"One day at a time, angel."

It's all he can give me, that I am sure of. And I don't know if I could even be with him after all this. For all I know, he could go to jail for kidnapping me, or worse.

The sound of sticky paint peeling off the floor makes him wince as he shifts. "We both need a shower," he says as he looks down at us.

"Last time you pulled me into a shower, you fucked me into a wall," I joke.

He licks his bottom lip. "Mmm. An even better reason to take a shower then."

"What is everyone going to think, Matías?"

"I told you not to worry about it."

"But I am worried. We don't know who could have just seen us as you had me pressed against the glass."

He shrugs. "I doubt anyone did."

I punch him in the arm, not that it causes him any harm, he's as hard as a concrete wall.

"Come on, little warrior," he says as he pulls me off the ground.

"Just because I'm small doesn't mean I couldn't kick your ass."

He chuckles. "I would like to see you try."

"I'll let my Italian woman out on you."

He raises a brow at me, then leans down and whispers in my ear. "I hope you do."

He wraps me in his shirt, then slides his pants back on. Both of our clothes covered in paint as much as our bodies. "Vinga."

He takes my hand as we walk out, surprising me. Luckily, we don't see anyone as we cross the lawn and walk back to the house. He pulls me through his room and into the bathroom.

"What language was that?" I ask him as he turns on the water in the shower.

"Catalan."

"Where are you from?"

He runs a hand through his hair. "I was born in England. But my mother is from Mallorca. I spent my summers there as a kid with my grandparents and aunt and uncle. Spanish and Catalan stuck from being immersed in it all the time."

"Do you still go to Mallorca? To see your family?"

He pulls on my shirt, pulling me into him. "So many questions."

"I'm just curious about you, Matías."

He raises a brow at me before answering. "No, I don't go back there anymore. Not after my grandparents passed."

I frown when I see the sorrow briefly flit across his

eyes. I decide to change the subject back to the original topic. "How many other languages do you speak?"

He shrugs as he starts to unbutton my shirt. "Four. English and French too. I know a little Italian but not much." He slides the shirt off my shoulders, his fingers outlining the paint on my body.

"I could teach you," I tell him as I look into his sapphire eyes.

His eyes drop to my lips. "I think you've already taught me a lot. When I make you come, you scream in Italian."

My eyes go wide. "No I don't."

He grins at me. "The fact I make you come so hard you don't remember what you say turns me on."

I roll my eyes at him just as he crashes his lips to mine. I suck his lip into my mouth as he picks me up and sets me on the counter. My hands move to his pants, shoving them off. He carries me into the shower and fucks me just like the night before.

17
MATÍAS

I run my fingers across my lips as I read the email in front of me. Alessia trusts me a little more with each passing day. But I want her full trust. If she trusts me more than her family, I can get us both out of the shithole we're in.

I asked The Partners to get a letter from her father explaining why he is doing this and why he hasn't spoken to her. I was surprised they followed through and gave it to me. It's fake but they wouldn't be where they are as an organization if they didn't make believable false documents.

I still haven't told them about Di Masio. I let them know the last hit was still useless. If it wasn't for the information Alessia gave me saying she recognized him the other night, then I would have told them. But I know how they work. Getting out is next to impossible, even when they claim otherwise. And I have a feeling this all ties together and I am being kept out of the loop. But I am just a lowly interrogator for them. I don't get to know why I am doing what I am doing most of the time. Just enough to get the information they need. But something in my gut is telling me I am being set up for something big. And not just for Alessia's kidnapping. So I will play along with them while I figure it out.

Demont left yesterday to do some recon and follow Di Masio. But he's had nothing of significance to report since then.

I hear a knock on the door of my office and see Alessia's head peek in. "You wanted to see me?"

Her hair is knotted on top of her head in some messy thing and her bangs wisp down over those spectacular whiskey doe eyes. She's wearing a white sundress I had put in her closet. She looks innocent in it and it makes me want to defile her.

I wave her over and she walks slowly to my desk. The only other time she was in here was when I felt her come on my fingers for the first time. The memory of her sweetness on my tongue. I make a mental note to eat her pussy out later. If she behaves.

I can tell she is nervous. I don't speak with her most of the day as I work. I would ignore her at night too if it weren't for my own needs that she seems to have no problem satisfying.

"I received an email from your father."

Her eyes light up as I say it and she quickly skips over to the desk. When she is within my reach, I pull her onto my lap. The need to touch her always present. I pull the email up and she leans over the desk to read it. I watch her as she does, her face dropping when she reads the words she doesn't want to see. The words I knew would make her upset. That her father cannot speak with her and cannot let anyone she knows speak with her in order to keep her hidden. I can see the questions fill her face. She remembers Di Masio coming that night. She believed he was there on her father's orders. But this trick of words will make her only trust me more. There are some things in the email, I have no idea what they mean, I can only guess words he used to tell her. Her eyes sad, she wipes away a tear when she gets to the end. But then she scrolls back to the beginning and reads again.

I let her read it as much as she wants. My hands gliding gently up her thigh. The feeling of her warm skin enough to make me hard but right now this isn't about my needs. It's about hers. And sex isn't an option when I know she will have a lot of questions for me. And I am only hoping she knows more than she thinks she does.

She stands up, pushing my hands away from her. "I'm so confused." She leans with her back against my desk, her arms folded over her chest.

I take the opportunity to slide into my chair so my legs are on either side of her and she's pinned to the desk. "What are you confused about?"

She wipes her eyes. I try to touch her again but she shakes me off. "Nicolas was there that night. I thought he came to rescue me. I-I thought you really kidnapped me. I don't know why you did, but I thought you were telling me lies this whole time."

I am, sweetheart.

"I don't know much. But I think Di Masio… Nicolas is the one your father is protecting you from."

"What?"

I decide to give her more, bait her with half-truths. "We think Nicolas is betraying your father."

She blinks at me several times. "Why... but... I don't understand." She pauses, and I let her think. "Who do you work for?" Her voice cracks when she asks me.

"Someone who has you and your father's best interests in mind."

She purses her lips, then turns back and looks at the email. "But he's worked for my father for years."

"Money and power change people."

She rubs her temple. "I remember him and my father arguing a few times. But I didn't think anything of it."

My hand goes to the back of her thigh. "Do you remember about what?"

She shakes her head. "No, I always walked away when he talked about business."

She bursts into tears and I pull her closer to me, enough that I lock my arms around her waist. "What's wrong, angel?"

"I thought you were a monster. That I was wrong for falling for a monster."

I run my fingers over her lips, not missing the words she said. "I am a monster. I never said I wasn't."

"But I thought you kidnapped me."

"Technically, I did." I pull her closer to me so she is forced on my lap. Her thighs on either side of mine.

Her hands land on my shoulders. "I shouldn't have feelings."

I lean up and press my lips to her neck. "Probably not."

"I shouldn't want you all the time."

"Mmm. Most definitely not."

"I... I don't know what to think."

I move my lips against hers. "Then don't think, angel. Just feel." I seal my words with a kiss and she goes limp in my arms. Her body giving in to mine as her arms wrap around my neck.

She pulls away and rests her forehead against mine. "What should I do?"

I push her bangs out of her eyes and cup her cheek. "Just let this play out. See what happens."

"Will you tell me if you find anything else out from my father?"

I nod.

"Okay."

I stare into her eyes, my hand still on her cheek when I hear a throat clear behind us. She jumps out of my lap so fast I chuckle.

"Am I interrupting something?" The hoarse cadence of Bastian's voice booms across the room.

I ignore him and grab Alessia's hand. "Go. I'll find you later."

She nods at me, then looks over at my brother. Bastian is intimidating with his broad shoulders and ever-present scowl. She glances back at me, then Bastian before scurrying across the room and slipping out behind him.

"New plaything?"

I chuckle. "You know I don't bring them here."

"Then who is she?"

I sigh as I rest my elbows on my desk. "What brings you here, Bastian?"

He sits across from me in one of the stiff leather chairs on the opposite side of my desk. He studies me as he crosses one ankle over his knee. He brings his elbow to the armrest, his fingers rubbing against his chin. I know he is trying to get me to break. I'm surprised when he flat-out asks me. "You are still working for them?"

I run my fingers along my bottom lip, facing off my brother is not easy. And I never win.

"They've been quiet, Matías."

"You got out. Of course you wouldn't hear from them," I snort and I know I just gave away my truths to him.

He's quiet as he watches me. His dark eyes the opposite of mine. Harder, more intense. "I talked to Ainslie."

I raise a brow at that. "You never speak to her."

He sighs. "She called me because she was worried about you."

I lean back in my chair. "It's nothing."

"Matías." His voice is stern, commanding. I hate when he acts like my father rather than my older brother. But the ten years between us have always given him that authority, especially since he's always been my boss.

"I'm paying off a debt." I speak quietly.

"Kilian paid our debts," he growls.

I shake my head as I glance over at him. "Don't be a fool, brother. He paid yours but he didn't pay mine."

I can see the defiance in Bastian's gaze but he rarely ever breaks his composure. "No, Kilian paid yours too. But you are foolish and you didn't want to get out. You wanted the power. And let me guess, you have none now. They wanted you to take Cameron. You failed. I can only imagine they dropped your rank."

I suck my bottom lip into my mouth, biting down to keep from exploding on my brother.

"You'll get yourself killed," he whispers.

I close my eyes, rubbing my hand over them as I tell him the truth. "I already feel dead so what's the difference?"

"I worry about you, Matías. You're my brother and despite everything we've been through, I do love you."

"Don't." I clench my fists against the chair, my voice rising with every word. "Don't act like you care about me. You never have."

"I've always cared about you." His words are soft and I hear his honesty in them. "I've forgiven you for what happened two years ago. Cameron's forgiven you—"

"No she hasn't."

"Matías, you need to learn to trust me. I'll help you get out."

I groan in frustration. "It's no use. I've learned to deal with my fate."

"You replaced one addiction for another." His words were blunt.

I know he doesn't know about Alessia and my addiction to her. He's talking about my fighting. "It helps clear my head."

He shakes his head at me. "Bernardo talked to me. He's worried too. It could kill you."

"And so could my debt to The Partners. At least I feel something when I fight."

He doesn't say anything. Just stares at me with those dark eyes.

"Did you come here to tell me to stop fighting or to talk business?" I ask, in hopes of changing the subject.

He studies me. And I know he knows more than he is telling me. "Who is the girl?"

"You don't want to get involved, Bastian."

"I became involved the second I walked through that door and found her on your lap."

I run my hands over the crease of my brow. "The Partners will get you back in their grip."

"I will do what needs to be done to get you out. I've always said that."

"We tried that once. It didn't work." My answer short.

"What do they have you doing, Matías?"

I look away from him, my gaze focused on the pool outside.

I hear him stand up, the click of his wingtips on the hardwood floor as he walks around my desk and leans against it. "Let me help you."

"I'm working on it myself, Bastian. Just like you thought you had something to atone for, this is my own repentance for my sins."

I glance over at him and his head is down. "I'll stay out of this as much as I can. Promise me that you are really trying to get out."

I nod. "I'm working on it."

"What can you tell me then?"

I stand from my chair and walk over to the window. The sun is shining on the deck and I am surprised Alessia isn't outside tanning. I see her there most days before she heads to the art studio. "I was tasked to interrogate people who went against their orders."

I hear Bastian sigh behind me. "I was worried that's what they made you do."

"Twenty people, Bas. That was all they asked of me." I run my hands over my face. "I was on number eighteen and I was setup. I got away before the police found me."

"And your punishment?"

Of course he knows how they work, he was involved with them for ten years. "I kidnapped her. Under the guise of protection based on her father's request."

"Who is she?"

I swallow and look over at the concern etched on Bastian's face. "Alessia Calvetti. Daughter of Lorenzo Calvetti of—"

Bastian nods. "Calvetti and Sons. They owe The Partners money?"

I shrug. "That's what I'm guessing, I've been kept out of the loop."

"Lorenzo got involved with them, as I was getting out the first time. He's a shady businessman."

"I think there is something more going on. He has an assistant who is close with the whole family. Nicolas Di Masio. I think he may be getting involved with the Mafia, turning on the family business."

"I'll look into it." His hand lands on my shoulder. "They don't have their eyes on me like they do you. It's safer for me to investigate. Use my resources."

"What about Cameron?"

"What about her?"

I face my brother. "If word gets out about your involvement, they could try to take her."

He shakes his head. "I won't let that happen."

"Bastian, I can't be the one that causes her life to be put at risk again."

He shakes his head at me. "It was never your fault, Matías. I never should have made you feel like it was. The second I felt attached to her, when I knew I needed her to be mine, the swift eyes of The Partners caught on."

He has no idea I needed to hear that. That he didn't blame me for the events that nearly ruined his life two years ago. I sag in relief.

"Matías, I've already lost one brother. I don't want to lose you too."

I nod at him, it's the first time in years I felt like he truly was my brother, believed in me, and felt the need to protect me as his own.

"Be careful with Alessia. She is fragile."

I look toward Bastian in confusion.

"You don't know what they are planning, what they will do to keep you tied to them. The Partners will stop at nothing to have a Montford under their name. And I wouldn't doubt them using her as a pawn."

I nod in understanding. "She's already a pawn in this twisted game."

Bastian moves around the desk and heads for the door I notice is slightly cracked open. "Then it may already be too late. Especially if you have feelings."

Feelings? I don't have feelings for her. Yes, I like fucking her and claiming her body but feelings are something I have never allowed myself to have with any woman. But the ache in my chest just thinking about her makes me cringe, aware that I may be too late. I clear my throat. "Don't worry, brother. She is a job. But her pussy is a good distraction."

Bastian smirks at me. I know well enough that he thought Cameron was just a distraction too. "I'll call you when I have information on Di Masio."

He opens the door to my office, both of us stepping out, our conversation changing to Montford Hotel business when I see a blur of dark hair bounce around the corner.

Alessia.

No doubt she was spying.

Both of us hurry down the hall and see her open the front door. With a quick glance behind her, she picks up her pace.

I laugh as she tries to run. She didn't even think about putting on shoes.

"I take it she's tried this before?" he asks me as I pull open the front door.

I smirk at him. "I'm beginning to think she likes handcuffs."

Bastian lets out a deep chuckle as I run after her. My long legs have nothing on her short, petite frame and within seconds I have her swooped up and over my shoulder.

"Put me down!" she yells as she beats against my back.

I tsk at her. "Angel, we've talked about you running."

"You kidnapped me!"

I don't answer her as I walk back to the house and Bastian walks over to his SUV, his bodyguard by the back door.

"You can't keep me here! I heard what you said! It's all lies!" she hisses and screams as I slowly walk us back to the house. She tries to bite me but it's of no use through my custom-made suit. I smack my hand across her ass hard enough that Bastian's bodyguard winces.

"Good luck with that one." Bastian smirks as he slides into his car. "We'll talk soon."

I wave to my brother before heading back into the house, a hot-mouthed Italian screaming every obscenity I know of in Italian as I march her into my room.

I kick the door shut behind me, then lift Alessia off my shoulder and push her against the wall. My hips hold her in place as my hands secure her wrists above her head. "What are you doing, angel?"

"You can't keep me here!" she yells as she struggles against my hold on her, not that she will get loose with the hundred pounds of muscle I have over her.

"Remember last time you ran away?" I ask her, but she just spits in my face. "You're a liar."

I grunt as I push both of her wrists into one hand and wipe away the spit. "Why would you say that?" I ask as I cup her jaw with a featherlight touch, a contrast to the firm grip I have on her against the wall.

"I heard you. You took me. You're only pretending that it was for protection."

I run my hands down her throat, feeling the rapid beat of her pulse under my thumb. "I don't think you heard correctly at all."

She grunts as I tighten my grip on her throat. "I heard it all."

"So you were spying?" I ask her. I move my lips to her ear. "I thought you trusted me, angel."

"Never," she wheezes out.

I run my lips along her jawline, then up to her lips, brushing them over in a light kiss. "I think you like handcuffs," I tease as I step away from the wall.

She looks at me in confusion, her body relaxing as she tries to figure out what I mean.

I use it to my advantage as I turn her toward the bed and pull the cuffs out of a drawer. Before she can register what is happening, I have one cuffed around her wrist and the other latched to the hook at the top of my headboard. I never brought a girl here, but I kept my room prepared in case I found one worthy enough.

She shrieks when the cold metal hits her wrist. "Matías!"

I smash my lips into hers this time, forcing my tongue into her mouth, making her submit to me. She fights but she never bites, so I know I am winning the battle.

She rips her lips from mine. "You can't do this to me!"

I let her go as I rip her dress from her body. "According to you, you're my prisoner, so I think that means I can do whatever I want."

She shivers as cool air hits her exposed nipples, both of them coming to a hard point. I crawl over the bed and snap another handcuff around her wrist so she is at the mercy of my hands. Only her legs free. A devilish grin takes over my face as I look down at her. She tries to kick her legs at me but I hold them down as I suck a nipple into my mouth hard. She squirms underneath me so I pinch the other nipple with force, causing her to yelp.

I slide off the bed and walk toward the end, her ankles still in my grip. "Beautiful," I tell her as I take her in, hands cuffed above her, making her body into a Y. She arches off the bed, pushing her nipples into the air.

"You're a monster!" she shouts.

I use that moment to pull her panties off, leaving her completely exposed. "I've told you so many times that I am. I'm glad you remember now."

I then tie her ankles so she is spread eagle. I bite my lip as I take her in. My perfect angel a treat for me, spread out on my bed like dessert.

I decide to tease her and sweep my fingers through her exposed center, not surprised to find it wet. "I think she likes it," I say in a dark tone.

"Don't," she whimpers and I know fear has finally taken over.

"Maybe you shouldn't have tried to run away." She lets out a cry mixed with a moan as I shove two fingers inside of her, her pussy sucking them in. "I told you next time you tried to escape I would cuff you to my bed." I crawl over her and whisper in her ear. "I keep my promises."

Then I pull my fingers out of her and suck them into my mouth. "Delicious." I crawl off the bed and adjust my suit jacket and start to walk away.

"You can't keep me like this!" she shouts.

"Angel, you should know by now I can do whatever I want."

"I'll scream!"

I grab a remote from the bedside and turn on classical music extra loud. "No one will come."

I bend down and kiss her one last time, the essence of her still on my lips and now on hers. "I'll be back in a few hours."

I can barely make out her screaming as I shut the door behind me and lock it.

18
MATÍAS

I've been driving for hours. Part of me wishing I had a job to do so I could let out my aggression. The other part of me is itching for a fight. But this time not to feel something but to turn off my feelings. I don't know who I am anymore. I tell Alessia constantly that I am a monster. I figure if I convince myself I am worthless, everyone else will feel the same.

I don't know why I acted the way I did earlier. Treating her like I do my kills. My monster coming out begging to play. The part that tears at me the most is the fact I enjoyed it, enjoyed torturing her and leaving her naked and spread eagle on my bed. It leaves a sickness in my stomach. Have The Partners really turned me into such a vile creature that I have forgotten who I am? I should be able to separate the two sides of me but they have joined into one. After so many kills, I enjoy the power it gives me, the control. What I said I always wanted. Maybe it's some sick and twisted game from The

Partners. To turn me into the thing I wanted, but not in the way I wanted.

And now that power is taking over my personal life. Or I am losing control of everything.

I finally end up pulling into a dive bar on the outskirts of town. It's dark and boisterous. But I have a seat at the end of the bar in the darkest corner where no one can see me. No one can see a Montford falling apart.

I sip on my bourbon slowly as I let my thoughts eat away at me. The same thoughts that I try to drive out of my brain when I am fighting. But tonight I need them to level me, bring me back to my true reality. Not the one I am hiding in. But the one where I am a cold-blooded killer.

"How many have you had?" Demont's deep voice snaps me out of my thoughts.

I glance up at him, jaw clenched. "Not nearly enough."

He doesn't say anything but takes the seat next to me.

"You left her alone?" I ask.

"I think you put her in a safe enough place she won't get out."

I snort at that. "How did you know?"

"When I got back to the house, Lastra told me she tried to run and you took her somewhere, then left. I went looking for her and heard her screams from your room. Figured you got creative."

I nod but don't say anything. He doesn't need to know the length my creativity went. Or the fact I can still taste her on my tongue even after the drinks.

He orders a beer and we both sit in silence for a while as we drink.

"Did you find anything out?" I ask him finally.

He shrugs. "Not much. Di Masio is definitely up to something." He looks around the bar and his voice lowers, it's nearly inaudible. "I couldn't get close enough. He was definitely being protected by someone. And if my research is correct, it was a Mafia family. That was enough to keep me away."

"Merda." I run my hands through my hair. "Do you think they know?"

He shakes his head. "Calvetti has no clue. If The Partners know then—"

"I'm fucked," I cut him off.

"We'll figure something out."

I take a sip of my drink. "Bastian knows."

Demont looks over at me with a raised brow.

"He came by the house today wondering why I hadn't been working in the office. He saw Alessia."

Demont takes a pull from his beer, not saying anything.

I run a hand through my hair. "He's going to have his people look into Di Masio."

"What did he think about Alessia?"

"He's not an idiot. He knew I was still tied to The Partners."

"He needs to be careful."

I nod. "I told him not to help. To stay out of everything for Cameron's sake, but he wouldn't listen. He wants me to get out. And he is going to find a way."

"Your brother is a good man."

I nod. I am well aware of the type of man he is. One that is much better than me.

"So, what brings you here? It's been a while since you've come here."

I don't say anything and just swallow down the rest of my bourbon.

"I called Bernardo first. Figured that's where you would have gone. But he said he hadn't heard from you."

I clench my jaw as my mind filters back to the thoughts I had earlier.

"You don't have to tell me, Matías."

I crack my knuckles before resting my head in my palms in defeat. "I'm confused."

"About what?"

"You know. You know what she does to me, how she makes me feel. And I shouldn't feel it."

His hand comes down on my shoulder. "But you are feeling something. I know you fight to not feel emotions, to feel nothing but the physical pain it causes you. Maybe you should accept these feelings. Accept that you are changing."

"How did you do what you did when you had a family?"

He swallows down half his beer. "I loved my wife. My daughters. I would kill for them and that is exactly what I did. I risked my life for them every damn day. And she knew, my wife knew what I was doing, but that didn't change a thing. She still loved me."

I chew my lip as sadness comes over Demont's face as he remembers his dead family. "Did she always know?"

"That I was a mercenary?"

I nod.

He shakes his head. "No. I didn't tell her for the first three years we were together."

"And when she found out?"

His thick hand rubs his shaved head. "The woman nearly tried to kill me. Then remembered I killed people for a living. Used every curse word in the book then stormed out of our house. She was gone for a week. I was in shambles. I didn't know if I should chase her or see if she would come back."

"What happened?"

"I finally decided she was worth everything. I grabbed my keys off the table and ran out the front door and she was standing in the driveway." He pauses and closes his eyes. "They were my happily ever after until they were taken from me."

I'm silent after Demont's story. I know there are no condolences for him. He's lived with his burdens for long enough.

"I was forceful with her," I grit through my teeth as I switch the conversation back to Alessia. "I treated her like one of my jobs and then I chained her to a bed. I'm a monster and the only people that ever see it are the ones I kill. And I unleashed the monster on her."

Demont nods his head and finishes his beer.

"How am I supposed to face her? Whatever was happening between us turned to ice after what I did to her tonight."

"Maybe so, or maybe not. You won't know until you go back."

I glance down at my watch. "It's been nearly six hours."

Demont grimaces. "Then you should probably head back."

"And what of the monster?"

He shrugs. "Maybe you should unleash him. If you let him go, he might not come back."

19

ALESSIA

I know I shouldn't have been listening in to the conversation Matías and Bastian were having but I couldn't help myself. I accidentally didn't close the door all the way, it never clicked in place. So when I heard them talking about my father, I risked pushing the door a crack so I could hear the truth. Unsurprisingly, I found out what I believed to be true, Matías did kidnap me. The part that surprised me was I didn't seem to care that much. The last two weeks with him as made me grow feelings I shouldn't feel. But the words that were said about my father, those I could not and will not believe to be true. He isn't a shady businessman. He runs a reputable company passed on for generations.

Of course, everyone thinks the Montford family runs a reputable business and now I am beginning to think otherwise. The fact Bastian did nothing when Matías threw me over his shoulder when he spanked me in front of others. He just made a snide remark and got into his vehicle like kidnapping and holding people hostage is an everyday occurrence for the Montfords.

But curiosity got to me when he talked about The Partners. Who the hell are they and what do they have to do with my father? Not to mention the quiet words I heard about Nicolas. What is his part in all this?

All I got out of spying was more questions than answers. And now I doubt I will ever get them.

Now I am truly a prisoner. Handcuffed naked to a bed for hours. Hell, I don't even know when Matías will be back. I watched from his sheer black curtains as daylight faded to dusk and dusk turned to night. I screamed for half the time but as he told me, no one came.

I don't know what kind of sick, cruel joke he is playing on me but I will make sure he pays for it. I don't know how but I'll figure something out.

I twist slightly in the bed, my thighs rubbing against each other and I am forced to remember how he made me feel when he tied me up. The way he teased me and took advantage of me. The abrasive touch of his fingers. The way he forced his mouth on me. And I know he did it all so I would be left wanting as I lie here. So I would beg for him to give me a release when he came back. Anything to get rid of the want between my legs. It's been hours and the arousal is still there. I can feel the wetness between my thighs.

He's a bastard.

A monster.

Yet I want him now more than anything.

The blaring of the music makes me even crazier.

Knowing I can't hear anything outside of this room and no one can hear me. My throat feels raw from screaming. My wrists hurt from the metal around them. My shoulders sore from the angle he left me in.

I twist again to ease my muscles but that only causes wanton desires between my legs.

I groan as I turn. Not sure if I am doing it to be more comfortable. Or to get off.

Then my entire body freezes when the blaring classical music stops.

I don't hear anything for minutes. I almost want to scream for help but the sound of Matías's deep voice stops me.

"Ready to play, angel?"

20

MATÍAS

The words come out of my mouth hoarse, raw. Like I haven't spoken in hours. I only left the bar an hour ago but sat in my car for forty-five minutes contemplating Demont's words. Wondering if I let the monster out, unleash my fury on Alessia, if it will make the demons inside of me disappear. If the next time I kill, I won't be so cruel. Won't enjoy the feeling of blood on my hands and the pleasure I get out of the control, out of taking a life.

The slightest groan comes out of Alessia's lips. If I hadn't trained my ears so well on hearing the last few years, I would have missed it. The sound of fear. Terror. But I also noticed the lust in that groan. The need she no doubt will try to hide from me.

I smirk as I move to the end of the bed so I can take in my perfect angel. Her legs spread wide, her perfect pink pussy on display for me. I lick my lower lip as I see the arousal between her legs. I wonder if it's been there for the last seven hours?

My eyes graze up her body. Her back slightly arched off the bed, her pert nipples hard as diamonds in the cool air of the bedroom. Her breathing slightly erratic from the way her chest moves up and down.

I bring my eyes up to her face. Her beautiful face with sharp cheekbones and full rosy lips. Her bangs sit haphazardly over her whiskey-colored almond eyes as she stares right back at me.

I laugh when I see what I thought I heard in her groan. Fear laced with wanton desire.

"Have you been a good girl?" I tease.

She huffs, blowing her bangs out of her eyes. "Fuck you, Matías."

I chuckle as I shrug out of my suit jacket. "Mmm, sweet angel, I rather like that idea."

She struggles against her restraints as she curses at me in Italian.

I just smile at her devilishly as I remove my cuff links, placing them on the ottoman at the base of my bed and rolling up the sleeves of my dress shirt.

I grip her tied ankles, pulling her farther down the bed, knowing it will only arch her back more as I stretch her arms almost to the point of pain. "Now what shall I do with you?" I slowly slide my fingertips over her ankles and up her calves until I hit her knees. "You didn't try to escape so maybe you deserve the treatment of a good girl."

"Don't." She trembles as I glide my left fingers down the inside of her thigh.

I look up at her. "What's wrong, angel?"

I can tell she is holding back a groan as I bring my finger dangerously close to her center. "This is wrong," she whispers.

I draw my fingers back up her thigh to her knee as I ask, "What's wrong with this? Don't tell me it's because you think we shouldn't be together."

"I'm telling you no."

I glance back at her eyes and see anger. But I also see her asking for me to touch her in the glaze that's taken over. Her eyes slightly darker as I trace my fingers down the same path they just took. "I don't really feel like taking no for an answer."

She whimpers as my fingers move even closer to her center, enough to feel her heat but not close enough to touch.

I watch as she tries to squeeze her thighs together but her restraints keep her from moving. I can smell her need. My dick getting painfully hard. It's been hard since I walked into the room. I remove my hands from her legs and lean over her. I run my nose between her breasts before licking across her clavicle. I bring my lips to her ear, whispering things she won't understand in Catalan. I pull up to look into her eyes, a million emotions running through them. She may hate me for this but that is the better option than her liking it. Although, I wouldn't be opposed to that either.

"You called me a monster earlier," I say to her in a low tone, my lips inches from hers.

I watch her trembling mouth. "You are a monster." Her words barely audible.

"Then maybe it's time he came out and played," I growl.

She screams in fear as I say it, no doubt scared of whatever my plans are for her. But within seconds her screams turn into moans as I move down her body in one swift movement and suck her clit hard into my mouth.

I've only tasted her on my fingers before. Never like this. And she is sweeter than I remember. I grin against her center as I move my tongue through her slickness before pressing it inside of her warm, soaked pussy. I move back and forth to her clit as I revel in her moans of pleasure. My dick grows uncomfortable as I devour her but I need her begging for it before I fuck her so hard she'll see stars.

I feel her come against my tongue as she groans in pleasure. "Mmm." My lips vibrate against her clit. "I like when you come on my tongue, angel. It means you like the monster."

She freezes at those words just like I wanted her to, and then I push two fingers into her hard as I bite on her clit. Her screams are loud, raspy, entirely sexual and I almost wish I left the music on. Almost. I want everyone to hear her screams so that when she faces them tomorrow she flushes with embarrassment and I'll know it's because she will be thinking about all the vile things I plan to do to her.

"Matías," she yells. "You bast—" Her words are cut off as another orgasm hits her hard.

I pull away from her and kneel back on the ottoman, taking in the sight of my beautiful angel. I run my hand along the outside of my pants, along the rock-hard steel of my dick. I watch her lips as she sucks them into her mouth as she comes down from her high. I want those lips around my dick, sucking me in until she gags. I could fuck her mouth as she's chained up like this, let gravity take over as I slide down her throat. But I should save that for another time. When she is willing. She might bite my dick off if I force her to take it now.

Her eyes open and watch me as I slide off the ottoman and onto my feet. I slowly unbutton my shirt. Her eyes taking in my bare chest before sliding down to the tent in my pants. She's silent as I unbuckle my belt and push my pants and briefs down my legs. My dick stands at attention between us, thick and pulsing, precum on the head. I rub my hand up and down it, hoping to relieve any of the pressure, but it only makes my need more intense.

"Matías." My name falls from her lips.

I grin at her, devilish and menacing, as I crawl back onto the ottoman.

"Matías." Her words stained with fear as I rip the bindings from her ankles.

I grip her hips and push her up the bed, my grip hard and firm.

"Please," she pleads.

"What are you so scared of, angel?"

She swallows hard. "The monster."

I laugh, letting the monster completely take over as I flip her over onto her knees. She yelps at the movement. Her arms twisting above her head. Her shoulders no doubt in pain from the sudden change from the position she was in for hours. Her cheek is pressed against the sheets, her breathing erratic.

I run a hand down the back of her thigh while the other keeps her in place. My fingers then drag up the center of her, sliding between her ass cheeks, slightly pressing into the puckered hole.

She cries at my touch. I lean over her back and trail my lips along her jaw while I work my finger deeper into her. "You never told me if you were a good girl or not?"

She pinches her eyes closed. "I was a good girl."

My other hand slides from her hip and starts rubbing her clit. I can feel her need in my fingers, the way she pushes into my touch. I know she wants this, wants to feel all of me. I slip a second finger coated in her juices into her ass. "Angel," I whisper.

"Don't hurt me, Matías." Her words are muffled in the blankets.

"I would never hurt you."

She moans as I push my fingers farther into her. "Then pretend I was bad."

I roar as something snaps in me at her words. My angel is just as deviant as me. Playing the game. I pull my fingers out of her and slap my hand across her ass, smiling as it turns pink from my hand. I slap the other cheek and she yelps at the pain. "Bad girls deserve to be punished."

She only nods her head as I slap her a handful more times. Her ass growing red. I see her desire sliding down her thighs. I run my fingers through her slick folds and she whimpers at my touch, my name falling across her lips, begging for me to fuck her.

I grip her waist hard as I slam into her throbbing pussy. My dick sinking in all the way to the hilt. I pull out all the way to the tip and slam back in, my balls slapping against her with every powerful thrust.

"Matías," she screams in pleasure as I pound into her.

I grunt as I pull back and watch my dick slide into her wetness. But the view of her perfect ass has me wanting more than I'm giving her now. It has me wanting every part of her. Claiming every single inch of her as mine.

I pull out of her and she groans at the loss of me. I pull a bottle of lube out of the side table. I slip my fingers inside of her wet heat, then glide them to her tight hole. I slip one inside, pulsing it slowly before I add a second.

She whimpers as I fuck her ass with my fingers. My dick growing impossibly harder than it already was. I know I shouldn't do this. I know I should work her up to taking more but the monster is unleashed.

I pull my fingers out and drip the lube between her round cheeks, then coat my dick. I hold on to her hip as I press the head into her. She groans as her body resists me but I push farther in.

"Matías," she whimpers, an essence of fear on her lips.

I slap her across the bottom of her thigh as I push another inch into her tight hole. I groan at the feeling. My dick never feeling pleasure like this before. She groans as I pull out, then slide back in slowly. It feels so fucking good, I don't know if I'll be able to stop.

"It's too much," she mumbles into the sheets.

I lean over her back and slowly lick from the base of her spine up to her neck. My dick sliding in a little farther every inch I move up her back. "Maybe you should have been a good girl then?" I snap in her ear just as I push in until I'm fully seated inside of her.

She groans. A muffled ache of pain and pleasure but I feel the moment her body accepts my length. I watch as her eyes flutter shut, and she bites her lip, holding in the moan I know she wants to release.

"Good girl," I say, then pick up my pace as Alessia whimpers underneath me. Every thrust bringing me closer and closer to the edge. I reach around her body and pinch one of her nipples, her moan guttural, I can feel it in my dick. Then she starts to meet my thrusts, telling me not to stop.

"Does my angel like this? Does she like being fucked in the ass?"

Inaudible words slip from her lips and I pick up my pace. I feel my balls tightening as pleasure radiates from my core throughout my entire body. I reach around and pinch her clit then slide two fingers into her pussy.

"Fuck, Matías!" she screams so loud I am sure the guards at the gate could hear her.

I pull out and come all over her back, my body exploding in pleasure. I watch as streams of my cum coat her back and her red ass. I pump myself dry as Alessia collapses to her stomach beneath me. She groans and fights against her handcuffs. I could sit here and watch her. The monster in me enjoying the sight of her restrained and thoroughly fucked.

But when I see her wrists are rubbed raw, I curse and

free her. I pull her onto my lap before her shoulders collapse onto the bed. Her head falls against my chest as I rub her shoulders and then her wrists.

I press my lips to her forehead and she nuzzles farther into me.

"Was I a good girl?" she asks me breathlessly.

Fuck. I would fuck her again just from those words. My dick already stirring to life underneath her. "Very good, angel."

She lifts her head up and smiles at me. A smile so dazzling it takes my breath away. "Good," she mumbles before falling back on my chest.

I hold her tight. My mind empty of the thoughts that weigh me down. My only thoughts are about her and how the hell I am going to find a way to keep her.

21

ALESSIA

The warmth of a bath stirs me awake. I blink open my eyes as I feel Matías slide in behind me.

I don't even remember falling asleep. But then memories of the night hit me like a freight train. Matías letting out the monster. Me telling him to treat me like I was a bad girl.

I let him torture me, spank me, and fuck me until he owned me. I want to be mad at myself. In shock with what I just did but a smile blooms on my face. I feel thoroughly fucked and dirty, but incredibly content. He said it was a game and one I can get entirely used to.

His lips press against my spine. "Are you okay?"

"Mmm." I nod as his hands slide across my stomach. "Are you?"

He lets out the laugh I love so much, the carefree one I heard the other day in the studio. "Baby, you don't need to worry about me."

I lean back against his chest, my head on his shoulder, as I turn and press a kiss into his neck. "I've never done that."

He looks down at me. "I know."

"I liked it."

He smiles. "Oh, I know that too."

I slap at his chest but he catches my fingers, bringing my red wrist to his lips. "I hurt you."

"It's fine. It doesn't hurt."

"You're lying."

I shrug. "It will go away."

His eyes glisten with deviance as he looks at me. "Hopefully soon so I can restrain you again."

I blush at his words. "I'll make sure to be a bad girl."

His lips collide with mine and I can't help but swoon at the kiss. Swoon for this man who I should have no reason feeling things for yet I can't stop myself from my stupid feelings.

Then I remember why I was restrained to begin with and pull my mouth away from him. He must have felt the change in my kiss because his arms lock around me, holding me in place.

"You've been lying to me."

He sighs and rests his chin on my shoulder. "Yes."

I try to shift but his large frame has me completely in his control. "Why? Why do you do it?"

His fingers draw circles on my stomach and I squirm against him. I know he is trying to calm me but everything hits me like a brick wall with the truth. I am falling in love with the man who kidnapped me.

"Alessia, I really am trying to protect you." His words are soft. I almost want to believe him.

"No. You. Aren't." My voice staccato. He pulls me tighter into him and I am enveloped in his smell. I want nothing more than to get lost in it but I can't let myself keep doing this.

He presses a kiss into my jaw and I shiver. "The people I work for would not have treated you this way."

"Your brother?" I ask curiously.

I feel his head shake slightly against my shoulder. "No."

"The Partners?" I ask cautiously. I am almost afraid to let him know how much I heard.

He stiffens behind me. "How much did you hear?"

"Enough."

His grip loosens on me but I don't move. "I'm not a good man, Alessia. You know about the scandal that happened two years ago."

I nod as I stare at the wall in front of me.

"The Partners are not something you want to get tangled up in." He is quiet as his hands pull away from me completely. "Merda. It's already too late."

"Too late for what?"

His fist slams on the side of the porcelain tub, causing me to jump. Water splashes over the side of the bathtub and I hesitantly turn to face him.

"I never should have agreed to this," he mutters with his head down.

I can see the tension in his shoulders. I can see the weight of whatever is going on, dragging him down. "Matías?"

"I should let you leave. Run. Pretend you got away."

My fingers shake as I reach out for his hand, gripping

the edge of the bathtub. "Matías. Tell me what's going on."

He doesn't speak to me, just keeps muttering with his head down. "But if I let you go, someone will find you and I don't know what will happen to you. They won't treat you like this. They won't use your body. They—"

"You aren't using my body. I agreed to everything."

He ignores my comment and continues. "They will keep you locked up somewhere. A basement, a warehouse. They will kill you when the time is right."

Fear creeps into my veins with his words. "Who will?"

"But I can't keep you here. I can't keep doing this to you."

I grip his hand and pull myself closer to him. "Matías, I'm happy here. I like being with you. More than I should."

He looks up at me with those words. His blue eyes piercing into my soul. "You shouldn't."

I kneel between his thighs, my hands moving up to his square jaw. "I can't help the feelings that are brewing inside of me. I can't help the way you make me feel. And I know damn well I can't get out of this situation. But when I am around you, I feel safe."

His eyes close as he speaks. "I'm sorry that this is your life. I would never want anyone to be forced into mine."

I run my thumb over his bottom lip. "We can't change the past."

He shakes his head. "I know. But I should have never agreed to this. I should have let them kill me rather than harm someone so innocent."

"Then I would be just where you said. In a basement,

probably starving and tortured. Not sitting in a bathtub with you."

His hands splash into the water and wrap around my waist, forcing me to slide off my knees and wrap my legs around his hips. "The Partners are a criminal organization run by the most brilliant minds in the business world. My brothers got involved with them but broke free of them. At least Bastian did. It cost Thiago his life." He pauses and I can see the pain in his face. Almost like guilt. "It was my fault Thiago died. I wanted to be a part of it. I was brought in by a mutual friend. Thiago was pissed. He tried to get them to not accept me and it cost him everything."

I run my hands along the back of his neck. "You didn't kill him."

"My actions led to his death."

I can see the guilt eating away at him. This strong, powerful man that is being torn apart by his demons. Maybe that's why he fights, to fight his demons.

He changes the subject away from his brother. "After what happened two years ago, The Partners agreed to let me go once I fulfilled a contract with them."

"Kidnapping people?" I tease, to lighten the mood.

It brings a slight smile to his face. "You'll be happy to know that you are the only person I have kidnapped. I don't make a habit of kidnapping women and fucking them into submission."

I blush at his words.

"I don't want to tell you what they make me do though. I don't want to scare you."

"You already scare me."

His hands slide down my back to my ass and pull me closer into him. "Yet you're sitting on the lap of a monster."

I shrug. "I found your bloody clothes that night, Matías. I know it wasn't from fighting. I know that whatever it is you do isn't legal. But—"

"I kill people, Alessia," he says as his fingers grip my hips hard. "I kill people."

My eyes shut at his words. My hands slide down his chest and land in my lap. I don't know how to feel about hearing those words from his mouth, even though I suspected that was the truth. Yet I'm not moving, not running away. Because I know the man in front of me, the broken boy weighed down by the world, isn't a monster. And I hate myself for feeling that way.

We sit in silence. Him in shock that he admitted that to me. I can tell by the clench of his jaw, the loosening of his fingers on my hips. I don't know what to say. Don't know how to react to something like that. But it doesn't scare me away. He might scare me as a person. He's intimidating, strong-willed, possessive. But I know that his truth eats away at him.

I lean forward and press my lips softly against his, hoping to relieve the tension flowing through him. But he doesn't kiss me back. He pushes me away.

"Don't, Alessia. Don't make me feel something I know isn't real. Don't pretend that I am what you want." He runs his hand through his hair, then stares into my eyes with intimidation. "You think you want me. That you have feelings for me. You don't. You can't."

"Matías..."

"I kill people," he growls. "And I enjoy it."

I don't believe him but I choose not to say anything.

"Fuck. I've messed this all up. I should have done what they would have done. Locked you in a room with a toilet and a mattress. Fed you scraps. Ignored you. Let the guards deal with you."

"You did do that."

"And I'm a fool because I couldn't stay away."

I slowly reach my hand out to his cheek. "I couldn't stay away from you either."

"You should have."

I shake my head. "Remember when we met? In the club?"

"It wasn't a chance meeting," he grits.

"I know that now." I pause as I pull myself onto his lap, forcing him to feel what I feel. I almost laugh at myself. Comforting the kidnapper. I'm more fucked up than I thought. "But you can't deny the chemistry we had, that we still have."

"I never should have acted on it."

"We can't change the past," I tell him again. He doesn't say anything and keeps his gaze on the floor of the bathroom. "I'm sorry I ran earlier."

He grunts.

"Matías."

His head snaps toward mine. "I'm no good for you, Alessia. I'm a bad man. You deserve someone much more honorable than me."

"But what if I don't want the honorable man?"

He shakes his head. "I've brainwashed you."

I laugh at that. "I don't think so. Like I said, I've felt

this pull to you since the club. Maybe we didn't meet under the best circumstances but someday we would have crossed paths and that pull between us would still be there."

"Why are you perfect, angel?" he asks me with a soft voice.

"I'm not perfect. I'm falling for the man that kidnapped me."

"Falling?" he asks as his hands finally land back on my body.

I sigh at the feel of his touch. I crave it. "Yes."

"Maybe we were made for each other. We are both fucked in the head."

I smile at him. "Did you just tell a joke?"

His eyes shine as he takes me in. "That was the truth."

"Are you going to tell me more of the truth?" I ask.

"Not tonight," he tells me with a sly grin.

I feel him hardening underneath me, and I can't help but grind against him as I wrap my arms around his neck. "Tomorrow?"

His lips fall to my jaw, peppering kisses. "Unlikely."

"The day after?"

"Fuck, woman. I don't know. But you just told me you were falling for me and the only thing I can think about right now is fucking you into oblivion. Now shut up and kiss me."

I let out a short laugh before smashing my lips against his.

22

MATÍAS

I watch Alessia walk out of my office, my eyes drawn to her perfect ass. Fuck, this woman does something to me.

She came in here interrupting a work call dressed in one of my T-shirts. I watched her as she walked around the office, looking at the books on the bookshelf. She eventually bent over and bared her naked ass to me. I never ended a call so quickly. She smiled at me, then demanded answers about Di Masio's role in everything. I denied her the information and shut up her begging by eating her out on my desk. She was at least nice and returned the favor by sucking my dick. The woman knows what she is doing with that mouth.

I lick my lips, the taste of her still on them. My dick goes hard again. I wish I could follow her out of the office and tie her to my bed, the bed that she has been sleeping in the last few nights, but I have too many things to do today.

I spend a few hours signing off on contracts when my phone rings. I pinch my eyes shut when I see the name flash across the screen.

"Montford."

"Matías, so nice to hear your voice."

"I wish I could say the same, Charles."

He ignores my unpleasantry. "We need you at a meeting tonight."

"With whom?"

"Does it matter? You will be there. Or else we might make more amendments to your contract. Eight p.m. The Parlor Room." He hangs up the phone without saying another word.

I crack my knuckles in anger. I don't like being called to meetings. The last time I was forced to kill someone for no reason. And I have a feeling this meeting tonight will be much the same.

I glance at the clock and see it's nearing four. The Parlor Room is in Sanremo, Italy. A good two-and-a-half-hour drive. I could take the plane but the drive will clear my mind.

I answer a few emails, then head out of the office to find Demont. I'm not surprised that he and Alessia are playing their game of Risk. I watch her for a few moments before I interrupt. She must have gone to paint after leaving my office. A few speckles are on her face. Her hair is trapped on top of her head in a messy bun, held up with a paintbrush. The woman is fucking gorgeous. And she is mine. At least for right now.

She looks up at me and smiles, my chest aches. This woman who told me she was falling for me. Me, the man who kidnapped her. I couldn't believe it when she told me three nights ago. When I broke down and told her things I shouldn't have. When she tried to comfort me. Her, my captive. Maybe we are made for each other since we are both crazy.

"Demont. A word," I say, interrupting them.

He glances over his shoulder at me and nods, then follows me to my office. I make sure the door is shut behind us so Alessia doesn't try to listen in again.

"I have a meeting tonight."

"Do you need me to drive you?"

I shake my head. "No. I need you to watch over her. I don't trust anyone right now. I almost want to bring her with me."

"You think someone will try to take her again?"

I nod. "We still can't find anything on Di Masio. Not even Bastian's guy can pinpoint who the hell he is working for. I'm worried that this meeting may be a distraction."

"I'll up the guards around the house tonight."

"Thank you."

"I'll make sure she stays inside too."

I nod as my eyes drift toward the door.

"I'll keep her safe, boss."

"I know you will."

He walks back to the dining room, and I head to my own room. I change out of my Armani suit and into my all-black Tom Ford suit. I don't know what The Partners are going to want me to do tonight, but I much prefer wearing black when I might need to kill.

I am slipping my gun into my chest holster when I

hear the door creak open. I glance up and see Alessia walking toward me, her eyes focused on the gun.

She wraps her arms around me when she reaches me, her cheek pressing into my chest.

"Angel."

She looks up at me, her chin on my chest. "You have a job tonight?"

I raise a brow at her.

"You only wear all black when you have a job."

"How—"

"I've paid attention these last few weeks."

I sigh as I wrap my arms around her hips and pick her up. Her legs wrap around my waist. "Just a meeting."

Her fingers trace over my brow. "Will you be safe?"

I laugh. "Unlikely. But don't worry about me. I'm just your kidnapper."

"Matías," she cries. "You know you mean more to me."

I press my lips against her forehead. "I know."

"If something happens to you, what will happen to me?"

Her words strike me with a panic deep in my chest. I haven't thought about that. Haven't thought about the risk I take every time I do a job or go to a meeting. I know The Partners would take her. And I can't be entirely sure they would only lock her in a basement.

I press a kiss against her jaw and then bring my lips to hers. I kiss her passionately. Devouring her mouth. Memorizing everything about her lips just in case something happens so I can remember exactly how they feel. How they taste.

I pull away from her, our lips centimeters apart. I don't answer her question because I don't want to think about it. "Demont will be here. Please listen to him. And behave."

"Matías."

I can hear the pleading in her voice. I know she is worried about me. "Routine meeting, angel. I'll be back in a few hours."

"I'm worried about you."

I set her down and press another kiss to her forward. "Don't worry about me. I'm a monster, remember? No one will hurt me."

"Even monsters can be killed," she says sternly.

"I'll be fine."

I can see the fear in her eyes so I kiss her one more time before walking out the door.

I stand in the dark corner of a room in the back of a classy bar full of socialites and rich men. I am still wondering why I was called to this meeting. What my role is in whatever The Partners have up their sleeve. No one knows of my involvement with The Partners, that is how they work. They have a group of men that act as the faces but only a fool would believe they run the syndicate. They are all pawns, just like me.

I fold my arms over my chest as I lean against the wall. I know my face can't be seen. I know I am supposed to keep my mouth shut. I wasn't told a thing about why they wanted me here. I can only imagine it's to hear information. The question is whether it's to help The Partners or intimidate me.

Charles and Harris sit across the table from Lorenzo Calvetti and what I imagine is his brother, Gianno, and one of the sons. I see a resemblance to Alessia so maybe it's her eldest brother. Behind them, a few beefy guards and Nicolas Di Masio. I study him as the men at the table talk. Looking for anything that might give him away. But his face remains stoic as he stands in silence.

"We assure you your daughter is perfectly safe," Charles tells Lorenzo.

Lorenzo slams his hands on the table. "You kidnapped my daughter. How can I believe she is safe?"

Charles leans back in his chair, a smug smile on his face. "We aren't monsters, Mr. Calvetti."

Harris cuts in. "She believes you have her under our watchful eye. A threat was made against you. Don't worry, you sent her an email explaining everything."

"We could have worked something out. I would do anything for her," he replies.

"You could pay us the thirty million dollars you owe us," Charles says. "It's that simple. It was that simple from the start. All you had to do was pay."

"We don't have the money," Gianno cuts in. "We invested a lot in new freights."

Harris smirks. "You invested our money to grow your business. I guess that means it's our business now."

"This has been a family-run business for years. We will repay you as soon as the profits come in," Lorenzo says, slightly panicked.

"You had the profits to pay us back. You should have

done that before deciding to reinvest." He pauses as he stares at the two men, the younger one clenching his jaw, remaining silent. "If I remember correctly, we saved your little company from being indebted to the cartel when a shipment went missing. I am sure you wouldn't want those goons from the cartel threatening you again." Lorenzo visibly gulps. "You have one week to pay us."

"One week!" Gianno yells. "That's impossible!"

"I am sure you have some assets you can sell." A diabolical grin falls over Charles's face. "You wouldn't want your daughter to go missing from our protection, would you?"

"We'll find the money. We'll pay you. Just don't hurt her," Lorenzo practically begs. I have to hold in the grunt I want to make. The man is weak and stupid. Messing around with the wrong people. I learned my lesson two years ago, but I was also a lot younger than he is.

"Then I suggest you don't try to pull a stunt like you did two weeks ago," Harris commands.

"What stunt?" he asks.

"Oh, come on, Mr. Calvetti, don't play dumb with us. You somehow found out where she was and you tried to take her back."

My eyes glance to Di Masio and his eyes flick to the brother. Interesting.

"I—what—I have no idea—"

Charles cuts him off. "Don't play dumb with us. You killed some of our men when you tried to take her. You should owe us for that too but we are letting that slide."

"I don't know what you are talking about," he says. He looks over at his brother and his brother shrugs.

"Like I said earlier. I am sure the cartel would love to have you in their clutches again. Having a shipping company to use at their own disposal sounds highly profitable to me." Charles leans forward, his elbow resting on the table as he casually sets his chin in his palm. "They also might very much like your blood on their hands or the taste of your daughter. Of course, they might not be very gentle with her. But that wouldn't really be our problem now, would it?"

I fist my hands in anger at the statement.

"That's my sister!" the brother starts to yell. "Don't fucking touch my sister."

"Calm down, Angelo," Gianno says to him.

"Fuck this," Angelo says as he stands up forcefully, knocking his chair back as he does it. "I won't—"

I pull my weapon and aim it toward Angelo, just like the other three men beside me. He puts his hands up in the air.

"Sit down, Angelo," Gianno says to him calmly.

He grumbles but he picks up his chair and sits back down.

"Now I would be careful what you say, Mr. Calvetti," Charles says as he looks at Angelo. "I can assure you your sister is in very safe hands. Although, I can't guarantee you that your sister hasn't been touched by the man protecting her."

I grimace at his words. I know he is saying it as a threat to Angelo but it's also a threat to me. They know I've been fucking her. I chance a glance toward Di Masio and he is looking right at me.

"Fuck you," Angelo shouts.

"Angelo," his father says quietly to him before turning and facing the men on the other side of the table. "We will work something out. Just don't hurt her. She's my baby girl."

"The only thing we will work out is you paying us." Charles grabs his phone out of his pocket and dramatically flips through his contacts. "One call and she will be theirs. Of course, we could always sell her. That may pay off some of your debt. Pretty little thing like her. I am sure they could easily get a few million for her, more if she was a virgin."

I watch Angelo clench his jaw, fighting off his need to scream at Charles.

"Ticktock, Mr. Calvetti."

"Don't hurt her. Please don't hurt her. We just need more time." Lorenzo nearly breaks down in tears. I fight to hold back my words. I know I can't say shit or else it will come back on me.

Charles sighs dramatically as I watch him hit a contact on his phone list. "Time is something I unfortunately don't have." He starts to speak in Spanish as he talks to whoever is on the other end of the phone. A devilish grin crosses his face as he looks at the Calvettis sitting across from him. My nails cut into my hand as I hear the words he is saying. Disgusting, vile words about Alessia. About selling her to the highest bidder. Words I used last week to scare another man. But I don't think Charles is faking this.

Lorenzo looks panicked as he stares at his brother, who nods at him. "We will get you the money—" he starts to yell just as I let "She's safe" slip out of my mouth.

Harris spins in his chair and shoots me a look that I know might mean the end of my life just as Charles hangs up the phone, telling whomever he was talking to that the deal was off.

"Where is she?" Lorenzo pleads as he looks in my direction.

Charles cuts in. "She will be back to you if you pay by the end of the week."

"We will get you the money," Gianno answers.

Charles claps his hands together. "Now that wasn't so hard, was it?" He stands, signaling the Calvettis to leave. "We get that money and I won't need to finish the deal with my associate. He has a special taste for tiny brunettes, so I would make sure you follow through on your end."

Lorenzo nods and the group of them exit out the door behind them.

Charles turns toward me. "Follow them. We will deal with you later."

I step out of the darkness and nod as I slide my gun back into its holster.

I slip through the door they went through and take the back exit out of the bar. The alleyways are narrow in this coastal town, so I know they won't have parked in the back. I go to turn down the dead-end side street when I hear voices around the corner.

"We never should have gotten involved with them."

"We would have lost everything if we didn't."

"Because you've made poor business decisions ever

since Mom died. And now you have us caught up with them. Of all the people you could have asked for help, Father."

"Leave your mother out of this. This has nothing to do with her."

I hear Angelo mutter something under his breath but I can't quite make it out.

"Who would you rather have bailed us out?" Lorenzo asks.

"I don't know, but I sure as hell would have stayed out of the way of them. They are pure evil, more calculating than the Mafia."

Lorenzo sighs. "We had no choice, son."

"There is always a choice. You could have decided to not work with the cartel. What were you even thinking getting involved with them?" Hatred coats Angelo's voice.

"I thought it would bring us more money. It did. Until…"

"Fuck, Dad. You think that missing shipment was an accident? No, that's how they keep you under their reign. You never should have gone to The Partners for help."

"They promised so much."

"And now Alessia is probably tied up and being tortured somewhere. Do you even care about your daughter?"

"That's enough, Angelo." The voice I am guessing belongs to Gianno. "He knows what's at stake."

I hear Angelo mutter a handful of swear words and then a few doors shut before a car pulls away. I glance around the corner and see Angelo leaning against a sports car across the street, smoking a cigarette.

I walk in the shadows along the side of the building when Di Masio approaches him.

"Do you have a plan?" Di Masio asks him.

Angelo nods as he takes a deep inhale of his smoke. "I'm meeting with them tonight to see what they can do."

Di Masio nods.

"He never should have been left in charge when grandfather died."

"He was the older brother. But Gianno doesn't seem to know any better either."

"At least you are around to talk some sense into him when I can't be there." Angelo throws his smoke on the ground. "I just wish I knew where she was."

Di Masio nods. "Me too but I'm working on it. Let me know what you find out tonight."

Angelo nods as he gets into his car. Di Masio walks over to a waiting SUV across the street.

I head back into the restaurant and into the back room to find Harris gone and just Charles and his two goons waiting for me.

"Anything?"

I shrug. "Family drama. But Angelo told Di Masio something about meeting with someone tonight."

Charles nods like he couldn't care less about that information. "I have someone on him."

"Great. Let me know when you find yourself not in need of my services again."

"Leaving so soon, Matías? But I didn't even get to

talk to you yet about that lovely piece of information you so willingly gave me."

I clench my jaw but don't say anything. Just stare at him.

"It seems I was right in assuming you were fucking Alessia. I would even go so far as to say you may have feelings for her."

"Fuck off, Charles. She's just a piece of ass."

He nods as he steps closer to me. He's short and rotund and has to look up at me as he speaks but I know not to cross him. I know he holds more power than I do. "I couldn't care less what you do with her. But you nearly ruined the deal with Calvetti."

"He agreed to pay you."

"You spoke out of turn. You were to remain quiet."

I run my hands through my hair, trying not to be intimidated by this man at all, even though I know he only has to say one word for his goons to shoot me. "Why bring me here, Charles?"

He smirks at me. "Do you not know, Matías?"

I fold my arms over my chest and stare at him.

"To see if you would pass the test. And you failed."

"What are you talking about?"

"I don't like secrets, Mr. Montford. And it would do well for you to learn that." He waves his hand to the two men behind them and I know there is nothing I can do. I can't run and I can't fight back.

The first hit barely affects me. A right hook to the jaw I've felt numerous times.

The second hit to my gut reverberates through me. The pain seeping into my bones.

The third hit to my ribs makes the dull ache in my heart subside. The ache of knowing Alessia can never be mine.

The fourth hit knocks me across the eye. Memories of guilt fading away with my consciousness.

By the time the fifth hit to my side happens, I fall to the floor. Laughing as I spit blood from my mouth. The darkness I search for taking over as they kick and punch me over and over.

Once Charles is satisfied, I'm left a bloody mess on the floor as they walk out.

It's nearly two in the morning by the time I make it back to Saint Tropez. In hindsight, I probably shouldn't have driven. Should have stayed in Sanremo or had Demont take me to the meeting.

Crossing the border was enjoyable, with a swollen eye and bleeding lip. But luckily, they let me pass without question once they saw my name.

I walk into the house as quiet as I can, heading straight for the bar. I need a strong glass of bourbon. Not just for the pain, but to quell the thoughts that invaded my head as I drove.

I can't be with Alessia. I can't bring her more harm than I already have. Despite the feelings that I never thought would fester in my cold heart. The Partners know she means more to me than a quick fuck. And that puts her in more danger than she's already in. They can decide at any time that they no longer are in need of my services. Take her away from me. Or worse, they could use her against me. And I can't let her go through that. I can't let her become a pawn in this game. I've kept her safe from their clutches so far. But now it may be too late.

I sit out on the back deck and sip my bourbon. Contemplating how to play my cards. How to make it so she is alright. My life is already forfeit but if I can save hers, the sacrifice will be worth it.

The sound of her soft voice reaches my ears and I pinch my eyes shut. "What are you doing out here? It's nearly three in the morning!"

I keep my face from her because I know she will try to comfort me the second she sees the cuts and bruises. "Go back to bed."

"I couldn't sleep," she says as she walks closer to me. "I was worried about you."

I look over at her and see her wrapped in a blanket. "You shouldn't."

She steps closer to me and I see the recognition in her eyes when she notices the bruises on my face even in the dark of night. "You were fighting."

I shake my head at her. "I was being taught a lesson." It won't hurt to be truthful with her. It might make her leave.

"What kind of lesson?" she says quietly, a hint of fear in her voice.

I grip the glass in my hand. "The kind that people like me get taught when they misbehave."

"Matías…" her words trail off as she steps between my knees.

I can smell her lavender scent from here. My grip

tightening on the glass as I try to push the memories of what she smells like in my arms out of my mind. "Leave me alone, Alessia. I'm not your friend. I'm your kidnapper. Or don't you remember that? I'm a monster. You called me that yourself. Now leave me the fuck alone."

Her hand touches the side of my face. "You're not a monster."

"You don't know half of what I've done."

"You've told me enough."

"And I barely touched on just how sinister I am."

"I don't believe that about you."

I pull her hand away from my face. "Leave."

"No. Not until you tell me what's wrong."

I grip her wrist hard as I push out of my chair. I bend her over and push her chest into the table. My emotions and anger taking over. "I don't have to tell you shit."

"You're angry," she stammers as she tries to turn her head to look at me but my hand is holding her neck down.

"I'm just dealing with my thoughts."

"No, you are stewing in your anger and you're acting like an asshole."

"I am an asshole." My dick hardens as she presses her ass into it. I know this is turning her on.

"You only think you are."

I rip the blanket off her and pull her shorts down, then plunge my fingers into her without warning. A scream falling from her lips at the forced intrusion.

"You're only doing this to scare me," she growls. "And you didn't scare me the other day when you punished me."

"Fuck!" I yell as I make quick work of my buckle and pants, pushing them down just enough for my dick to spring free. I slam myself inside of her in one hard thrust.

She lets out a scream, her body not ready for me. But I just lean over the table and pin her hands behind her back as I pump into her. Her body at my mercy as I act like the monster I am. Her hips banging into the edge of the table with every thrust. I whisper in her ear. "You didn't seem to learn your lesson."

I fuck her hard against the table, but she doesn't resist. She just whimpers as I pull an orgasm out of her right before I come. I don't pull out this time. Not like every other time. Maybe it's to show her who she belongs to. Or my own need to truly mark her with myself.

I pull away from her and pull up my pants. She doesn't move. Just stands with her legs spread as she's bent over the table. I watch as our juices start to slide down the inside of her thigh. But I don't give her the man that she wants, the one who holds her after I fuck her. Instead, I sit down in my chair and go back to my drink. Thankful it didn't spill from the force with which I slammed her into the table.

"Go clean yourself up. I'm done with you for the night." My tone harsh.

She pushes herself off the table, pulling up her shorts and picking the blanket up off the ground. "You don't scare me, Matías."

"Leave," I command.

"I think you are scared of yourself." Her words quiet before she walks back into the house.

I stay outside until I see the sun start to rise. The bottle of bourbon I brought out nearly gone. I pinch my eyes shut as I rub my temples.

I finally stumble into the house and collapse into my empty bed. It's not lost on me that she slept in her room. Maybe my point did come across. I ignore the ache in my chest as I pass out.

23

ALESSIA

I haven't seen Matías in two days. I checked in on him after our argument on the deck and found him sprawled out in his clothes on his bed. No doubt he passed out drunk. He never came out of his room yesterday. At least that I saw. I spent most of the day in the art studio, then ate dinner alone and went to bed early.

This morning I woke up in a fit from that damn dream again. But nothing changed. I was still drowning in a dark pool, a crown that didn't belong to me on my head. I've been staring at a blank canvas for the last two hours but for some reason the dream is blocking everything from my head.

Or maybe the conversation with Matías.

Or my fucked-up life in general.

The more I try not to think, the more I get lost in my head. I want answers. Real answers. Not the half-assed ones that I've been given. I want to know what my father truly did. If he isn't the man I thought he was. If my brothers care that I am being held captive. What it will take for me to be set free.

Do I want to be free? Yes. But do I want to leave Matías? No. The answer is a firm belief deep in my soul. I know that I shouldn't feel things for him but the pull between us is so undeniably strong, I can't deny it. Maybe this was fate. A very messed up version of fate, but fate nonetheless that brought us together.

He makes me feel like the person I was before my mother died. Before I lost my best friend. Before I hid from the world behind my paintbrushes and canvases. Too scared to live. Now I realize I was too scared of dying. Too scared to let myself take risks. I didn't want a shortened life like my mother but instead my life turned into not living at all. It's fucked up that my being kidnapped made me realize that. Or maybe it was the wake-up call I needed. Being so close to death, being able to taste it on my tongue.

But Matías woke me from that internal cage. He sparked something so deep inside of me I never would have found it on my own. He brought out that spirited girl I used to be. And I know it's fucked up, he kidnapped me, locked me up. But he never did any of it out of hate or spite. I know he was protecting me from whatever forces are working against my family.

He thinks he is a broken man. One with his own chains keeping him from living. But he's not. I see it deep in those sparkling azure eyes when he laughs, when we talk about the past, when we talk about nothing at all. I can see the boy that he was trying to break through the shell of a man held down by burdens.

I love him. The thought not nearly as scary as I thought it would be. I love Matías Montford with all my heart.

But I don't think he will ever accept my love.

I finally give up on painting. My stomach rumbling from lack of food as I make my way into the kitchen. Claudette is nowhere to be seen but Matías is sitting at the kitchen island with another glass of bourbon in his hand. I wonder if he has stopped drinking since our argument.

I don't know if I can talk to him. Even though that is the only thing I want to do. Talk to him, make sure he is okay, feel his arms wrap around me. But I don't know if he is ready to face my honesty. I don't think he could handle hearing those three words I want to tell him.

I turn to leave, figuring I'll just find something to eat later but he must have felt my presence.

"I'm sorry about the other night. You deserve better than that. Better than me."

His words cause an ache in my chest.

"I shouldn't have treated you that way." He runs his hands over his face. "I shouldn't have done any of the things I've done to you."

I see the regret etched across his face, a sadness and despair that I don't think he ever lets anyone see. I slowly walk up to him, my heartbeat speeding up with every step I take.

He turns to face me when I get close. His hands

trying to reach for me but he pulls back at the last second.

I nod toward the glass on the table. "Have you been drinking since the other night?"

He shakes his head. "No."

"I haven't seen you."

He looks down, his shoulders sagging. "I went to the office. Slept there last night. I-I couldn't face you after those vile words I said to you. After I treated you like you meant nothing."

My heart aches at those words, knowing I mean something to him. "I forgive you."

His head snaps up. "Why? Why forgive me when I treated you like a whore?"

I step closer to him. "Because I know you didn't mean it. You were drunk, angry."

"I took my anger out on you."

I nod as I take another step closer to him. "You're angry with yourself." His fists clench but I continue. "I see it in everything you do, Matías. The life you are living. You say you need to do the things you do as a penance for The Partners but I think you do it, you like it, because it's reparation for your soul."

He swallows as I let out the words he needed to hear. His words are soft as he asks, "How do you know me so well?"

I shrug. "I don't. I… sometimes I just think… I can see past your stormy eyes and into your soul. The man that you've hidden away. The man that deserves so much more than you give him."

His head falls to his chest as his hands wrap around

my hips, pulling me between his legs. "I don't deserve you."

I run a hand through his hair. "Yes, you do."

He looks up at me. A million thoughts and feelings in his eyes, but he doesn't say a word. Just stares at me with those eyes I could get lost in every day.

I study the bruises on his face. The healing cut across his cheek as I run my fingers gently over it. "Why do you do it, Matías? Why do you fight?"

He sighs deeply. "So I can shut off my feelings of guilt and shame."

"Does it help?"

He shrugs. "Temporarily. The physical pain makes my brain shut off my thoughts."

"But not in the long run?"

He shakes his head.

I take a deep breath before I ask him my next question. Afraid the answer will be the same. "Is that why you fuck me the way you do? To shut off your feelings?"

His eyes snap up at me, a burning lust shining through them as he pulls me closer to him. "Don't ever think that, Alessia. Don't ever think that I touch you to turn off my mind. It's the opposite. I fuck you to allow myself to feel. Every single touch of my fingers along your skin, the sounds you make as I give you your deepest pleasure, the look in your eyes as I make you fall apart. Those make me come alive. You make me feel alive."

I gasp at his words just before I crash my lips into his. My hands grip into his short hair as his tongue slides into my mouth. I can feel every emotion electrifying through us, like lightning. I'm caught in a storm I don't want to break free of.

He pulls away and we are both breathing heavy. Our eyes locked on one another. My heart rate beating fast as I let the words slip from my mouth. "I love you."

His eyes fall closed at my words. Fear runs through my veins as I build up a wall, getting ready to push away his rejection. But instead he opens his eyes and grips my face. "You make me feel honorable. Redeemed. Like the man I once was. You're my deliverance. My salvation. And every touch, kiss, hell, the air you breathe brings me closer to redemption. Closer to letting myself feel like I can love you in the way you deserve." He pauses. "I want to say those words to you. I want you to know that deep down in my dark soul, I believe you are the woman for me but I worry about the consequences. Of what that would mean for you, bringing you into a life like mine. You deserve more than me, angel. So much more."

"What if I don't want more?" I ask as I hold back tears.

"Then I would say you are a fool." The intensity in his eyes weakening with those words.

I run my fingers on the top of his thigh, my head down. "I think they say something about fools falling in love."

His fingers lift my chin. "I don't care what they say. But I'll try my damn hardest to be that man for you. If you are willing to take the risk."

"I would risk my life for you, Matías. Don't you see that?"

The words must break something in him. He picks

me up, wrapping my legs around his waist. "I think you are a fool."

"A fool who fell in love with a monster."

He nods as he presses his lips to my own.

"But you are my monster. Maybe you should let the monster come back out to play."

His lips kiss down my neck as he carries me to his room. "There is no monster tonight."

He tosses me on the bed, the monster a gentle beast as he worships my body for hours.

24

MATÍAS

I lean back against my headboard and watch her sleep. Her dark hair fanned across my pillows as soft snores come from her mouth.

I don't know what I've done to deserve this woman. She accepts me despite everything working against me, against us. I worry that it's some version of Stockholm syndrome. That she only thinks she is in love with me due to some chemical imbalance in her brain.

Maybe that's what I want to think because I know I am no good for her. She said she was a fool to fall for someone like me and I know she's right. But I don't give a shit. When I look into those honey-colored eyes, all I see is love. Or what I imagine love is. I never let love into my cold heart. Never gave anyone the chance. But the way she looks at me, it's the way Thiago used to look at his wife. The way Bastian looks at Cam.

And she told me she loved the monster inside of me. I don't know how anyone could love that. He's cruel, sadistic, violent. But she asked for him. She craves him as much as I do.

I run my fingers down her arm. This woman is more than I ever could have asked for. She shifts from my touch just as my phone rings on the side table next to my bed.

I glance down at the number and a scowl takes over my features. I lean over Alessia and press a kiss to the top of her head before sliding off the bed and grabbing the phone.

I click the bedroom door shut behind me. "Montford," I answer.

"Matías, so good to hear your voice."

"Charles, how many times do I have to tell you to quit with the fake greetings?"

He clears his throat. "Someone is in a mood today. Has Alessia gotten sick of your dick?"

I clench my fist as I walk into my office. "What do you want, Charles?" I ask, ignoring his last remark.

"A deal has been made with Calvetti. We should celebrate with a dinner tomorrow night. Bring the girl."

It's only been three days since we threatened Alessia's father and I find it strange that the family somehow came up with the thirty million dollars they owe The Partners. Something isn't adding up. "Yes, sir." It's all I can say.

"Maybe give her a nice fuck one last time."

I fake a laugh. "I'll give her more than one."

He chuckles into the phone before rattling off the details and hanging up.

I want to shoot the man in the head. He has ruined my life and my brothers'. He is the scum of the earth, yet he acts like he holds so much power when I know for a fact he has no power in The Partners. I've thought of a hundred ways to kill him, and I have even more reasons to do it, but I know it will end with a bullet between my eyes if I act on my instincts.

I lean back in my desk chair, thinking when it hits me that I truly only have a day and a half left with my angel. Because I don't know what will happen after this. The chance we get to be together so slim I don't even try to hope for it. Mostly because of the feeling in my gut about that call. Something was off and tomorrow may be the last day I breathe.

I make a few calls and then head back into my bedroom. I hear Alessia in the bathroom and find her brushing her hair. I wrap my arms around her from behind and watch us in the mirror.

"What?" she asks me.

I raise a brow at her.

"Why are you looking at me like that?"

I don't answer her and instead press my lips to her neck. "Get dressed. Grab a swimsuit." I smack her ass, then walk into my closet.

"What do you mean get dressed?" she asks me as I pull on a pair of shorts.

"We're going out."

"Out?" she asks with the cutest confused look on her face.

"Yes," I say shortly as I pull a white T-shirt over my head.

"Like out of the house?"

"That would be out."

She starts a sentence a few times before finally saying, "But I'm your prisoner."

I step into her space, grabbing her chin with my hand and lifting her gaze to mine. "Angel, you know you're more than that."

"I… but…"

I drop my head until my lips touch hers. A soft kiss unlike all the others we've shared. "You'll be with me the whole time. So you are still mine."

"But you are going to let me walk around freely?"

I want to fuck that cute little confused look off her face but I hold myself back. "I could keep you handcuffed the whole time if you want." I lean in and suck the lobe of her ear into my mouth, then bite hard. "I know how much you love it."

I pull back and find a blush creeping up her neck.

"Ten minutes."

"Where are we going?"

"You'll see."

She eyes me cautiously before walking out of my room to her own. At least the one she uses to keep her clothes in.

I push the gas to the floor as we fly out of my neighborhood in my Bugatti. We zip around the city, my hand on her thigh. This need deep inside of me to touch her as much as I can today because after tomorrow… I don't want to even think about after tomorrow.

I pull up in front of an old, unmarked brick building.

Two gas lanterns hang outside the archway that leads to double wooden doors.

"What is this place?" Alessia asks as she opens her door.

I smirk at her but don't answer as I climb out of the car and walk around to meet her.

"Matías?"

I grab her hand and pull her toward the wooden doors. "Don't trust me?" I ask, with a hint of humor in my eyes.

"I'm beginning to wonder if I shouldn't," she says cautiously.

I laugh as I pull her into my side and press my lips to her head. "You probably shouldn't."

"Ass," she mutters under her breath in Italian.

I press in a code to the pin pad next to the doors and pull them open and lead us into a dark hallway.

"Did you bring me to a sex dungeon?" she asks, and I burst out in laughter.

I slide my hand down her ass and grab it. "You'll know if I ever bring you to a sex dungeon, angel."

She looks up at me through her bangs. "Wait... I was joking. You wouldn't—"

"Don't pretend you wouldn't like it. The monster would have his way with you," I whisper into her ear.

She bites her lip, the faintest flush hitting her cheeks. "Oh."

I push open the dark glass doors in front of me. "Don't worry, this is the opposite of that."

I pull her through the door. The room is dark with soft lights spread through the floor.

"What is this place?" she asks me as she walks farther into the dark room, letting go of my hand.

"Go step onto one of the squares of light."

She looks back at me and in the dim lighting, I can see the look of confusion on her face. But she does as I say.

When she steps onto one of the squares, lights come on above her head and shine onto the wall in front of her, lighting up a piece of art on the wall.

"Is that a Benicia piece?"

I walk up behind her. "Yeah."

"How? This has been privately owned for years. People have been asking for it to be moved to a museum..." she trails off as she takes in the brilliance of colors. She steps off the light square and the lights shut off on the painting.

I see her shadow move across the room to another square and she gasps as another painting lights up. She jumps around the room, moving from square to square as she takes in the paintings. Her face pure joy and awe.

"I... I don't even know what to say."

I walk up to her, a smile on my face as I see her smile. "Friend of a friend. This is his private collection."

"These paintings cost millions."

I shrug. "I'm friends with rich people."

"He just keeps this here for himself?"

"He has parties here every now and then. Private showings at times."

Her hands land on my chest before sliding up and around my shoulders. She steps to her tiptoes before kissing me with soft lips. "Thank you."

I don't say anything. I don't know what to say. I've never in my life done something like this for someone. I wasn't even sure if she would like this but I felt that she needed to see it.

I pull her into me, deepening the kiss, my tongue sliding between her lips. She moans into my mouth as she presses herself into my body. My dick throbs at the taste of her, the feeling of her needing me as much as I need her. But she pulls away before I can take things further.

She tugs on my hand and drags me to one of the light squares. "Stand here."

I raise a brow at her.

"Get your mind out of the gutter. I just want to look closer at the paintings."

I stand on the square lighting up the first painting she looked at. She steps all the way up to the canvas, studying the lines and brush strokes. I am sure she is taking mental notes. "You know the reason he did this with the lights was so no one touched the canvas."

She looks back at me, rolling her eyes. "I'm not touching it."

We spend the next hour going from painting to painting, her directing me to each light square. When we finally get to the last painting, she walks up to me, her hands on the buckle of my pants. "This was amazing."

"I'm glad you enjoyed it." She smiles at me and my heart clenches. I pull her hands away from my belt. "There will be time for that later."

She pouts and I am tempted to slam her against the wall and fuck her between these paintings I know nothing about. But I hold myself back, grab her hand, and head to the door.

"Where to next?" she asks as I open the passenger door on the Bugatti for her.

She slides into her seat and I lean down. "So many questions today."

"I don't like surprises."

"Too bad."

I shut her door and walk over to the driver's side. I pull us out onto the road, my hand back on her thigh. Her fingers wrap around the top of my hand. I look over at her and she is staring at me. I see that love in her eyes she told me about last night. I grip her thigh as feelings pulse through me, beating so hard in my chest I feel it may burst. What has she done to me?

When we pull up to the marina, Alessia gets giddy next to me. "Are we going on a boat?"

I snort. "Uh, yeah."

"What?"

I shake my head at her. "Nothing."

"I've missed the water. I used to sit outside every morning on my balcony drinking coffee and looking at the sea."

Her words hit me in a way I never expected. I pulled her from her life, from the peace that she had in Positano. Her quiet life of painting and solitude.

She presses her palm to my cheek. "Matías."

I look over at her, giving her a weak smile before I pull away from her and get out of the car. I grab the bag she brought out of the trunk.

"I haven't been on the water in so long. My brothers

had a small yacht, but they moved it from Naples to Palermo. Bianca's family has a sailboat but we rarely ever used it. I miss it. I love being out on the water."

I watch her as we walk down the dock, her excitement palpable. Her eyes widening the farther we walk as the yachts get larger and larger. When we get to bay thirty-six, her jaw drops open. "This is yours?"

"Nah. Too flashy for me. I wouldn't waste my money on this."

"You have a three-million-dollar car," she deadpans.

"Touché." I step onto the yacht where one of the deckhands waits for us. "This is Bastian's. He isn't one for flaunting his money. But he spends a lot of time on the water. So this was one of those things he splurged on."

"This is like a two-hundred-foot yacht. I would call that more than a splurge."

I grab her hand as she steps onto the deck. "It's three hundred and fourteen feet. Like I said, flashy."

"Mr. Montford, it is nice to see you again. Can I get either of you a drink as you settle in?"

"Daniel, I've told you to call me Matías. Mr. Montford is my brother."

He nods. "Apologies, sir."

"I'll take a bourbon." I turn to Alessia, who is taking in the high-end features of the outside deck of the boat. "Alessia?"

"Vodka and grapefruit please."

"Feel free to roam around. I'll bring you your drinks."

"No need. We'll meet you on the front deck in ten minutes."

He walks away and I turn to Alessia. "Come, let me give you a tour of this obnoxious boat."

"Do you use this often?"

"No. Bastian doesn't trust me with his things." She gives me a strange look but I ignore it and continue. "He made an exception for me today."

I guide her through the doors leading to the living quarters of the ship. I point out the inside bar and dining area and then up the stairs to the master bedroom. It leads out to its own private deck. I watch her as she walks through the sliding glass doors to take in the view as I set her bag down on the bed.

"This is incredible," she says as she turns toward me.

I lean my shoulder against the open glass door. "Wait until we are out on the water."

She gives me that dazzling smile and I can't help but give her a smile of my own. She saunters over to me and wraps her arms around my neck. I pull her into me and meet her lips as they reach for mine. I don't know what will happen after tomorrow. But I need these moments with her. These memories. Because if I die tomorrow at least I will die a happy man.

I pull away from her. "Let's change and head to the front deck so we can head out."

"Okay."

She goes to pull away but I pull her back in for another kiss. My lips needing hers. Needing as many memories as I can give her. I stop before I turn it into more.

I quickly change into swim shorts, then sit on the bed and watch her. The fluid movement as she pulls off her dress. The way her hair falls down her naked back. The roundness of her perfect ass. Her head peeks over her shoulder at me.

"If you keep looking at me like that, we will never make it downstairs."

I shrug. "What can I say? You're mesmerizing."

She rolls her eyes at me. "You're creepy."

A low chuckle comes out of my mouth. "Angel, I just like to stare at what's mine."

She slips off her panties then walks over to me, coming between my legs completely nude. "Well then by all means stare some more."

I run my finger over her hip bones, over the bruises I left there from my fingers. "Mmm, I want nothing more than to do that but we will never leave this room."

"You're no fun," she says as she turns away.

I slap her ass hard, leaving a bright red mark. "You'll regret saying that later."

"You never know, I may say it again."

I growl as I pull her arm and drag her back between my legs but she pushes against my chest. "Let me get my suit on."

"Or you could go naked."

She rolls her eyes again as she steps out of my grip.

We spend the afternoon out at sea. Alessia looks happy on the water. And I wonder if this thing between us works, where we would live. Would I move the offices of Montford Hotels to Naples or would she want to live with me here? Maybe I could buy a house closer to the water so she can look out at the sea as she paints.

"What's on your mind?" she asks as she joins me at the railing, looking out into endless blue.

I've waited long enough. It's time I tell her what's going on. But I wanted this day of just us. A day where it didn't feel like she was just a job, but truly mine. A day where I get to feel what it would be like if this was real.

Her hand glides up my arm and I pull her in front of me so she is against the railing, looking out. I cage her in and kiss her neck. I lean into her ear. "You get to go home tomorrow."

She leans back against my bare chest, her long hair tickling my abs. "Is that why you brought me out here today?"

I brush my lips against her sun-kissed shoulder. "Yes."

She spins around, her hands on my chest. "What about after?"

"I don't know." I step into her, pushing her back against the railing. "I needed today."

Her fingers run down my abs. The energy around us turning melancholy. "What about us Matías?"

I sigh deeply, trying to find words to say.

She's quiet as she asks. "What aren't you telling me?"

I stare off into the water behind her. I can't tell her the truth. That I am not likely to walk out of that meeting tomorrow. That my fate is death.

Instead, I push back a loose strand of her hair and cup her cheek. "Maybe in another life, angel." Then I press my lips to hers, crushing everything inside of me to her, hoping she can understand all the pain I feel from what I know will happen. I hope she understands that I love her more than I've ever loved anything in my life. And that she will be the last thing on my mind when my fate is sealed.

She pulls away from me, her eyes forlorn. "I don't accept that."

"Alessia, you know there isn't another way."

"Why? Why can't there be something for us after. Why do we just have to forget about everything that happened between us."

"I kidnapped you, Alessia. There isn't much—"

"On orders from some stupid crime organization that think you owe them your life. It wasn't your choice, Matías. But this"—she points between the two of us—"us, this is your choice. This is my choice. You are my choice, Matías. Every damn time."

"Things don't work that way."

"Then we find out a way to make it work."

I step away from her in frustration. She doesn't understand I have no control. I run my hands through my hair. "If I could find a way, I would," I say quietly.

"I'm not giving up on us."

I feel her hands on my back before I hear her. She wraps her body around me as she steps in front of me. "There is no other choice for me."

I rest my chin on her head as I pull her tight against me. My heart swelling at the thought of this woman willing to fight monsters to keep me.

25

ALESSIA

I feel the cold of the chains on my wrists before I look down and see them. Their grip pulling me into the dark, viscous water below me. I don't even inhale as I feel the restraints pull me under, beneath the quicksand of blood and into the depths of the frigid, cold, dark water. I know I can't scream, I know I can't do anything but let the chains pull me deeper and deeper into the abyss. The water's frigidness a blanket, almost like it's calling me home. Like this dream is meant to tell me something I should already know.

I wait for the heavy crown on my head to fall like it does every time. But as I am pulled deeper and the light completely disappears from the surface far above me, the crown stays put, the sharp edges of it piercing my skull. I wonder if all the blood I fell through at the surface was mine. My kingdom bleeding around me.

For the first time, my feet hit soft sand. Then I am suddenly standing in a cold room, soaking wet, but out of the water. The white nightgown nearly see-through as I stand barefoot on the dirty floor.

I wonder if this is real. If my reality has blurred with my dreams. If I am awake or dreaming.

I let my eyes adjust to the dim lighting when I see a body on the floor. I cautiously walk toward it, the chains on my wrists breaking free. I gasp when I see my father's dead body on the floor. I lean over and touch him to find his body ice cold, like he has been dead for a while. His eyes are open and staring at the ceiling, fear still evident on his face.

I hear a soft moan coming from a dark corner of the room. I edge along the wall, the dark of night keeping me from seeing the body hunched on the floor against a wall. But as I get closer, a sliver of moonlight hits the man's face and I scream as I run to the man that owns my heart.

Matías sits slumped against the wall, blood flowing out of bullet holes in his chest. I reach his body and the crown stuck on my head comes tumbling down, clattering across the cement floor of the room. I drop to my knees and grab his hand. He's mumbling angel over and over. I grip his face, bringing my lips to his. "I can't lose you," I say.

He gives me a weak smile. "You already have." His hand goes limp in my own and the scream from my mouth fills the room in agony.

"Angel, wake up. Angel." Matías's voice is in my ear, his rough hands on my body as I blink awake into the darkness of his room. "Shh, it was a dream. Just a dream."

I can't find my breath as I grasp for him, needing to hold on to him. To feel him so I know he is real and alive. He pulls me into him, his hand making gentle strokes along my naked back. "It was a dream, angel."

I grip his arms tighter as tears crest my eyes. "It always feels so real."

"The dream? Have you had it before?"

I nod.

"Do you want to talk about it?" His words are soft as his lips press against my forehead.

"I—it's just so strange. It's been haunting me for months."

His hand cups my jaw as he runs his thumb over my lips. I look into his blue eyes and I can't help but tell him. I tell him how it started, how it's progressed over the months, but I don't tell him about the change in this one. About the part where I see him and my father dead.

The dream felt like an omen. A sinking feeling deep in my stomach as I think about tonight. About being freed, seeing my father, and hopefully finding out the truth.

Matías walks up to me as I slip on a pair of Valentino stilettos.

"You look beautiful."

I give him a weak smile as I brush my loose curls over my shoulder. I'm wearing a Saint Laurent long-sleeved white dress that hugs all of my curves and ends at my knees. The back is completely open until right above my tailbone. It's embellished with Swarovski crystals. The thing is stunning and I would have bought it for myself. Demont gave it to me earlier in the day, along with the heels. I'm still trying to figure out why we need to go to some fancy dinner. And why I needed to be handed over to my father. I would much prefer if I could just be dropped off at my home in Positano, or even my father's estate in Naples.

"This is ridiculous. Why do we need to do this?"

Matías shrugs. "The Partners have their way of doing things. And they like to make a show of things at times to set an example."

"It's dumb."

He chuckles as he reaches for a tie. "At least I get to see you in this dress. I knew it would look perfect on you. But now all I want to do is take it off you."

My thighs clench at his words. "You picked it out?"

His hand comes to my jaw. "You think Demont picked this for you?" He shakes his head as he runs a hand down my arm. "Baby, I know your body better than anyone. And I would only pick the best for you."

He presses his lips to mine and I don't want to forget this feeling. He pulls away from me and I fix his slightly crooked tie. "Is this the end for us?" I ask him quietly.

"I don't know."

I watch as he opens the safe and pulls out a gun, sliding it into the back of his pants before pulling on his jacket.

This dinner is pointless and ripe with tension. My father isn't even here. Nicolas Di Masio is. I find it strange that he was tasked to get me, not even one of my brothers decided to show up.

It's just Matías, Nicholas, and a man by the name of Charles and another named Harris. They say they are business acquaintances of my father but I know they are with The Partners. Matías told me as much. He also told me to pretend I know nothing.

We are back in Monaco at some ritzy place. Matías's hand is on my leg throughout the entire dinner. I can feel the tension in his body. His hand tightening whenever Nicolas looks at me a certain way. I barely know the man. I know he is close with my father but that's the extent of my knowledge on him. But the way he is looking at me creeps me out and I know Matías feels the same way.

Charles seems to not shut up, blabbering on and on about who knows what. My mind is muting most of his words out. I'm too focused on figuring out what the hell is going on. When I asked about my father, Nicolas said he was occupied with other business. I wish I could step away from the table with Matías, see if he has figured anything out, but I know that would only cause suspicion. So I sit uncomfortably silent.

"Well, this dinner was delightful," Charles says as a server removes the last of the plates from the table, my food barely touched. "But as Harris and I have somewhere to be, let's get this show on the road, shall we?"

Nicolas stands up from the table. "Let's go, Alessia," he demands.

I clench Matías's hand. "I don't understand why I am

going with you. I could just find a way home. Go back to Positano if my father or brothers aren't here."

Matías lets go of my hand as Nicolas rounds the table toward me. "I have orders to retrieve you. Let's go."

"Retrieve me? I'm not some object," I hiss at him.

"Don't be difficult. Let's go." His eyes bore into mine. "Or do you want to stay with the man that kidnapped you?"

"I-I just want… I want to talk to my father."

"I'm bringing you to him, princess." His tone demeaning.

I glance sideways at Matías but he's looking at the other men at the table, paying no mind to me. I swallow hard, knowing my fate is not with him, no matter how much I want it to be. I slowly stand from the table and feel my heart breaking as I step away from Matías and closer to Nicolas.

Nicolas grabs my arm and pulls me quickly toward the back of the restaurant. "You're hurting me," I tell him as he pushes open the kitchen door.

"Keep moving, Alessia."

I stop. "Where are we going?"

"My car is in the back."

"I don't trust you."

He growls and pulls me into him. "I'm not the man you shouldn't trust. I saw the way you looked at the man that kidnapped you."

"He didn't kidnap me, he was protecting me under father's orders," I lie.

Nicolas pinches my side. "Don't be naive. You know that man kidnapped you. Now move."

"No," I yell. The kitchen workers barely looking up as I struggle against Nicolas's hold.

He curses in Italian, then I feel the hard press of cold metal in my side. He leans into my ear. "I would watch that mouth of yours. Now move your ass or I will shoot you. My instructions didn't specify if I needed to deliver you dead or alive."

I bite my lip hard as I listen to him and walk out the back door of the restaurant into a waiting SUV, worried that I'm going into a worse situation than the one I've been in.

26

MATÍAS

I watch her leave with Di Masio. A man I don't trust. A man who holds more secrets than me. I could tell the second we were close enough to the table, I could see Charles and him talking. Like they were old friends. Meaning he works for him. But from what I've overheard, Di Masio is working with the mob. Crossing The Partners is a bad idea. And I just let the woman I love walk out of my life with a man that has a huge target on his back.

I close my eyes as I remember the conversation I had with her right before we got out of the car.

"You know how I feel about you, Alessia."

"But you won't say the words," she says with her eyes focused on her lap.

"I-I don't want to say them. Not yet. Not until I know you are safe. Until I know we can be together." I don't want to tell her that I doubt I'll make it through the night. Maybe it's selfish of me to not say those words, for her to at least know how I feel before we

never see each other again. But I think it will only hurt her more. To have loved and lost than for her to never think I loved her at all.

"What's going to happen in there?"

I grab her hands and squeeze them. "The Partners will make everything seem normal but there will be hidden meaning in everything. Pretend you know nothing. Stay quiet. Don't let that sass out."

She nods and I hope she understands as much as she can. A tear falls down her cheek and I brush it away with my thumb.

"For what it's worth," she whispers. "I would take a bullet for you."

I pull her into me tight, letting our hearts beat in sync, knowing this is the beginning of our end.

"Well, Matías, your assignment is now complete."

My eyes snap up to Harris. "Does that mean I am free? That I have fulfilled my debt to you?"

Charles chuckles. "You are free to go, Matías."

I clench my jaw. "That is not what I asked."

Harris stands from his chair. "We will be in contact, Mr. Mont—"

"Actually," Charles says with a smirk on his round face, cutting off Harris. "I have one more assignment for you. Then your debt is paid."

Harris looks over at him with a curious look on his face, like Charles is going against the plans laid out by their bosses.

"I was just given word about something. Meet us in an hour. I'll text you the address."

"Charlie," Harris hisses. "What are you—"

Charles gives him a look that shuts him up. And they both walk away.

I watch as both of them walk out of the restaurant. Something does not feel right about any of this. The way Di Masio seemed to know them more than they let on at that meeting earlier in the week. The way he was looking at Alessia. And that look in his eyes when he grabbed her and left.

And now Charles wants me to meet him somewhere for one more job. I think I might very well be walking with open arms into my own death.

I head out of the restaurant, my hand in my pocket, gripping the locket I stole from Alessia's apartment. I meant to give it back to her yesterday. But I couldn't. Not when this is the only thing I will have left of her.

My thumb runs over the engraving on the back. What I now know says *a warrior chooses her own fate*. Just like those words tattooed over her hip.

Maybe I should have let her fight. Let her take a bullet for me. Because if I know my angel at all, I know she is the fiercest warrior of them all.

Demont walks into the warehouse with me. He never does. He always stays outside, but he has the same feeling about this as I do.

I've been here before, one of The Partners' many properties they use for finding out answers the hard way.

We walk down the hall until we reach a door on the left that I know leads to the interrogation room. A guard stands with his arms crossed at the door. "Mr. Vanguard said only you can go in."

I look over at Demont and nod and he takes his place across from the door.

The guard opens the door and two men are roped to chairs with black bags over their heads sitting three feet apart. I see no blood and no weapons, meaning whoever is in those chairs has been left for me.

"Matías." Charles's voice echoes from a corner of the room. "So happy you made it."

"What am I doing here?" I ask, anger laced in my voice.

Charles claps his hands together and smiles as he walks into the center of the room where one dim light bulb hangs. "Well, you seemed to think you were free of all your debts earlier when you handed Alessia over." I notice one of the men in the chairs twitch at the mention of Alessia's name. "But your contract clearly stated, twenty kills and from my count, you are only at nineteen." He walks around the two men tied to the chairs, a jovial look on his face. "And since you seem so anxious to be free of our grip on you, I thought, why not give you your freedom tonight! And to make this even better for you, I'm giving you a choice. Don't say I never did anything nice for you." He laughs as he stands behind the chairs, his hands gripping the top of the black bags. "Now who will it be? Option number one?" The bag comes off the head of one of the men and I immediately recognize Lorenzo Calvetti. "Or option number two?" Angelo Calvetti sits in the chair next to him.

I look up at Charles and that annoying smug look on his face. "Let me guess, they didn't pay."

"Ding, ding, ding." Charles's sarcasm rings through

the room. "And his poor brother tried to put all the blame on Lorenzo, such a pity that even as he was begging for his life, he was blaming his brother for everything. No honor. No oath. A wasted bullet if you ask me."

I snort. "And who did you get to pull that trigger?"

"I can't reveal my secrets just yet, Matías." He turns toward the two men. "Now please find out what you can. But you only need to kill one. Brother dearest of your dear lover or her father? You know, I heard she is a daddy's girl. But I am sure you like to play that game too."

I keep all the emotion off my face as Charles taunts me. My eyes flick over to Lorenzo and I see flames of anger in his eyes as Charles references the relationship I had with his daughter. Not to mention he knows I kidnapped her. My identity with The Partners no longer a secret. "Why choose when I can just kill them both?" I ask nonchalantly.

"Oh, by all means, do what you want. I'm just here to watch the show."

I look at Charles and try to read the meaning behind his words but his dead eyes give nothing away. The man is a psychopath. I wouldn't be surprised if he had killed someone out of pure joy.

"So what have they done besides not pay you? Seems rather simple to recoup your fees."

Charles smiles a cynical smile, his white teeth look like weapons. "Seems that someone here has been talking to the Mafia, trying to find a way out of our deal by getting tied up with someone else."

"Which family?" I ask. Not that I know much of anything. I only know the Mafia families and The Partners do not get along. They will never work together for reasons I'll never know, nor do I care to know.

"Well, that is one thing we would like to find out."

I nod at Charles as he walks across the room and leans against a wall. "Proceed."

I roll my eyes as I face Lorenzo and Angelo. A shiver runs through me as I cut off my emotions and turn into the monster. I shut off my mind and don't think about how this is Alessia's family in front of me. I understand the game now. Charles knows I have feelings for her, and he wants to destroy us by making me kill her family.

I turn their chairs so they face each other, so they have to watch the other as I put them through hell. I question them, torture them, and yield no answers. Their mouths shut tight even though I can tell they are communicating with their eyes. Blood drips from their faces, bones crunch as I crush them. I try to keep my feelings away from Alessia. To not think about how this is her family I am torturing, who I am going to kill.

I interrogate them for over an hour, yet neither of them breaks. I'm tired of the game and I pull my gun out and point it at Angelo, hoping it will get his father to give up information.

"We aren't working with the Mafia," Angelo wheezes, then spits blood at me.

I scratch my head with the barrel of the gun. "You know, I want to believe you but the thing is I overheard you talking to Di Masio about meeting with them."

Angelo glances at his father quickly and I notice the slight shift of Lorenzo's eyes.

"Di Masio?" Charles finally cuts in. "You never told us, Matías."

I look over to where Charles is still leaning against the wall. "I was putting the information together." I know The Partners are going to be pissed that I kept information from them but I'll deal with that later.

"Nicolas has nothing to do with this," Lorenzo talks for the first time.

"He has everything—" Angelo starts to shout but gets cut off by a look from Lorenzo. Maybe Calvetti has more balls than I thought he did.

I pace around the two men. "Now who do I need to kill to get the other to talk?"

"You aren't going to kill either of us," Angelo spits out.

"And why's that?" I ask with annoyance in my voice.

"You have feelings for Alessia. And you've had your dirty hands all over my sister but she would never be with someone who kills people. So you won't touch us."

I smirk at him. "She knows what I do."

He looks at me in disgust. "She is too innocent for that. You hide behind the facade of a billionaire but you are a cold-blooded killer. She could never love someone like you."

I laugh, hoping the anger flowing from his mouth will let out more secrets. I lean over his shoulder and whisper loud enough in his ear so Lorenzo can hear as I look him in the eye. "Too late for that. She already told me she loves me. She loves it even more when I have her tied up and at my mercy, kind of like you are right now."

"You are a monster."

"And she loves when the monster comes out to play. Begs me to spank her, to pound into that tight pussy of hers, to shove my cock—"

"Enough!" Lorenzo yells.

"Dad, you can't—"

"You want to know the family? I'll tell you. Just please don't talk about my daughter like that."

"Dad," Angelo warns.

"We needed an out. The money wasn't there. The debt—"

"Di Masio brought us in. He is the connection to the family. Don't listen to my father, he's lying."

I look over at Lorenzo and see anger flare in his eyes. I take that moment to knock Angelo in the back of the head with the handle to my gun. He slumps in his chair and blood dribbles down his neck from the blow. Not enough to kill, but enough to incapacitate so his father can talk.

"Now, Mr. Calvetti, what were you saying?"

We are interrupted again by a scream. A scream I know all too well.

"Angelo," Alessia yells as she fights against the hold Charles has on her, as he pulls her out of a back room and toward me.

My heart clenches when I see the look on her face. Utter terror and hatred, so much hatred toward me. Charles lets her go, and she runs to her brother.

"He's not dead," I tell her. "Just unconscious."

She looks up at me, tears in her eyes. "How could you?"

"I had no other choice," I say quietly. I hate that she is seeing this part of me. She knew, but it's completely different when you see it happening.

"Is this the man you love, Alessia? A killer? It's crazy what can happen when you get locked in a place with such a good-looking man." Venom laces Charles's words.

"Charles," I warn.

"Oh, come on, Matías, this is classic."

I ignore Charles and walk over to Alessia. She bangs her fist into my chest and I let her, needing to feel the physical pain. I'm silent as she lets out her anger, my fists clenching as she does it. My own anger boiling in my veins. I glance over at Lorenzo and his eyes are on me, vengeance written in them.

"Angel," I whisper as my arms wrap around her.

Tears flood from her eyes as her fists stop hitting me and she grabs on to my shirt. I glance over at Lorenzo with a smug smile. He looks like he is ready to scream.

"Enough of the games, Charles," a voice comes from out of the dark corner of the room. "I have better things to do with my time."

I blink in surprise as the man walks into the light. A man I haven't seen in two years. A man who is supposed to be dead. Clearly, he isn't.

"Kilian," I say in shock.

He looks over at me. His baby blue eyes shine as he smiles at me. He rolls up the sleeves of his dress shirt. "Matías. It's been a long time."

"How?"

He shakes his head and walks over to Lorenzo. He places his hands on the arms of his chair and leans into his face. "Give us the damn name, Mr. Calvetti."

"Not until he gets his hands off my daughter."

Kilian glances back at me and I nod as I step away from Alessia.

"Now tell me," he growls.

"Promise me that she will be safe. That—"

"I am not in the mood to be making deals. Now tell me what family you have been working with or else I'll kill you just like I killed your brother."

No wonder Charles didn't want to say who killed Gianno. Everyone thinks Kilian is dead but apparently he has been deeply involved with The Partners. I wonder if Bastian has known all along.

Kilian sighs when Lorenzo keeps his mouth shut. He quickly pulls his gun from his chest holster, turns and shoots Angelo in the center of the head.

A clean shot.

A death shot.

Alessia screams as blood splatters across her white dress. I wrap my arms around her waist when she tries to reach for her brother. She slumps into my back as her legs give out.

"Well, that didn't go as planned." Charles laughs as Kilian lowers his weapon. "Now how am I going to get Matías to make a decision? He had just one more kill to make before he was out of our clutches."

"Charles." Kilian's voice threaded with power.

"Stand down, boy. This is my operation. Not yours."

"And I'm here because you are taking too long."

"Well then, your father should have brought that up with me."

Kilian rolls his eyes, but walks away from Lorenzo and gestures for Charles to continue.

"Now we told Matías he could be free of us if he killed twenty people. He's at nineteen. Now since he can't choose between the father and the brother. I guess he is going to have to choose between daddy and his lover." He walks over to us and picks up a piece of Alessia's hair. Her body tenses in my arms. I want to grab my gun and shoot Charles in the head. "Or we can find a different way to pay the debt the Calvettis owe us and I'll let you off the hook, Matías. She is such a pretty thing. I bet we could get a lot of money for her. I heard the Arabian cartel lord is looking for a new plaything. Too bad she isn't a virgin."

I fill with rage at the thought of her being sold as a sex slave. It was the one thing I never let myself get involved in with The Partners. I didn't care about money laundering, illegal gambling, or drugs but I stopped at the trafficking.

I look over at Kilian and see him on his phone, looking bored as ever. I wonder how deep he is involved with The Partners. The way Charles talked to him, it made him sound as if he was ranked high. But no one knows anyone's ranking. For all I know, Kilian could be running the entire black market. I know his family has been involved with The Partners for years, longer than when Thiago and Bastian joined, but it always seemed like Kilian joined with them.

"So Matías, what's it going to be?" Charles asks me.

"You aren't selling her."

"I was hoping you would say that. Now it gets even more fun."

I look at him, panic settling into my stomach, knowing I am not going to like what he has to say.

"One kill. One kill and the freedom you've wanted from us can be yours." He looks at Lorenzo and then at Alessia. "Who shall it be?" He taps his finger against his bottom lip. "Her or her father. The choice is yours."

Alessia pulls out of my grip and steps toward her father.

"You'll either lose her or she'll hate you."

"How is this relevant to anything?" Kilian asks from where he has moved to, leaning against the wall.

"Matías has a payment to fulfill."

Kilian looks at his nails. "I think he's paid his dues."

"You have a soft spot for the man."

Kilian shrugs and looks up at Charles. "Maybe so, but he's done enough. You've had him under your thumb for two years. He could have been done after six months but you've been stringing him along."

Charles glares at Kilian, then goes back to talking to me. "Make a choice, Matías. Alessia or her father?"

"I'm not killing either. There is no merit to either kill."

"Merit?" He chuckles. "Since when have you killed for merit. I know you like the power. The feeling of taking another man's life. I've been told so. I've seen it."

I look at Alessia, who is kneeling beside her father, whispering something to him. Harris walks up behind her and pulls her away, pushing her onto her knees, his grip in her hair as he holds her head up to me.

"Kill me, Matías. My daughter deserves a happy life," Lorenzo resigns.

"Daddy, no!" Alessia cries out. She attempts to reach for him but Harris's hold is too strong.

"Let him kill me, Alessia. And you can live your life away from this despicable man. He will get what's coming to him," he snaps at me.

I look toward Alessia, tears falling down her blood-splattered face. I knew this would happen. I knew I would be put into a position that would never free me. Maybe I could get free of The Partners but only to be a prisoner to my own regret.

I clear my throat and point the gun toward Charles. I hate the man. He has made my life a living hell. What he has turned me into. The monster I try to hate. A man not worthy of anything. But he just tsks at me. We both know it would be a stupid move.

My eyes glance toward Kilian and he shakes his head at me.

"Matías, do you really think that would be a good decision? You kill me, then one of my men kills you." Charles walks closer to me. "Has love made all the Montford brothers weak? First Thiago giving his life for his wife and his unborn child. Then Bastian for that woman who worked for him. And now you. The kidnapper falling for his captive. The thing with that storyline, dear Matías, is that as soon as she is free, the spell between you two will break. She'll run home. Leave you with a broken heart and a body full of rage. She will forget about you."

I clench my fists at Charles's words. Knowing them to be true. That there will never be a future for Alessia and me. I knew it before tonight. I've known it since the first time I touched her. But she was the forbidden fruit and I've never been one to follow the rules.

I see her whispering I love you and my heart clenches. Despite everything, she still loves me. This woman I love more than anything. A woman who taught me what my heart needs to beat. A woman I would give my own life up for.

I turn the gun toward my head, and a bloodcurdling scream comes from Alessia. I glance at her and see her struggling on the floor to get to me. But what choice do I have? I glance at Kilian and he mouths the words safe, then glances at Alessia. I take a deep breath and cock the gun.

Just as I go to pull the trigger, a shot rings out across the warehouse. I barely register the chaos as pain flies through my shoulder, causing the gun to fall from my hand. I look down and see blood running from the wound where I was hit. I blink a few times at the shot that stopped me from pulling the trigger.

"Kilian, you are ruining the fun," Charles whines.

I look over at Kilian and see the gun in his hand. The man stopped me from killing myself.

"Enough!" a booming voice silences the room. "What the hell is going on here?"

Charles's face goes pale as he looks at the man who walked into the room. "Mr. Bancroft, we-we were just on the verge of—"

"Where is Di Masio?" the man I recognize as Kilian's father asks.

"He's around somewhere."

Harris chimes in. "He was in the holding room with Alessia before we brought her in here."

Mr. Bancroft nods toward the men that walked in with him and they walk toward a back room.

"What does Di Masio have to do with this?" Charles asks.

"He is the one that brought us in with the family," Lorenzo answers.

"Di Masio can't be the problem." Charles's words rushed from his mouth. "He has worked for me for ten years."

"He's not here," a man shouts from the back room.

"Find him," Mr. Bancroft commands, then turns to Charles. "Mr. Vanguard, you have a lot of explaining to do."

Charles pales. "I don't know what you are talking about."

"To not know that one of your men was working with the Mafia the entire time. I thought you were smarter than that."

"I swear I didn't—"

Mr. Bancroft draws his gun and aims it at Charles. "Or is it that you have been working with them as well? Giving away our secrets. Using Mr. Montford here to find out information. Peculiar, that the shipments you've been in charge of are the ones that have been going missing."

"Coincidence," Charles stutters. "There has been a lot of tension in Italy—"

"Enough of your excuses. Tell me the truth."

"I don't know—"

"The family is—" Lorenzo cuts in but before he can say what family it is, shots ring out across the warehouse. A bullet hitting him directly in the head.

I pick up my gun with my unwounded shoulder and rush toward Alessia. She reaches for me just as a bullet flies past her head. I pull her toward her brother's dead body to use as a shield. I flip her between me and her brother's body just as a bullet nearly misses her stomach and pierces my thigh.

She clutches at me, tears falling from her eyes and I know she saw her father die like her brother. Shock covers her face just like the night she was almost kidnapped from me.

Demont comes running into the room and he grabs Alessia from me. "I'll get her out of here."

I nod at him, then look up to where the shooters are above us. The lights in the room are dim and the moonlight barely gives way to the catwalk above us. I rip a piece of bloody shirt from Angelo's dead body and make a tourniquet for my leg.

I hear Kilian shouting at his father. Then watch as his father aims his gun at Charles, who is just standing in the room, no bullets hitting him.

"You gave us up," Mr. Bancroft shouts at him.

A sinister look comes over Charles's face. "You didn't give me the position I asked for. The one that would lead this syndicate to even more wealth and power. So I found someone who would give me what I wanted."

Mr. Bancroft laughs. "You think the Mafia is willing to give you what you want? You want a seat at the table. You want to sit next to me and lead. The Mafia is a family and they will never put an outsider at their table. You are a foolish man, Charles."

"I'm a businessman."

"And a poor one at that," Mr. Bancroft says just as he fires his weapon.

I see Charles whip his own gun out just as Mr. Bancroft fires his. Two shots ring out louder than any of the rest in the room. In fact, all other gunshots seem to cease as I watch Charles fall to the ground, a bullet between his eyes.

Then I feel it. The struggle for my own breath as pain rips across my chest.

I blink as my knees collapse underneath me. I look down and see the blood leaking out of me. I touch it in shock. I let it drip down my arm. It's thick. Viscous. But it doesn't have the same effect coming from me as it did for others.

Alessia breaks free of Demont and runs toward me as I slump to the side. My vision waning as I watch the battle fading before me.

"No, no, no." I think I hear her screaming. My vision fades in and out, but I don't miss when she picks my gun up off the floor. My angel turning into my warrior. She aims at the rafters above, shooting at whoever is shooting at us.

I use whatever strength I can find to dig the locket

out of my pocket. My fingers grazing the engraving one last time. "My warrior," I wheeze as I reach for her.

She looks down at me and sees the locket in my hand. She drops the gun and reaches for me. Her hand clasping around mine.

"You get to choose your own fate," I choke out.

Her hands feel like an angel as she grips my face. "Don't leave me. Matías, please. You can't die. You are my fate. You can't…" Her sobs bring me comfort knowing her love is flowing from the tears as they drop on my face.

My breathing slows, and the pain disappears. Her lips land on mine until I start to cough up blood. She pulls away and I see my blood on her mouth. The streaks of red almost like art.

I think I feel her hands on my chest. Her cries getting softer as I fade away.

It takes all the effort inside of me to find her hand. And even more to whisper my angel before everything fades to black and I find the peace I've been searching for my whole life.

27

ALESSIA

The cool wind blows through my hair as I look at the cedar coffin in front of me. A priest says words in the background but I barely focus on them. My heart shattered into a million pieces. I finally understand the dream. It was almost prophetic. The loss and pain building up to reality after all these months. And now all I am left with is an emptiness in my heart. My soul lost, looking for answers it may never find.

I glance up and see one of my brothers staring at me, anger laced across his face. Maybe he is mad that I am not crying. Or that I did nothing to save father or Angelo. But what was I to do? I was just a pawn in a game I can't make sense of. Just like Matías was a pawn.

The priest talks about the love of family and how it heals even the most devastated hearts. But my heart is hardened now. My brothers and cousins upset with me for not trying to save anyone. Yet they aren't mad at the two men being buried in the ground today. Men who decided illegitimate business practices were the best way to make money. Tying themselves up in the criminal underworld. There was nothing I could have done to save this family.

Bianca grips my hand as they lower my father's coffin into the ground. All I can picture is Matías finally dying. He's been in a coma for a week. And I can tell by the look on the doctors' faces that they don't think he will make it. The bullet barely missed his heart, punctured a lung and his liver. The wound in his leg millimeters from his femoral artery. He lost too much blood. And they worry about the low oxygen levels to his brain before he got to the hospital.

I haven't left his side for a week. Only today for the funeral of my brother and father. My uncle's body still hasn't been found, not that I care. But my cousins do. Maybe that is why they are upset with me. That I have ignored my family this whole week when we should be grieving together over our loss. But my heart doesn't care. Not after none of them came looking for me. Not when they knew something dubious was going on.

No, my heart is with the man that kidnapped me. That protected me. That took a bullet for me.

My heart lies where it truly should. With the Montford family and all their secrets.

And I would choose them again and again.

I've gotten to know Bastian, Cam, and Ainslie over the last week. Cam and Ainslie there to comfort me. It's almost stifling but Cam says she understands my pain. She told me about how Bastian was gone for two months. Kept in a prison and tortured by The Partners for the fun of it. His punishment wasn't like Matías's and Bastian seems to still be upset with himself for the life that Matías got thrown into.

But it was fate how both our lives turned out. If he hadn't been handed such a cruel punishment, our paths may never have crossed and I never would have met the man that made my heart beat again.

I remember the words Charles said to him, those cruel words that I would leave him once I was free. At the moment, I thought I should. That I should go back to the life I had known, the one where I spent my days and nights alone in a two-bedroom apartment with the sound of the sea and my collection of paints. But that time with Matías made me feel alive. At the beginning, it was the fear but then transformed into so much more. Every day I spent with Matías, the relationship I built with Demont. They feel like family. More than mine ever has. I realized that day in the warehouse just how much Angelo and my father were shielding me from. The way they treated me since Mom died, a way to blind me from the truth. My father told me in the warehouse that night to run and change my name, forget about our family. I pleaded that I would do anything to save them. And he told me I wasn't needed. It broke my heart. How could a man that cared about me so much, that I loved so much, tell me to hide? Tell his only daughter I wasn't needed? I would have done anything for my family but at that moment I felt lost and alone. The cold look in my father's eyes was enough to make me want to rip the gun from Matías's hand and shoot him myself.

It's why I'm not crying today, nor have I shed one

tear over the loss of my father. I realized I was only a burden to my family.

"Do you want to go?" Bianca pulls on my hand.

I blink and look around me. Most people have scattered. The ceremony over. Both coffins six feet under. I look at her and nod.

"Let's go then."

Demont is by my side the second we start moving. I glance over at my brothers and both of them stare at me with vengeance in their eyes. "Ignore them," he says softly. "They won't accept the truth from you."

I hold my head high as I walk out of the cemetery. I know Demont is right. I know they don't want to believe what I tried to tell them a week ago. Their denial is overwhelming and there is nothing I can do. I was left with nothing. My father's will giving the business to my brothers and cousins.

I climb into the car, Bianca right behind me. "Are you sure you want to fly back to Saint Tropez with me?"

She laughs. "I have some words for that man that kidnapped you."

A few days after the warehouse, when Matías was stable on machines, I finally called her. I broke down in tears as I spilled everything that happened to me to my best friend. She said she thought I was finally living my life. That I ran away with Matías after that night in the club. I thought she would be angry but since she is crazy, she thought it was romantic, I fell in love with the man who kidnapped me.

"We don't know if he will ever wake up."

She squeezes my hand. "For you, he will."

I walk into his hospital room, the beeping of the machines a sound that now haunts my dreams. Cam is asleep in a chair and Bastian is sitting in the chair next to Matías's bed.

"How was the funeral?" he asks me quietly.

"I never should have gone. I can tell my family is done with me."

His dark eyes look up at me. "Don't worry about them, Alessia. They are going to be indebted to The Partners for a long time. You are better far away from them. A war is coming. It's best you are as far away as possible."

"They had no idea."

Bastian looks over at Cam as she sleeps. "That's the price you pay. The price I paid. The price Matías paid. They find a way to weasel into every aspect of your life and ruin it from the inside out. You are free of them. We all are now."

I nod. "Has anything changed with him today?" I ask, changing the subject, my hand going to the locket around my neck. The one Matías had, the one he gave back to me as he lay dying. The locket that has more meaning now than before.

He shakes his head.

Tears threaten to fall down my face. "Do you think he will ever—"

"He'll wake up," Bastian's voice commands the room. "He has to."

"He loves you, you know."

Bastian raises a brow at me.

"I know about your past. I know about the things that ruined your relationship. Matías blames himself for Thiago."

"He shouldn't."

"You both shouldn't. It was Thiago's choice that day."

"You are a good woman for him," Bastian says as he turns back to look at his brother. "You see the good in him that I don't."

"He doesn't see it either." I sigh. "Maybe, if…" I correct myself. "When he wakes up, you two can finally mend your relationship. It's not worth wasting time hating each other."

"I don't hate him. I hate that I got him involved—"

This time I cut him off. "He got himself involved."

"We were both young and stupid."

"That's life." I shrug.

"Do you—" Bastian's words stop as he looks behind me.

I hear the door shut, but don't turn around to see who is behind me.

"Did you miss me, you old bastard?"

"Kilian," Bastian says in surprise.

"I came to check up on him."

I turn and look at the beautiful blond-haired man who shot my brother. I thought I would feel anger but I don't. Because he is also the man that made sure Matías was safe and got to a hospital.

"Under orders, I presume?" Bastian asks.

"Perhaps. Or maybe I just missed you."

A smile crosses Bastian's face. His smile seems rarer than his brother's. "Fuckin' wanker. You trying to get yourself killed?"

Kilian shrugs. "Showing up in a hospital is the least of my worries."

"I'm sure you—"

"Kilian!" Cam shouts, cutting off Bastian, pushing past me and jumping into Kilian's arms. "You're alive!" Tears stream down her face.

"Relatively," he says ominously.

"Let's talk elsewhere," Bastian says with a nod toward his brother.

I watch the three of them walk out of the room. So many questions in my head about that man and his role in everything. Because what I saw in the warehouse that night has me thinking he is much more important than he is letting on.

I take a seat next to Matías, wrapping my hand around his. I brush the overgrown pieces of his hair out of his face, they never seem to stay put. My fingers trace over his brow and along his jaw. I brush them over his full lips before leaning in and placing my own against his. I miss his kisses, the way he claimed me with his mouth and his teeth. The way he dominated me in ways I never thought I would like. And now I worry I will never feel again. His rough hands pressing me into a wall or forcing me to my knees. His dirty mouth whispering all the things he will do to me in my ear. His thick cock claiming my body as his own.

My tears fall onto his cheeks as I hold my lips against

his, wishing I could breathe life into him. Or trade my own for his.

"How are you holding up?"

I turn and see Ainslie, Matías's sister-in-law, standing in the doorway. I shrug as I sit back in my chair, my hand wrapped firmly around Matías's hand.

She walks into the room and sits in the chair across from me. "I worried this would happen to him. I told him so a few weeks ago. Told him he needed to get out."

"You saw him a few weeks ago?" I ask.

She nods. "He came to see me. He was stressed about something but I never asked." She snorts. "More like I knew he wouldn't tell me."

I count the weeks on my fingers and realize it was around when he kidnapped me. But I don't tell her. I don't know how much Bastian lets her know. "He likes to keep his secrets."

She chews her lip as she looks at him. "He does." She sighs, then looks back at me. "Sometimes I feel like I raised him. When his parents divorced, his mom didn't see him often. He lived with his dad but he was always working. When Thiago and I started dating, I saw how much he needed a mother in his life."

"He never told me," I whisper.

"He wouldn't have. Like you said, he likes to keep his secrets."

I nod and look back at him. This man I have given my whole heart to. A man with secrets, but he let me in, let me see who he was.

"You're what he needs, Alessia." I snap my gaze to her in confusion. "He needs someone to support him, love him. I can see it in your eyes. See that you love him more than anything."

She squeezes his hand, then stands and walks toward the door. "Don't lose hope. If you love him that much, I can only guess he loves you more. He has a huge heart but only a few get to see it."

She walks out of the room and a tear slides down my cheek. I tell myself to be strong. Not just for myself, but for Matías too. I hope my strength will pull him through this.

I lean forward and rest my head on the bed next to his hand. My fingers slowly moving up and down his arm, willing him to wake up.

I know I'm dreaming. There is no way this is real. Matías and I are on Bastian's yacht. Making love on the deck, the sun beating down on us. I am happy. Happier than I've ever been.

I bring my hand to his cheek as he slides in and out of me and I see a sparkling diamond on my hand. I smile, knowing that I'll soon be Mrs. Alessia Montford.

But then the sky darkens, gray storm clouds rolling in from nowhere. The ring melts off my hand and Matías fades away. I scream for him. But nothing happens. Giant waves crash against the deck, knocking me over. I run toward the living quarters but find the place deserted. I realize I am alone on the boat in the middle of nowhere. I collapse to the ground as I feel the water pulling the boat under.

The sound of beeping stirs me awake. But not the sound that haunts my dreams. This is different. More terrifying.

"Alessia!"

I hear my name and it sounds like Cam's voice. But I try to fall back asleep. Try to get back to the dream where I was happy.

"Alessia!"

This time I wake up as someone pulls me out of the chair I fell asleep in. My hand falling away from Matías as I realize the beeping sound is the emergency sounds of his machines.

He's crashing.

Cam's arms are around me as I am pulled against a wall, doctors pushing us out of the way as they try to save the man I love.

"No!" I scream.

"Shh…" Cam whispers in my ear. "They will save him."

"You need to leave," a nurse says to us.

"I'm not leaving. I can't leave!"

Cam tries to pull me out of the room. "We have to."

"I can't let him die alone. You don't understand. He can't die alone," I cry out as I am pulled from the room.

"He isn't going to die," Cam says in a soothing voice.

"I can't leave him!" I shout as I pull myself from her arms and rush toward his bed. But a nurse pushes me away just as I hear a doctor say no heartbeat. I collapse on the ground, my heart shattering into a million pieces as I watch Matías die in front of me.

"Get her out of here!" another doctor yells.

"No," I whisper. "Don't… he can't…"

Thick arms wrap around me and lift me off the floor. I fall against a hard chest I recognize as Bastian, crying so hard that I can barely see through my tears.

He brings me into the private waiting room down the hall from Matías's room. I bury my head in his chest as tears leak down my face. My hand wrapped tightly around my locket. Bastian holds me tight as Cam grips my hand. Bianca runs her hands through my hair as I try to breathe. But panic has set in. My chest caving in as my soul is ripped apart.

There is a commotion in the room as I try to find my breath. The sound of his mom, dad, and Ainslie speaking. Cam mumbling words of promise. Bianca crying as she grips my arm. I grow lightheaded as I scream at the top of my lungs. Bastian's arms never letting go of me. Cam's grip tight on my hand as we all deal with the loss I feel in the marrow of my bones.

I feel a sharp pinch in my arm and then everything fades away. The pain, the tears, the gut-wrenching agony.

I close my eyes and pretend I am back on the yacht with Matías, smiling at me as he holds my hand.

I wake up, unfortunately. Surprised to find I am still wrapped in Bastian's arms. I wait for the panic to set in again but it never comes. Maybe my heart died with Matías and I am nothing but stone.

"There you are," Bastian says to me as I blink my eyes open.

Cam is sitting next to him with an arm wrapped around his thick bicep. Bianca is on the floor in front of me, tissues and water in hand.

Cam brushes her hand down my face. "You had a panic attack. They may have given you a little too much Valium to calm you down."

"Matías," I croak.

"He…" Bastian starts to speak just as a doctor walks in.

I scramble out of Bastian's lap and nearly fall over Bianca but she gets up in time to steady me on my weak legs.

"Ms. Calvetti, Mr. Montford," the doctor says with a solemn face and I know. I just know. "Matías's heart stopped beating. Twice."

"No." The words fall from my lips. Bianca squeezes me as I feel my knees about to give out.

"But we got him back after the third try."

Relief floods my body as tears stream down my face.

"He's asked for you, Ms. Calvetti."

My jaw drops to the floor. "He's… he's awake?" I stutter.

The doctor nods. "The electric current from the AED must have reset his brain. It's been known to happen a few times."

"I… can I…"

"One visitor at a time, right now. I don't want too much commotion around him."

I barely let the doctor finish before I rip my hand out of Bianca's and run down the hall to Matías's room.

A nurse is leaning over him as I push open the door

to his room. I stand frozen in place as I look at him. Color in his cheeks for the first time in a week. He doesn't notice me at first. Too busy paying attention to the nurse that is redressing wounds and checking vitals.

But he must feel my presence. His sapphire blue eyes snap toward me and that one look has me rushing around to the side of his bed.

"Leave," he commands the nurse. She doesn't say a word and walks out of the room. I can't help but giggle. My monster just woke up from a coma and yet he still radiates power and control.

I hover at the side of the bed. Not sure what to do. I want to smash my lips to his. I want to jump on him and straddle him and claim him. But I know I can't do any of that. Instead I reach for his hand.

"Angel."

That one word brings tears to my eyes. I never thought I would hear it again from those lips.

"Don't cry," he says softly as he pulls me into him, my ass falling onto the bed. "Why are you crying?"

"I thought I lost you." I wipe my tears as I stare into his eyes. My mind a mess as I take in every single detail of the man I love. "I-I was so scared."

"Baby, it takes more than a bullet to take me down."

"You nearly died!" I yell at him.

He pulls me against his chest with more strength than I thought he would have. "Angel, I would kill the reaper himself to get back to you."

I grab his face and bring it to mine. My lips crashing into his with such force our teeth clink together. But he doesn't pull back. He lifts both his hands and grasps my face. I feel him wince from moving his injured shoulder but he doesn't stop. He devours my lips as his tongue slides against mine.

We only stop when he pulls back an inch. "Fuck, it hurts."

I notice my chest is pressing into his side and try to pull away but he doesn't let me go.

"Don't leave me ever again, Alessia."

I look at him in confusion.

"Do you know how hard it was to watch you walk away from me in that restaurant? To see the look on your face in the warehouse. I thought you hated me."

"I could never hate you. I love you." I trace my fingers over his lips.

He presses kisses to them. "Angel, I never thought I could love someone. I thought my heart was dead. It belonged to the monster in my soul. But you love the monster too."

"The monster is a part of you, Matías." I pause and link my fingers between his. "I don't hate you for what you did in that warehouse. It was part of your job, your contract. I understand that it's part of you. I don't hate what you did to my family. It doesn't matter what happened that night. My family is dead to me. I have a new one now."

A smile peeks up in one corner of his mouth. "A new family, huh?"

I smile back at him. "Yeah."

"I love you, Alessia. Every hardened part of me."

I slide in closer to him, careful of his wounds. "You love me, huh?"

"Undeniably."

I lean in and press my lips to his chest, just above his heart. We spend the night lying in his hospital bed. Even after Cam and Bastian disobey doctor's orders and join us in his room. Then we spend the night talking. Just talking about nothing. And I almost feel like we are on that yacht watching the sunset.

28

MATÍAS

I spent another week in the hospital before they released me. That night we returned home, Alessia and I spent hours in bed, her riding me into oblivion. Doctors told me I needed to wait two weeks before sexual activity but I couldn't keep my hands off her for two minutes after we got back into the house.

And the last few days have been peaceful. She and I tangled in sheets. Sitting naked out on the deck, swimming in the pool. It's almost surreal. Like I am waiting for the other shoe to drop. But maybe that is me and the way I have ingrained so many things into my soul. I never thought I would deserve this. A woman who gave up her family to be my family. My angel. My warrior.

Bastian and Cam visit us each day. My relationship with him rebuilding to what it should be, what it's never been. We have a lot to work through. A lot to deal with from our pasts and it will take time. Cam and Alessia believe we can have a normal life. I overheard Cam telling Bastian one day that it could be like he dreamed. I am not sure what she meant, or what Bastian wishes for our family but I can only hope it's peace.

Despite me waiting for something horrible to happen, peace is something I have been feeling. Like the turmoil has calmed, the worst of the storm over, and now it's smooth sailing from here on out. As long as I have Alessia by my side, I know it's something I can truly have.

Alessia decided to move in with me. I told her she didn't have to. That we could find somewhere else, somewhere closer to the sea, since I know how much she loves the view from her apartment in Positano. But she just shrugged and said maybe someday. She is keeping her place there. We can use it when we visit my hotel in Naples or when she needs to get away for inspiration. As long as she is always by my side, I couldn't care less where we live.

"Matías." Alessia walks into my office, where I have been trying to catch up on work.

I bite my lip as she walks in. She has on tight-ass leggings that I know make her perfect peach ass look good enough to eat and a black crop top that shows off her flat stomach and ends just below her tits.

"Get that look off your face. I am not here for that."

I chuckle as she rounds my desk. "You sure about that, Angel?" My hands reach for her ass and squeeze but she bats them away.

"You have a visitor."

"Who?"

"Kilian," she says softly.

She has been asking me the last week about Kilian

and his role in everything. But I have been reluctant to answer. I am not sure how to answer. I know in time I will have to tell her. But the memories with him are too much. The mistakes I made under his encouragement too raw for me to face right now. "I'll be right out," I tell her.

She nods and leans down to kiss me on my cheek before heading out of my office. I watch her ass as it leaves. But my head is too consumed with thoughts of Kilian to enjoy the view.

I answer a few emails and then roll out of my office. I've been confined to a wheelchair. The bullet to my leg causing a lot of damage. I'll be able to walk again soon. Be able to work out my leg muscles and regain my strength. But the doctors want me to stay off it until the muscle tissue heals more.

I enter the living room and find Alessia curled up on the couch and Kilian perched on a stool.

"For a dead man, you seem to be walking around with the living just fine."

Kilian smirks at me. "Everyone has secrets, Matías. And mine run deeper than either you or Bastian know."

"You saved my life." Alessia had told me how Kilian made sure I didn't bleed out on the floor of the warehouse. Ensured I was taken to a hospital that would get me the best care.

"You're in a wheelchair. Can't say I did that good of a job." He shrugs.

"It's temporary."

He nods. "That's an interesting piece of artwork," Kilian says as he looks at the panel of glass I had removed from the art studio, the one with Alessia's naked figure pressed into it in paint. I had the glass removed and hung two days ago.

I look over at Alessia, a blush rising from her chest up her neck and to her cheeks. "What can I say, I like abstract art." And I like the self-portrait of Alessia bound in ropes even more. It's now hanging in our bedroom.

Kilian glances at Alessia and snorts, no doubt piecing together how that piece of art was made. "I'm here to let you know The Partners have terminated their contract with you. You no longer are indebted to them."

"I find that hard to believe," I say with a straight face.

Kilian sighs. "You helped uncover a mole in our organization. We are grateful to keep our place at the top of the black market and the criminal underground."

I look at Alessia, my love, and wonder what she thinks of all this. "You sure we are actually safe, Kilian? Because I've heard this narrative before."

Kilian runs a hand through his blond hair. "As a courtesy to the Montford family, I am personally overseeing your safety. All of you," he says as he glances to Alessia. "But we may need a favor or two in the future."

"So never fully free." My words harsh.

He shakes his head. "That's business, Matías. You know that. But I will personally fight like hell to make sure your family is never put in harm's way again."

The conviction in his voice leads me to believe his role in The Partners is much higher ranked than he has ever led Bastian or myself to believe. But I don't ask questions. Questions only lead to a path I am trying to stay clear of.

"And what of the Mafia family that learned some of your secrets?"

Kilian looks at me, a gaping smile on his face. "I get to hunt them down now."

I smile at him with the diabolical smile I came to love when I let the monster break free.

Kilian stands up and heads to the door. "It was a pleasure seeing you again Ms. Calvetti." Alessia gives him a short smile. He turns to me. "I'll be in touch if necessary."

"Goodbye, Kilian."

He walks out of my house without another word. I stare at the door for minutes until I feel Alessia's hands on my shoulders.

"You are free, Matías. But what does that mean for your monster?"

I know she saw that smile on my face at Kilian's words of hunting. I know she understood what that meant to Kilian. A small gesture telling him I was willing to let the monster out if he needed it.

I grab her forearm and pull her down into my lap. "I'll just have to find other ways to let the monster come out to play." I snag her bottom lip between my teeth and bite hard.

She pushes her hands against my chest. "I think you need to heal more before that happens."

"You think I can't find a way to fuck you into submission while I am slightly incapacitated?"

She shakes her head. "You'll hurt yourself."

"Oh, angel, you have no idea what I am capable of."

"Is that a threat?" she asks as her cheeks flame.

I push out of the chair, standing on my feet, fighting through the pain that shoots through my leg. The grip she has around my neck tightens as I slowly make my way down the hall to the bedroom.

"Matías, you shouldn't be walking."

I grunt as I push open our bedroom door. "And you shouldn't be talking." I toss her on the bed and pull the handcuffs out of the bedside table. "Now take your clothes off and spread your legs."

She bites her lip at my words but makes quick work of taking her clothes off.

"The monster is ready to play."

EPILOGUE
MATÍAS

Three Months Later

"I don't understand why we couldn't stay at your hotel tonight. It's absolutely gorgeous," Alessia whines as we climb the stairs to her apartment.

"Because it was the grand opening and while the party was fun, I feel like we would have had no privacy there."

She folds her arms over her chest, pulling down on the red lace fabric that barely covers her tits. "You have an executive suite there that is just for you. There would have been plenty of privacy."

"Well, maybe I just like it here at your little old apartment instead."

She huffs as I unlock the door. I pull her in behind me and press her against the door as I shut it. My lips crush hers, my body pressed against every inch of her.

She moans into my mouth as she shifts a leg and wraps it around my hip. "Not so upset we are here now," I joke.

"We could have already been fucking if we just stayed at your hotel."

"I have better plans for you here."

She pulls away from my lips and I bend down to kiss her neck so she can see behind me. "What the hell?"

I pull away from her and let her step past me as she takes in the apartment. Her giant mural is hanging in the living room, the self-portrait of her that haunted her dreams for months. Candles scatter the floor, bringing the only light to the room.

"You had it hung?" she asks me.

"It has such a deep meaning to you. One that you still feel to this day. One that changed both of our lives. I thought it deserved to be here."

She squeezes my hand. "It's perfect here. The entrance to my own personal gallery."

I press a kiss to her neck just under her ear and she shivers at the touch. "What's with the candles?"

I shrug.

She spins around. "Matías, what are you planning?"

I slap her ass hard. "Maybe you should just follow the candles and find out before I have to punish you."

"Maybe I want to be punished."

"Woman," I moan as I run my hands over my face. "Would you just listen to me for once?"

She pokes my chest but then turns around and follows the candles that lead through her baroque-style apartment. When we get to the balcony, a bottle of champagne sits chilling on a glass table. Small jars of paint around it.

"What's all this, Matías?" she asks me curiously.

"Celebrating the grand opening of a new hotel."

She rolls her eyes at me. "So you wanted candles and champagne. Unlikely." She points to the paint. "What's that for?"

A devious smile takes over my face. "It's a surprise."

She purses her lips at me. "You know how I feel about surprises…" she trails off as I walk up to her, wrapping my arms around her waist, my chin resting on her shoulder.

"I do. And I will never stop surprising you."

"I swear one day you are going to kidnap me just for fun."

I press my lips into her shoulder. "Now that isn't a bad idea."

She grunts and steps out of my arms, her fingers tracing the paint jars. "This isn't my table."

"I know. I had it replaced."

"Matías, that was an antique. You better not have—" She spins around and stops her words when she sees me on one knee. "What are you doing?"

"Telling you to marry me, angel."

"Is that supposed to be a proposal?" she says with sass as she throws her hands on her hips, mumbling Italian under her breath.

"No. I am not proposing anything. I am telling you to marry me."

"I don't get a choice?"

I laugh. "Have I ever given you a choice?"

"You're such an asshole." Her eyes widen as I chuckle. "Oh my god, you want me to marry you and you are laughing."

"I don't want you to marry me, I am telling you to."

"What if I say no?"

"You won't." She throws her arms in the air and goes to storm off but I snatch her around the waist, pulling her down onto her knees in front of me. "You want to be punished?"

She purses her lips. "Are you going to punish me until I agree to marry you?"

That cynical grin takes over my face. "Baby, you don't understand. We are a done deal. The monster and his angel. You have no choice. There is only us. And you know it."

Her arms land around my neck. "You didn't answer my question about the punishment."

I see a darkness flash through her eyes. The same darkness that lives in mine. "I am sure I can find a way to bend you to my will, to force you to agree with my demands."

"Will you tie me up?"

My hands slide down the back of her thighs and under the hem of her dress. "I will bind your whole body in ropes."

"Will you gag me?"

My fingers slide up the inside of her thigh, teasing her as they graze so close to her center. "With my cock."

"Will you spank me so hard you leave handprints?"

I squeeze her ass as I let a finger ever so slightly touch

the heaven between her thighs. "Hard enough to make you cry before I fuck you so hard I break you."

"Then will I be yours?" she asks on a moan.

"You already are."

She leans in and presses her lips to mine, gripping my hair and grinding against me. "Then I suggest you put that ring on my finger and do everything you just said."

I throw my head back in laughter as I scoop the ring box off the ground. I slide the large black diamond onto her finger, and my heart skips a beat as I see it there.

"A black diamond?" she asks as she runs her finger over the stone.

"A reminder of the monster you love."

She looks up at me with those doe eyes and I get lost in them. "No, I love the man that's in front of me. The man who would rip apart the world for me. The monster is just an added bonus."

"I don't deserve you," I say as I skim my hand over the ring.

"Well, too bad because you just claimed me as yours and there is no way I am taking this ring off."

I chuckle as I press a kiss to her hand. "An angel and a devil can fall in love."

"I might have to paint it."

"You should. With our bodies. On that glass table."

She smiles at me as she understands. "The greatest love story ever told."

"I wouldn't go that far," I tease.

"Don't ruin my moment." She cups my jaw. "Now take me to bed and do all the things you just promised me. We'll save the table art for the sunrise."

I chuckle at my deviant little warrior. "Angel, I'll do worse."

She laughs as I pick her up and carry her inside. The angel that claimed my monster as her own.

The End

Want to know Kilian's fate?

Pre-order REDEMPTION now!

Sign up for my newsletter to find out what's coming next!
Sign up here
Want to be the first to know about sneak peeks and exclusive content?
Join my reader group!
To keep up with my upcoming releases and sales follow me on BookBub.

ALSO BY TORI FOX

The White Creek Series
Missing Pieces

Broken Pieces

Forgotten Pieces

The Broken Lyrics Duet
The Ghost of You

The Fate of Us

The Partners
Atonement

Repentance

Redemption

(Coming 3/31/22)

Other novels
Desolation: A Salvation Society Novel

Burnout: An Everyday Heroes Novel

ACKNOWLEDGMENTS

This book came out of nowhere. I never had any intention of writing more books in this world after Bastian's story but readers were asking and I knew I had to do it. Not to mention, I felt such a connection to this criminal underground I created. I was going through a lot of crap when I was writing this book and I think it played a huge role in how the story turned out. It's darker then anything I have written. But I had so much fun going dark. It let me get out emotions I was keeping buried deep inside. It helped heal me through a rough time in my life and now I almost don't want to go back. I like the dark side.

Thank you so much to my partner in crime, the pea to my pod(cast), and one of the best people in this writing community, J. Akridge. You are full of positive energy and bring a smile to my face everyday. Keep being you, boo!

Autumn and Mary, I am so happy you stuck with me as betas on this book. I cannot wait to keep working with you both!

Juliana at Jersey Girl Design, thank you for making my cover so sexy!

Ellie at My Brother's Editor, thank you for polishing up the hot mess I send you and making my words pretty.

Thank you Give Me Books for helping promote the heck out of this one!

To everyone that has been on the podcast, you all motivate me daily to write more, write better, and work harder.

Tom Ford brought Bastian and this entire world to life all from me smelling a fragrance one day. Well, Matías exists because of him too. I know you will never see this, but Mr. Ford you inspire me everyday.

To my husband, thank you for letting me live my dream.

Thank you to all my readers. There wouldn't be books if it wasn't for you. I cannot wait to share more stories with you!

ABOUT THE AUTHOR

Tori Fox is the author of romantic suspense and contemporary romance with a little bit of angst and a whole lot of sexy. When she isn't writing, you can find her listening to true crime podcasts as she tends to her plants or singing along to pop songs as she drinks champagne. Tori lives above the clouds with her husband and dog in the Rocky Mountains.

You can find Tori on Facebook, Instagram, and TikTok @ToriFoxBooks

For the latest news and releases visit
torifoxbooks.com

Made in the USA
Monee, IL
04 December 2021